Free Throw

Michael Chin

AmErica House
Baltimore

Copyright 2001 by Michael Chin.
All rights reserved. No part of this book may be reproduced in any form without written permission from the publishers, except by a reviewer who may quote brief passages in a review to be printed in a newspaper or magazine.

First printing

ISBN: 1-58851-166-9
PUBLISHED BY AMERICA HOUSE BOOK PUBLISHERS
www.publishamerica.com
Baltimore

Printed in the United States of America

*Dedicated to Jean Chamberlain,
Megan Grenier, CJ Johnson,
Zie McGregor, Eileen Ryan
and Mike Scalise*

Chapter 1

Ray Penner was high school basketball in Florida. About thirty years ago, he was a 6'3" forward, who it was said could hit any shot, from anywhere on the court. During his senior year, he had averaged over thirty-six points, twelve rebounds, and nine assists per game, including the time when he set the Lankford High School record for most points by a single player in a game with fifty-seven.

Penner became one of colleges' most highly recruited students of his time. He ended up going to Arizona. I don't really know the specifics, but some how, during his second game there, he hurt his back. He played just a little for a few more games, before it was decided that he wasn't, and probably never would be, capable of playing competitive basketball again.

Upon hearing the news, Penner dropped out of college, and disappeared. Some say that he got a new haircut, and a name change, and is still living out his life somewhere, right to this very day. Others insist that he put a bullet through his head. For quite a while now, there have been a lot of people trying - unsuccessfully - to find him.

However, regardless of what has become of him, I've always been fascinated with Ray Penner. When I was in the seventh grade, I found an old sports section of a newspaper in the attic of my home. On the front page of it was a picture of Penner, standing alone, about to shoot the ball. Beads of sweat streamed down his face, and, according to the caption, he was about to drain a free throw.

***

I received the invitation to Karen's birthday party in mid-August, during the summer between my freshman and sophomore years of high school. We weren't the closest of friends at the time, but we both hung out with the same crowd, and so, I phoned her to accept the invitation, before I thought about the consequences of my actions.

"What do you mean, 'the consequences'?" Carrie asked me. She was sitting there in the kitchen, writing a poem or something, and I hadn't really thought that she was listening all that much to what I was saying.

FREE THROW

Carrie and I had a different relationship from most siblings. Whenever I had a problem, it was almost customary for me to go to my big sister for a chat. I never knew for sure if she was really paying attention, though, since more and more she had been spending her time writing, and not really focusing on the our conversations.

"I was getting to that," I said. "You see, I kind of forgot how Karen is, like best friends with Alicia,"

"A-ha. The plot thickens,"

"Uh... yeah," I never knew how to respond when she started using literary terms or anything. It wasn't really my field of expertise.

" 'Uh... yeah'? What's that supposed to mean? We are thinking of the same Alicia, right?"

I only knew one Alicia - Alicia Harris. During the previous winter, my yearlong crush on her reached its climax, when I asked her to accompany me to the school's Winter Formal dance. She gave me a traditional 'Sorry, but I'd rather just be friends' answer - a response that just didn't satisfy me. This, of course, led to that day after the rejection, when I persisted. I waited by her locker before first period, with a bouquet of flowers that I had picked up at some florist shop earlier that morning. When Alicia approached, and saw me standing there with the flowers, I caught a glimpse of her smiling.

Naturally, I took that as a good sign. When she arrived at her locker, I asked her, "Would you please reconsider?" and she just broke out laughing. It wasn't just giggling. She stood there - laughing - for at least a minute or so, before I dropped the flowers and walked away. From that point on, she hadn't hesitated to make cracks about what had happened, and she seemed to get progressively more abusive as time went on.

Anyway, I went on in my conversation with Carrie, "Yes, we're definitely talking about the same person,"

"Okay, so what are you planning to do?" she asked, while adjusting her red spectacles, and looking at me for the first time in the conversation.

"I don't know. I guess I'll still go to the party... I'll just try to avoid her," I said, as I bit into an apple from the fruit basket on the counter.

"How many people are you expecting for there to be at this party?"

"I don't know..." I said in between bites, " Ten, eleven, twelve people... probably something like that,"

FREE THROW

"Hmm... good luck avoiding her for long with a small crowd like that," She looked down and started writing something down. For a while, the only sounds came from the crunch of the apple between my teeth and sound of her pen pressed against the paper. I despised moments like this... when she poked those little holes in my logic. I hated it because I could never come up with any counter-arguments; and half the time I think she just brought up things like that to show off her intelligence. Most of all, though, I hated it because she was always right.

"So, what have you been writing?" I changed the subject.

"Nothing good," she said, a bit agitated, and then tore the page she was writing on from her notebook.

"It's just that I've seen you writing a lot lately... I was just curious..."

"No... that little... outburst had nothing to do with you. See, I've wasted most of the summer already just sleeping and watching television. This is time I could be using to write that novel,"

"What novel?"

"The one I've been *thinking* about writing for years, but have always been too lazy to actually work on at all,"

" Oh... *that* novel," I smiled. She glared at me. "Oh, come on, Carrie, stop taking things so seriously. You're seventeen... you're going into your senior year of high school in less than a month. Just live a little,"

"Maybe you're right... I don't know. I just want to get *something* done," She paused. "Can I get a bite of that apple?"

"Here, take the whole thing," I lobbed it to her. She stumbled back a bit, barely caught it, and glared at me. Carrie wasn't exactly the most coordinated person in the world. "Sorry," I said quickly.

She took a couple small bites, before tossing the apple in the garbage. She then stood up, walked to the fridge, and took a carton of ice cream from the freezer. "What about that diet?" She was really just a little chubby, if anything, but abusing her self-consciousness was among my favorite hobbies.

"Ah, screw it. Swimsuit season's just about over... it's not worth it anymore," She grabbed a bowl from one of the cupboards, and an ice cream scoop and spoon from a drawer. It was odd - I mean, when I talked to her, she was perhaps the most mature adolescent I knew. But when I looked at her; maybe it was the red glasses, or the little ponytail, or the freckles, or

FREE THROW

the combination of all that, but she just *looked* like an overgrown eight year old.

"Want some?" she asked.

"No thanks," I started to say something else, but then the doorbell cut me off. "I'll get that," I said, left the kitchen, and headed for the front door.

"Hey, what's up?" I said, when I saw that it was Chris Brady standing outside.

"Hey," he said. "I was just wondering if you'd be interested getting your butt kicked in a game of one on one at the park," He moved his basketball from hand to hand in front of him.

"Sure," I said, "Just a sec," I turned around and hollered to Carrie, "I'm going to the park for a while. I'll be back by six,"

With that, I stepped out the door, and started the walk to the park - about two blocks away. Chris lived right down the street from me, but it was the park where we had met a couple years before.

At a time when just about every kid who knew the difference between a three-point shot and a dunk had his or her own hoop, Chris was one of the few people besides myself who still went to the park to play ball. For him, it was because his parents perceived basketball as his main distraction from his schoolwork - perhaps justifiably. For me, it was because my parents simply didn't see the point of buying one, when I could just take a five-minute walk and play at the park for free.

One way or another, we ended up both playing by ourselves, at the park on the same summer day once. His ball got stuck - lodged between the side of the rim and the backboard, on his side of the court. I let him borrow my ball to knock his back down, and then we started shooting around together. After that, we began coming to the park a lot together to play, and eventually started talking about our lives, and what was going on with each of us. He was a year younger that me, which made things awkward at first. But, after a while, we both got used to it. I'm not sure when exactly you could draw the lime, but at some point, we just became best friends.

Another thing that connected us was our desire to play for the Lankford High School varsity basketball team in the coming school year. I hadn't made the cut the year before. I was determined not let that happen again.

FREE THROW

"All right, I'm calling this one. Off the backboard and in," Chris said as he lined up for a three-point shot. Contrary to his beliefs, he fired an air ball, which I caught on the way down.

"In your hands was what I meant, of course," he said.

"Oh, of course," I answered, before tossing in a short jump shot. Chris and I had very contrasting styles on the court. He could do a lot of flashy dribbling and passing, but had a great deal of trouble with his shooting. I had extremely good shooting most of the time, but my ball handling wasn't quite up to speed.

"Oh, so you don't believe me? Is that what you're trying to say?"

"Yeah, that's pretty much it," I said bouncing the ball. "Now, if you want to shoot a three, this is how ya do it," My shot went off the backboard, off the rim, and fell out.

"A-ha... so when I'm going to miss a shot, I should make sure it goes off the backboard, then off the rim, and then out?" he said sarcastically as he picked up the ball.

"Hey, my shot was a lot closer than yours,"

"It so very was not,"

"Look, you airballed... I hit the rim..."

"No, no, no. You see, my shot was right on target. Only, a gust of wind blew it back. Meanwhile, for your shot... man, that ball should've stopped and asked for directions to the hoop,"

"Big words for a man with so little game,"

"You did not just diss my game,"

"How could I diss your game? You have no game!"

"Well, I guess you'd be the authority on having no game, you know, since you've lived your entire life that way,"

I laughed for a second, and was about to reply with another comeback, when I got distracted by someone behind Chris. "So," I said, "Any news about Erin lately?"

"Hey, now don't go switching subjects here..."

"No, seriously. Anything new in the romance department?"

"Naa... not really. Same old, same old. I obsess over her... she doesn't even know that exist. You know, the usual," he paused. "Why do you ask? Have you heard anything?"

"No... but, hey, I did see her not so long ago,"

"Really? Where?"

9

FREE THROW

"Well, right about... over there," I said, pointing behind him. He turned around, to see her jogging there.

"You couldn't just tell me that she was behind me?!"

"It's so much more fun this way," I smiled, as he threw the ball at me. I caught it, and went on, "Come on, seriously, go and talk to her,"

"Ha ha, no," he said, and took the ball back from me. "But thanks for trying. You're a real pal,"

"Come on, what are you so afraid of?"

"What am I so afraid of?! What am I so afraid of? What I'm so afraid of, is what will inevitably follow my going and talking to her,"

"What do you mean?"

"I'll look like a jackass... that's what I mean," he said as he banked in a close range jump shot.

"How are you going to look bad? You just go and talk to her. You have a nice conversation. Then it's over. Everybody's happy. No jackasses,"

"Yeah... it sounds great on paper, but the fact is that as soon as I start talking to her, my entire vocabulary will be reduced to two words: 'um' and 'uh'. And technically, I don't think that 'um' and 'uh' are even considered words. So, not only will I look like a jackass, but I'll also look stupid. I'll look like a stupid jackass. And besides... naa, forget it,"

"No, wait, 'besides' what?"

"Na... it's nothing,"

"Come on, man. If you don't tell me what's on your mind, I can't argue against it,"

"Look," he sighed. "It's just that we're... different kinds of people. I mean, she's going to be a senior next month... a high school *senior*. Meanwhile, I'll just be a freshman..."

"So you're telling me that the only reason you don't think that you're right for each other is that she's older?"

"No... that's just a part of it. I mean, she's popular, and so incredibly hot. How could I ever even think about seriously pursuing her? It's a lost cause,"

"Listen, I totally understand where you're coming from. But I don't agree with your conclusions. You like her... and... and that's all that matters. And besides, maybe she likes you too. Remember that old saying: 'opposites attract'?"

FREE THROW

"That's not just a saying - it's a cliché. And do you know why it's a cliché? Because pathetic losers like me always say that to themselves in an effort to kid themselves into believing that they could ever get their dream girl,"

"But you can never know for sure until you give it a try. Look, she's jogging around this way. You can talk to her now," He didn't say anything; he just stared at Erin. "If you want, I can come with you... you know, I'll make sure you don't say 'umm' too much," He wasn't laughing. He just kept watching her.

"Hey, Erin, wait up!" I called. She kept going.

"See that? She didn't stop," Chris started. "That's about as clear a sign as you'll get of her not wanting to talk to me,"

"Don't give me that. She probably just didn't hear me. Come on, let's go catch up to her,"

"I'm just asking out of curiosity, but, how much crack exactly are you on?"

"Just enough to make me want to do this," I smiled. "Come on, I'm going over there, and having a chat with her, whether you come or not," I turned around and began running towards her. I heard Chris coming along behind me.

I slowed down so we were at the same pace. "Glad you decided to come join me," I said.

"Yeah, yeah, yeah," he mumbled back. "Here, you wear this," he added, handing me his cap.

"Why?"

"'Cause I don't want to wear it in front of her. It's disrespectful, or something. And someone has to wear, it or else we just look like dumb people who carry baseball caps around," he said while he attempted to smooth back his dark hair.

"All right," I said, "But just remember that I'm doing this for you, man,"

We continued our jog in silence for a few moments. "Ha! Ya see that?" I said as we got closer, "She's got her Discman. That's why she couldn't hear me before,"

Chris ignored the reassurance. "All right, what should I say to her?"

FREE THROW

"Hey, I know," he jogged around to the other side of me, so he was the farthest from Erin. "You can start the conversation, and then I'll join in,"

"Heck, no. I don't know Erin any better than you. Actually, I probably know her even less. So no. But hey, that is something to start with... introducing yourself... and me," I switched sides with him again. "All right. Here we go," I whispered as we had come to being only a yard or so away,"

"Hi Erin," he said when we had run up to where we were beside her.

"Oh... um, hi," she said. That was all that she said. Chris looked at me. Things weren't looking good, admittedly, but I wasn't about to let him give up that easily.

"Keep talking," I whispered.

"Um, so, you go to Lankford High, right?" Chris asked.

"Yeah," she said.

"Cool. That's where I'll be going when school starts.. you know, in September. Uh... my name's Chris... Chris Brady,"

"Um.. nice to meet you," she said hesitantly. It was clear that she was surprised, and unsure of how to act in this situation. It had always amazed me that for all the time Chris had virtually worshipped Erin, he had never actually had a real conversation with her, prior to this.

"Oh, and this is my friend, Mike Weaver," he said to her, tilting his head towards me.

"Hi," she said.

"Hi," I said back.

"So... um.. uh..." Chris started, and I elbowed him. "Uh, so what are you listening to?"

"Oh, just some old Simon and Garfunkel music,"

"Oh... Simon and Gar... Gargoy... uh... yeah... uh, those guys. I listen to them all the time," he said. I was about ready crack up, right then, but resisted the urge.

"Oh really?" she smiled. "That's kind of a surprise... they're not that popular these days,"

"Oh, but they're.. uh... timeless. You've got to love that stuff,"

"Hey, mind if we slow down for a second?" Erin asked as she slowed down to walking.

"Of course not," Chris said.

FREE THROW

"So," Erin began, "What's your favorite Simon and Garfunkel song?"

"Oh, I don't know," Chris said, "I mean, there's so many... uh... hey, Mike, what's your favorite?"

"I don't know. I don't think I've ever really listened to their music," I said, completely calm.

"Oh," Chris didn't say anything for a few seconds. I knew that he'd be ready to kill me later, for leaving him hanging there. However, for the moment, I just enjoyed myself, watching this comedy unfold before me. If Chris weren't my best friend, or if it weren't Erin that he was talking to, I wouldn't have been able to stop myself from breaking into fits of laughter. He went on, "Well, I forgot the name of it, but it goes kind of like, 'Bum-bum, bum, bum," he started putting together a sort of melody, apparently completely at random. "Bum-bum-bum-bum, bum, bum-bum, bum," he kept going for almost a full minute.

"Oh, is that 'Mrs. Robinson'?" Erin spoke at last.

"Yeah, right, that's it," He let out a nervous laugh as he spoke.

We talked for a while, probably somewhere from fifteen to twenty minutes. Then Erin glanced at her watch, and said that she had to be headed home.

"Oh, what time is it?" I asked.

"It's about quarter after five, or so," she said after a second glance at her watch.

"Oh, then I'd better be going too," I said.

Chris began, confused, "But you only told your sister that you'd be back by six..."

"Sixteen after five... that's right," I laughed. "So I guess I'll leave, and *you* can walk *Erin* home,"

"Oh..." he started, and realizing what was going on, said another, quicker, "Oh," before finishing, "Well, I... umm... guess that we should be going,"

"Okay," Erin said.

"Catch you guys later," I added and walked away from them, and back to the park. Chris had left his ball there, so I knew that he would be back for it, and then we could talk about what happened.

In the mean time, I shot around for a while. Most of my shots went in, but that wasn't enough for me. I still had to try that one thing, that I had

FREE THROW

been trying since I first started playing basketball, but had never been successful at.

I looked all around to make sure no-one was watching, and then, starting at just a little past the three-point line, I sprinted toward the basket, clutching the basketball like a football. Finally, as I neared the hoop, I jumped up, into the air. This was my attempt to fly - well, at least dunk.

The ball slammed hard against the bottom of the backboard, and flew out of my hands. It then bounced and rolled to the half court line, before falling out of bounds. It didn't take so long for me, however. I landed flat on my back, on the grass behind the backboard.

I lay there for a moment, thinking of how stupid I was to keep trying that. It didn't help matters when I rose to my feet, and saw that I wasn't alone.

Standing right on the half court line was Mr. Nicholes. He was one of the high school janitors - a middle aged man with long brown hair and a beard. He was quite tall, and his shadow stretched out so far that it nearly reached me where I stood.

"Ya gotta stick with what you know, kid," he said. I held up my right hand - sort of signaling to him that he could pass the ball to me. He shook his head, and then right from where he was standing, he released a high arching jump shot, with perfect form. The ball barely even rippled the net on the way in.

I just stared at him for a moment, in disbelief. He shrugged and walked away. I dribbled around for a while. I wondered if it had just been a lucky shot... but he had shot with such confidence... like he *knew* that it would go in.

So, finally, I walked over to just about where he had been standing, and put up a shot of my own. I didn't hit rim, net, backboard, or even the post, holding the basket up.

"Air-ball!" I heard a voice from behind me yell, like the audiences often do, when it's provoked at real games.

"Yeah, but you wouldn't believe what just happened..." I started.

"Look, it can wait, man," he broke in. "This thing with Erin... I think it might actually have some chance of working out somewhat agreeably!"

"Hey, what happened?"

"Well, nothing really, but we talked and stuff, and it's not like I thought it was... she's not that different or anything,"

14

FREE THROW

"So," I smiled, "Ya gonna be asking her out?"

"No! Well, not yet at least. I don't want to screw things up before they even get started. I gotta give it some time,"

We went on talking right up until about six o' clock, when I really did have to be getting home. So, we walked back to our street. I remembered back, just a year or so ago, when we used to always ride our bikes for that trip. Chris outgrew his, though, and never bothered to get a new one. I wasn't about to keep riding mine around, when he didn't. So, we had both become accustomed to just walking.

Chris and I stopped when we got to my house. "You doing anything tomorrow?"

"Well, I've got Karen's birthday party tomorrow night, but other than that I'm free,"

"Cool... maybe we can play some more then,"

"Sure thing,"

"Mike, your dinner's getting cold!" My mother called from inside. She's always been the type to be loud and outgoing; almost like she was trying to embarrass me.

"Well, I guess I'd better be going," I said to Chris. "Catch you later,"

"See ya,"

Chapter 2

Ray Penner was never afraid when he stepped onto a basketball court. As he said in an interview that I read, "No matter how big or bad the other team looks, there's always a way to beat them. And if my opponents don't have weaknesses, then I'll just raise myself up to there level. I'll surprise them. When things look bad, something will always happen to make them better,"

***

It was about ten minutes after I arrived at the party, when Karen welcomed in Alicia. Her curly red hair reached halfway down her back, significantly longer than it had been when I'd last seen her. She was followed in by another girl, who was very pale, with dark brown hair that didn't quite reach down to her neck. I was standing far across the room at the time, and that, coupled with the stereo's booming, made it impossible to hear what was being said between any of them. It appeared as though Alicia was introducing Karen to the girl who came in with her. Whatever was happening, all three soon joined the rest of the party, Alicia and the girl being the last people to arrive.

My friend Greg Highman soon changed the direction of my attention, with a swift blow to the back of the head with one of the balloons used to decorate the party.

"Hey Weaver!" he said, smiling as I turned around.

"Now you must die," I replied, snagging a balloon of my own from the wall. He took off his glasses, knowing what was coming. The series of balloon hits from each of us went on for a while, before we called a truce. "I could use a drink, how 'bout you?" I asked, out of breath.

"Sure," he answered, and we strolled to the corner of the room where the cooler was located. We each removed a can of coke, and took a few sips.

"So, let's see," Greg then started, "One, two, three, four, five of us guys. And then there's one, two, three, four, five, six, seven chicks. I like these odds!"

"Hey, don't forget about that girl over there on the couch," I put in.

FREE THROW

"Make it eight!" He put his hand out for a high five, which I gave him. "You know who she is?" he continued in a moment.

"I was about to ask you the same thing. I saw her come in with Alicia..."

"Well, of course you'd notice Alicia..." he interrupted, on the verge of laughter.

"Shut up, man," I said. "Seriously, though, I haven't got a clue about who she is,"

"Why don't you go talk to her then... tell me what you find out,"

"Now, hold on a second; you're the one who wants to know about her so bad... you should go talk to her,"

"Walk with me for a moment," he said. I wasn't sure what he had in mind, but I followed. As we neared the couch, where she sat, all alone, he re-began, "Now, you're going to talk to her," Once had finished speaking, he used his strength advantage in shoving me down next to her. He then turned and engaged another one of the guys in conversation, as he walked away.

Having suddenly appeared next to her, I realized that I ought to say something. "Umm... hi, I'm Mike," I stuttered out, extending my hand.

She looked at me for a little bit, and then smiled and shook my hand, saying, "I'm Pepper,"

"Pepper? Like the... food... thing?"

"No," she laughed, "Well, maybe actually," I must have looked somewhat confused, because she went on to explain, "You see, my parents wanted me to have name that stood out, you know? Like when I'm applying for college, or a job, or something - they'll, like, have to remember my name. Anyway, I guess they just thought up 'Pepper'. Maybe they were eating at the time. Anyway, it's kind of a pain sometimes... because I always have to explain it to people... like this. But, I guess it'll be good for me in the long run. And I don't really *have* to explain it to pe..." she broke off and giggled, "Sorry, I guess I was kind of babbling... I've been known to do that from time to time,"

"That's okay," I smiled. "So, what brings you here.. I mean, I haven't seen you around before,"

"Oh, I just moved into town. You know Alicia over there?" I nodded. "Well, she's my cousin, and she thought I should start getting out some... you know, meet some new people before school starts, so she brought me

FREE THROW

along with her to this party. It's kind of pointless really, though. I mean, so far I haven't talked to anyone... except you that is," She paused. "I'm sorry, but what did you say your name was again?"

"Mike... Mike Weaver,"

"Oh my gosh... the Mike Weaver who asked out Alicia last year?"

"That would be me," I said quietly. I'm sure I was blushing.

"Well don't worry. Alicia didn't say anything really bad about you or anything. Actually, I thought buying her those flowers and all was really kind of sweet..." she stopped and then started to laugh. "Well, I guess I'm the one blushing now,"

I smiled. "You know..."

I was interrupted by Karen's voice. This came as quite a relief, since I hadn't really been sure what I was going to say - I had just been trying to fill in blank space. Anyway, Karen shouted, "Hey everybody, now that everyone's here, you wanna start the party games?"

"Yee-ha!" Greg exclaimed. Over the past year, it had become habitual for each gathering someone in our clique held, to include at least one of the 'party games', usually starting with our favorite - spin the bottle.

"What's she talking about?" Pepper asked wearily. "Or do I not want to know?" We both laughed as the others pulled up folding chairs from around the room and formed a circle that included the couch.

"You'll see soon enough," I replied. I sat back, as everyone got settled.

Another one of the girls broke in, "Okay, the first round is hugs, the next is a kiss on the cheek, and third round is kiss on the lips, all right?"

"And handshakes for same sex," Karen added.

"Can't we skip the first two rounds?!" Greg smirked.

"You always say that," another guy entered, and then paused for a moment, and said with a smile, "Not that I mind,"

"Come on guys, let's just start at the beginning... we've got plenty of time," another girl interjected. "Now, it's Karen's birthday, so I say she should spin first," She grabbed an empty Mountain Dew bottle, resting beside her, and handed it to Karen. In a moment, the game had begun.

In the first round, not much happened. I ended up shaking hands with Greg, and then had to spin the bottle myself. I scanned the room, clutching the cold plastic bottle in my hands. With a twist of the wrist, my fate was decided. I knew who I wanted the bottle to land on. Even though I'd just

FREE THROW

met her, I already felt these strong feelings toward Pepper. It wasn't like anything I'd felt before. Corny as it might sound, I think it could have been love at first sight - or at least at first conversation. However, there was no room for misinterpretation when the bottle stopped spinning. It was pointing squarely at Alicia. At first, it was reassuring when Alicia didn't really hesitate. However, when I did, she said, "Come on... we all know that you want this," The room erupted with laughter. I quickly hugged her and sat down, embarrassed.

"Aw... Weaver, that was so sweet..." Greg said sarcastically, and I punched him in the arm.

It wasn't until round three, when things started to get interesting again - at least for me. Pepper shook hands with another girl, and then had to spin. And it was quite a spin, as it went for nearly half a minute, before stopping on me. It had still been very early in the round at that point - this was the first kiss. "Weaver, Weaver," the guys started to chant.

It took a little time for me to really figure out what was going on. When I turned to face her, she slipped in a little grin, and then closed her eyes, and tilted her head to the right a little, so her hair just grazed her black tank top. I closed my eyes, and tilted my own head in the opposite way. We got closer and closer, before, all of sudden, Karen burst in, "Wait guys!"

I opened my eyes and realized why we had been cut short. It was the sound of footsteps, coming down the stairs. Soon enough, Karen's mom was present. "Hold on a second, kids," she said, smiling from ear to ear, as she walked into the kitchen, which was adjacent to the room where we sat. I noticed the Mountain Dew bottle, still resting on the floor. Most parents wouldn't exactly approve of this activity, so I started to get up to grab it. I was too slow, though. In an instant, Karen's mom had reentered, birthday cake in hand. Soon, all of us realized the situation.

Karen bolted up. "Here Mom," she said, "Let me help you with that," As she spoke, she moved right between her mother and the bottle. I extended my leg, and in a flash, had kicked the bottle under the couch.

***

I didn't get much of a chance to reflect on my feelings, or on what had happened, until my sister was driving me home.

20

FREE THROW

"I don't know," she said, "I've never really been one to believe in love at first sight. Do you honestly think you love her... so soon?"

"I think so. I mean, with Alicia, or anyone before that, it just wasn't the same feeling, and it didn't come so fast. I know that it happening that quickly might just seem like evidence that this isn't real. But..."

"Hey, look, you don't have to explain all this stuff to me. It's me, remember? I've always been a romantic at heart... even though I haven't had all that many great romances to speak of. You know, Matt's been great. He's probably the only guy I've been involved with who I would even consider saying it was love with. And even then, I don't really think so," She fell silent for a moment, and then went on, "Look, if you're really serious about this, you have to talk to her,"

"But I did..."

"No! Not just two seconds of talking. You need a real conversation. If it really is love, then you've got to find out if she loves you too, right?"

"I guess," I said. We were silent for the rest of the ride. I had a lot to think about by that point.

***

I only saw Pepper one more time before school started, and as much as I hate to say it, I would've just assumed skipped this meeting.

It was Friday night, when my parents and I went out to eat at some Italian restaurant - my sister was working at the time. While we were waiting for a table, I looked around the place, and saw Pepper, along with two adults, who I assumed to be her parents.

Because my mother's actions can often tend to lead to great embarrassment, I almost wanted for Pepper not to see me. However, I hoped to be seated close enough, so that I could see her. And, in that respect, I got my wish. We were seated at the table directly next to theirs. Worse yet, due to our respective seatings, we ended up directly opposite each other. She'd only have to look up to see me, and I still lacked confidence.

But then, the minutes started to just fly by. When about five to ten minutes had passed, I started to look at her. At first, it was just quick peeks. They evolved into stares. Meanwhile, I struggled to overhear the conversation for their table.

FREE THROW

"So, I think that you should really try to make some new friends here, already," her mom said.

"Look," Pepper started, "School hasn't even started yet. There's plenty of time,"

"But there are those mixers at the country club your father and I signed up for. There are always a few teens around..."

"I don't know," Pepper said. "I mean, I'm sure it's really nice, but I'd really feel kind of out of place there,"

"You know," her father spoke at last, with a smile, "I've noticed that boy over there looking at you..." Immediately, I put up my menu, in front of my face. I wondered if it was possible for me to have worse luck.

"Well don't *look* over there, Pepper. You'll just scare him off... wait, see, now his menus up in front of him... you've already done it..."

Pepper broke in, "He's right there. He can probably hear every word we're saying. Now will you guys please just be quiet,"

I didn't think it through particularly well, but I wanted to make it seem like I couldn't really hear them, so I put the menu down.

"Mike!" Pepper exclaimed.

I looked up as if she had surprised me. "Oh, hi Pepper," This was the first point of the evening when I could really look at her, without the worries of being caught or anything. It sound pretty corny, but the way she looked right at that moment, was about the most beautiful thing I can ever recall seeing.

"Mike," My mother started, interrupting my thoughts, "Why didn't you tell me you had your friend over here," She took a deep breath. "Well, we can't be rude; we'll have to join them," Suddenly, she vaulted to her feet, and started pulling our table towards theirs. "Well come on Stan," she said to my father, "Help me!" He acquiesced. I couldn't believe that she was doing this in public - much less directly in front of Pepper.

Pepper's parents kept saying things like, "That really isn't necessary," and "Oh, you don't have to do that," - polite ways of saying, 'Stop it, you creeps.' My parents ignored them, though.

The sound of the table being dragged across the hardwood floor was deafening. I was sure that my parents would be arrested or something. However, once they had brought the tables together, they just sat down like nothing had happened, and no-one even reprimanded them.

FREE THROW

The parents all introduced themselves and all. Pepper's folks seemed a bit frightened. Judging by their discussion of the country club and such, I guessed that they were fairly high-class people. Pepper seemed to just be kind of amused, as she wouldn't stop smiling.

Their family had already been close to finishing their meal, when we began ordering. They were polite, though, and sat there for an extra hour or so with us, though both of Pepper's parents seemed mildly upset.

At the end of the evening, I whispered to Pepper, "Sorry about all that,"

"Don't worry," she said, "Everybody's parents do stupid things," It was kind of reassuring, but I still felt terrible about that night.

***

With school coming soon, I decided to invite a few of my friends to the park for end of summer basketball playing. Chris, Greg, and Steve showed up on that hot August day. We were in the middle of a game of horse, when they arrived.

They were four boys, the biggest and probably oldest of whom looked to be about my age. Two of the others looked about a year or two younger, and one couldn't have been much over eight or nine. They stood at the side of the court, just watching us play for a while. It was a bit disconcerting, to say the least.

After a little while, we loosened up again. Things were fine, until Greg, most likely out of pure luck, made a shot from three-point range, by just tossing the ball behind his head. Steve was to go after him, and being the only non-basketball player, he had endured his share of ribbing through the whole day, and was getting more of it then. Knowing that the shot would be virtually impossible for him, he just flung the ball behind his head, with all his might. It careened off the backboard, and didn't land until it had reached center court. From there, it bounced and rolled over to the guys on the sideline.

That biggest one of them, a fairly muscular, black individual, palmed the ball, and then, with the rest of the guys, walked toward us.

"Wanna have a game?" he asked nonchalantly.

"What do you guys say?" I asked, turning to my friends.

"Yeah, let's do it," Greg blurted out.

FREE THROW

"I'm in too," Chris said.

"Come on guys," Steve began, "We don't have to play a game,"

"Oh come on, don't be a chicken" Chris said. "It's just a little game of basketball - and it's not like we'll be passing to you anyway,"

"Yeah, come on, Steve," I said, "Let's just play them,"

"All right," he said, "But don't blame me for anything that happens out there,"

"Well that's the attitude I like to hear!" Chris said, somewhat sarcastically. "So let's do this thing,"

"Yeah!" I said, and high-fived him.

"Yeah," Steve said, with far less enthusiasm, and the game began.

***

The game wasn't going well for us. We started out respectably, until they caught on to the fact that Steve wasn't going to take, much less make, any shots, and stopped guarding him.

The opposition didn't have that much talent, though. It was the guy who had challenged us, who they called 'Kahn', who was carrying the team. I recognized him once the game began - he had been an exceptionally good player at Jorles High School the previous year, and nearly led the team to a state championship. He had a complete game, excelling at shooting, ball handling and rebounding. I can only assume that he was a good passer, though he didn't do much of that in this game. We ended up guarding each other for most of the game, and he seemed to enjoy that, at one point dunking hard over me, and taunting, "Beat that, little man!"

On our next possession, Steve missed a shot, Kahn grabbed the rebound, and he dribbled it down court himself. This time, we decided to leave that eight-year-old kid open, as Greg and I double-teamed Kahn. Seeing the open man, he threw toward him, yelling, "Brian, catch this!" Chris was able to anticipate the pass, and stole the ball. He sped down court and I sprinted after him - if nothing else, I was faster than Kahn.

Chris was still a little ahead of me, and spotted the fact soon. When he reached the foul line, he bounced the ball backward, to me, through his legs. I rose up with it, and for a moment, thought about dunking. I didn't like the idea of potentially embarrassing myself by falling short, though, so I settled for a finger roll.

FREE THROW

"Yeah, Weaver!" Chris shouted, and gave me a high five. Kahn snarled. I smirked.

However, that was among our last bright spots in the game. Soon enough, a kid from Kahn's team was yelling, "Game point!" as he made his way back down court after being scored on. To no-one's surprise, he passed to Kahn. Then, with his back to the basket, Kahn threw the ball behind his head to a teammate. He faked a lay-up, and then returned the ball to Kahn, standing just past the three-point line. He turned so his back was to the basket again, and threw up his shot, backwards.

The ball swished through the net. "Gee," Kahn said, "That shot didn't seem so hard to me," After a moment he added, "Hey, good game, little boys," as he and his friends walked away. It was a disappointing loss, but I knew that I had much more important games on the way. Winning and losing wouldn't really matter until school started, and I was on the varsity team.

Chapter 3

Ray Penner said in an interview once, that he loved it when school was in session. This was mostly because it meant that the basketball season was on the way. But he also said that he like meeting new people checking out girls and just seeing what happened. He likened the first day of school to being given a hard foul on the basketball court. It could be disastrous - causing an injury or something. However, if someone's prepared, calm, and takes things as they come, they can make the best of their situation - and make the free throws.

***

On the first day school, I met up with Steve outside of the building, before class. "Hey man, what's up?"

"Oh, hey Mike. Have you seen the new girl yet?"

"Which one?"

"The one right there," he pointed off in the distance. " 'Bout an inch shorter than me, short brown hair, great legs..."

"You mean Pepper?" I broke in.

"Why? Do you know her?"

"Well, yeah, she was at Karen's party a couple weeks ago... you know... the one you forgot to go to..."

"Dang... I always miss the important stuff. So what's her deal, man?"

"I don't know too much about her... she just moved into town, she's hot..."

"You can skip the obvious the stuff,"

"Well..."

"Hey, what's going on Mike?" Chris said, coming up from behind me.

"Hey Chris! Oh, Steve, you know Chris, right?"

"We've met," he said. "Now, back to that new girl..."

"I'm telling you, I don't really know anything worth speaking of... but I'll say this much... I'm pretty smitten,"

"Smitten?" Chris started, "I am so going to pretend that you did not just use that word,"

27

"What's wrong with smitten?" I asked.

"Hey, guys, kill the debate," Steve said. "I think I might be a tad smitten myself,"

"Well I saw her first..."

"Yeah, but I saw her body, and I'm experiencing some serious smittenage right now..." Steve broke off, as he was bumped into.

"Whoa... sorry," said the guy who had bumped into him.

"Holy crap," Chris replied, when he first looked at him. And I have to say that his statement was warranted... the guy was seriously tall - easily over seven feet. "Uh... how's the weather up there?" Chris asked.

"Just the same as it is down there!" the giant fired back, and hurried away.

"Looks like that girl's not the only new kid in town." Steve said.

"You shouldn't have made fun of him," I said, looking at Chris.

"Hey, I didn't mean anything by it... it just seemed like something to say..."

"Look who else is here..." Steve said. I turned to see Alicia and some of her friends walking our way.

"I think that I can finally say, that I'm honestly over her," I said.

"Wow... this is truly a noteworthy occasion," Steve started. "But I suspect this will last all of five minutes..."

"I'm serious man, I've moved on..."

"Hey, I'll see you guys later," Chris interrupted, and then ran off toward Erin, and started talking to her.

"Well, it would appear that someone else is smitten too," Steve said.

"Yeah, he's got it pretty bad for that girl,"

"And he doesn't realize how incredibly out of his league she is?"

"Hey, he's giving it a shot..."

"Hey Mike!" came a voice for behind me. I turned, to see that it was Karen, walking alongside Alicia.

"Hey Karen," I said, and followed with, "Hey Alicia,"

"Alicia just rolled her eyes at me as they walked on." Steve began, "What's the word I'm looking for? It rhymes with witch..."

"Be kind."

"Why? I thought you said you were over her..."

"Yeah, but... getting *over* someone is a gradual process. I mean, you could say that a couple of months ago I was under her. Then, up until recently I was right on the same level with her. Now, I'm on top of her... and boy, did that ever come out wrong..."

"Well, hey, while you're on top of Alicia, I think I'd like to be on top of Pepper, myself,"

"First of all, this little metaphor has already been taken too far, and secondly... gee, vulgar much? You haven't even met her yet,"

"Yeah, but I have a sixth sense about these sort of things... I get the feeling that she's something special,"

"So do I,"

"Well, buddy, at least this'll be interesting..." He stopped as the first bell rang.

"Guess we should be going... wouldn't want to be late for homeroom," I said sarcastically.

"Yeah, right. So where's your room?"

"Umm... I think it was 312,"

"Oh, cool... me too," he said as we walked towards the school.

The bell rang just seconds before we entered the classroom. A short woman with brown hair and glasses accosted us. "Since it's the first day of school, I'll excuse you both from tardies. Now go find an open seat, so I can take attendance,"

"Yes sir!" Steve shouted, and saluted her like a military officer. Some of the people around us laughed, while the teacher simply glared.

Apparently, Steve and I were the only ones who were late - leaving a very small number of seats available. We walked along the room together, in search of a place to sit. As I passed by Pepper, she recognized me, and smiled. "Hey, I think this seat is open," she said, gesturing to the spot next to her.

I smiled back, and made my way to the desk. However, as I pulled out the chair, Steve slipped in, saying, "Oh, cool. Thanks man," he added, to me. Pepper shrugged, and I gave a little smile back. Steve waved as I walked away.

Looking around the room, I saw only one other open seat - right next to Alicia. At the time, she was looking the other way, talking to one of her friends. I looked desperately for another seat. However, the teacher noticed this, and took it upon herself to say, "Young man, there's an open chair right next that girl over there, with the red hair,"

FREE THROW

I covered my face with my hand. "Thank you," I said, and lethargically made my way over to the desk. As I sat down, Alicia kind of slid away from me in her chair.

"Now class," the teacher began, "Remember we're you're sitting, because this will be your assigned seat for the rest of the year," Steve smiled widely at me, as I ran my hands through my hair in frustration.

***

My third period class was gym. After Mr. Resont had handed out locks to everyone he picked two guys a random from the roll call sheet, and appointed them as captains for a game of basketball.

"You pick first," he said to Greg. I had played with him the previous year, on junior varsity. He had played at the small forward spot. He scanned the class, and stopped when he saw that same giant I had encountered before school started. "Whoa, I'm taking this kid!" he exclaimed, as he pointed at him. "Man, how freaking tall are you?" he asked, when the big guy arrived next to him.

"7'9"" the giant answered, shyly.

The other teams captain was Brad Davies. He had been a reserve point guard for the varsity team the previous year. He had good all around skills, and selected Greg's brother, a senior, named George. He was also a basketball player. "You're done, man!" he joked with his brother.

"We'll see about that," George called back.

I was selected next, by Greg. I was curious about how well the tall guy standing beside him would play. Height was surely an advantage in the game, but it would never be the only skill necessary for basketball success.

In a few minutes' time, the two teams had been fully selected, with eleven players on each team. "All right," the gym teacher hollered in his creaky voice. "We'll start out with the first five guy that were picked, then it'll be three on three for the remaining six. If there's any fouls, I'll be calling them - not you. You wanna get smart with me, and you'll end up in the office," He gestured towards Greg. "You picked first," he then pointed towards Brad, "So your team gets first ball,"

Brad inbounded the ball to the George. He dribbled up court, and was able to lose the guy guarding him with a quick crossover move. That wasn't the only obstacle for him, though. The 7'9" player loomed over him as he

FREE THROW

neared the paint. Still that proved to be no problem. George used a not too spectacular shot fake which drew the big guy up in a block attempt. Then, as his opponent neared the ground, he launched a fade away jumper from just past the free throw line.

The shot glanced off the back of the rim, from which the giant jumped above all others for the rebound. He then dished the ball off to a Greg. He dribbled down to the top of the key on the other side of the court, where he passed it to me. I drained the short jumper.

"Good rebound!" I called to the big guy.

"Thanks, nice shot," he replied as we slapped a high five.

In about twelve minutes, the first squad game was over, and the second teams began to play. We had given our team a six-point lead, myself scoring the game high eleven points. But the real secret to our success was the tall individual who had blocked seven shots, and snagged a total of fifteen rebounds by my count. My only question was that he never took a shot himself - he had always passed off as soon as he got a hold of the ball. I mean, with his height, he should have been able to dunk easily - maybe without even jumping.

I made a point of it to sit beside him on the bench, and it was there that I started my first real conversation with him.

"Hi, I'm Mike Weaver," I said, holding out my hand. He looked wearily at me, and then responded.

"I'm Travis Ribalow," Following this statement neither of us talked for a moment. Then, he continued, "You're a really good shooter,"

"Well, I've practiced a lot. I noticed that you didn't shoot any. How come?"

"Just not my style. I usually can't get 'em in, so it's a waste trying,"

"You should still be trying out for the basketball team this year. I saw you grabbing all of those rebounds, and making a ton of blocks. A team can always use a guy like that,"

"I don't know..."

"Hey, the try-outs aren't till next month. Just think about it,"

"Okay," he agreed.

We were both headed to the same Global Studies class for fourth period, so we walked together. On the way, we passed by Karen at a drinking fountain. "Hey Karen," I said, as she lifted her head. "What's going on?"

"Nothing much... same old, same old. How about you?"

"Ah, nothing really. Oh, hey, I'd like you to meet a friend of mine. His name's Travis... Travis, this is Ka..."

"Yeah, we already met a couple classes ago," Karen cut me off. "Math, right?"

"Uh... yes, yes it was," he stuttered.

"Um... yeah." Karen went on, to fill the silence. "So, where are you guys going?"

"Global Studies," I answered, without enthusiasm.

"Oh, woo-hoo," she said sarcastically. "Well, I'm going over to the science wing, so I guess I'll see you both later,"

"Yeah, see ya," I said, as she turned, and walked the other way. I turned, and started to walk to our class. I stopped when I realized that Travis was no longer with me. I walked back to him, to see that he was staring after her. "Umm... shall we be going?"

"Oh... uh... yeah," he said, and we resumed our walk to class. "So, you... uh... know that girl?"

"Yeah, we're friends,"

"Okay, because I'm finding myself seriously attracted to her. She's nice, and so... what's the word I'm looking for?"

"Hot?"

"Actually, I think I was angling more toward beautiful, but, yeah, hot works. So, is she involved with anyone?"

"No. She's available,"

"Great! Of course, I really have no idea what I should do, but great in the sense that there's a small, sliver of hope there,"

"Oh, come on, you just have to talk to her, get to know her, and if you still like her at that point, ask her out,"

"But, you see, girls don't exactly go for... you know... freaks, like me,"

"I think you're selling yourself short..." I trailed off, and then went on, "Sorry, bad choice of words. But still, you won't know until you try, right?"

"We'll see," he said, not sounding reassured at all.

***

FREE THROW

At the end of the second day of school, I exited the building, and saw Chris immediately. He wasn't alone, though. He was, once again, talking with Erin.

"Hey," Carrie came up from behind me. "I'm ready to go whenever you are... would your friend Chris want a ride?"

"Na... he looks busy," I chuckled.

"Wait a second, is that Erin he's talking with?"

"Yeah... you know her?"

"Uh.. yeah. We'd better be going,"

"Huh? What..."

"Look, I'll tell you about this in the car," she said, and then started walking. I followed after. It sounded like there was something seriously wrong - the way she was talking.

"Okay, so what's up?" I asked, once we were inside.

"I have study hall with Erin," she started. "And today, the teacher let us just hang around and talk and stuff,"

"Uh-huh,"

"And I overheard her talking with some of her friends. Chris came up,"

"Oh, great! What did she say?"

"It wasn't so great,"

"What do you mean? What'd she say?"

"Well, she started talking about there being some guy who just wouldn't leave her alone. She said it was like he was following her, or something, and kept talking to her. Then someone asked her what this guy's name was, and surely enough, she said Chris Brady,"

"Oh, man! This is gonna kill him,"

"I take it Chris is rather fond of Erin..." Carrie started.

"That's an understatement. He's liked her for almost a year now, and he's just started talking to her."

"Well, you know, Erin doesn't really seem to be the most likely person to go out with Chris. Maybe he shouldn't *be* trying to talk to her so much. I mean, he's probably just annoying her more and more with every word,"

"Yeah... the whole her not being within his reach thing was an issue before, but Chris figured it was worth a shot... and I kind of encouraged him," There was a short pause before I went on to say, "Well, I guess I'll tell him the news later."

***

"Are you sure she said that?" Chris asked, as he put up a long jump shot.

"Sure as can be. Carrie doesn't kid around about this sort of thing,"

"Man! So what am I supposed to do now?" he grabbed his own rebound, and dribbled around.

"You've got to give her some space..."

"I've got to give her some space? We were standing her just a week ago, and you were saying all that stuff about how I had to talk to her. Now it's 'give her some space?'"

"Look, I know it's tough to accept. But, Erin... she's an unusual case..."

"No kidding,"

"Come on... right now, she's probably thinking your overbearing and obnoxious. You've got to prove her wrong. Do nice things for her..."

"Like what? Meet her by her locker, with a bouquet of flowers..." he smiled.

"Hey, we all make mistakes," I smiled back. "I don't know what you should do. Let her borrow a pen or something. Something subtle... but, you know, nice,"

"All right, I'll try. But, anyway, how are things going with you and that Pepper girl,"

"Things are going no where. I never even get the chance to talk to her..."

"How about lunch. She's in the same period as us, right?"

"Yeah, but she sits at the same table as Alicia... I can't do anything with her around..."

"Hey, we've all gotta make some sort of sacrifices,"

"Yeah, we'll see,"

***

FREE THROW

At around five o' clock on the first Saturday after school started, Carrie told me that her boyfriend, Matt, would be coming over, to meet the family and have dinner that evening. At about 5:30, a worn, gray Oldsmobile with a dent the size of the crater in the front, driver-side door, pulled up in our driveway. Out stepped Matt. He was tall and lanky with hair that was a really light shade of brown, and a pale skin tone. His face was that of someone three or four years younger than his true age.

He strolled up to the front door, and pressed the doorbell. Carrie scurried over to him, and let him inside. I detected a hint of nervousness - this being Matt's first meeting with the family. They had been going out for about a year at that point, and Carrie had always kept him away from our house, weary of my parents' behavior, as well as being afraid that they would disapprove.

We all sat, talking in the living room, while we waited for dinner to be ready. Matt seemed nice enough, though I got the distinct impression that he was a nerd. I'm not the type of person to label someone, just because they're smart, or unusual. But I got the impression that Matt was the sort of person who spent all of his free time sitting up in his room, calculating pi.

I soon found out that there was more to him, though. Just, not much. "I'm a major Star Trek fan," he said, proudly, and proceeded to list his entire inventory of Star Trek paraphernalia. Carrie looked at him; one of those 'Please shut up.' looks. She knew how I thought, and knew the impression that Matt was making.

After a while, my mom and dad went into the kitchen to work on supper. Then Carrie went to the bathroom. So, conversation with Matt was left up to me. "So," I began, attempting to fill the awkward silence, "What kind of music do you like?"

"Soundtracks,"

"A-ha," I wasn't sure what to say. *Soundtracks*? Since when was that a genre of music?

"What type do you like?"

Here came the moral dilemma. Be nice, and just answer honestly, or have fun? I was about to tell him that I liked TV theme songs, when I heard the bathroom door open. As Carrie returned to the room, I said, "Mostly alternative stuff, and little hard rock,"

FREE THROW

Shortly after, we were called into the kitchen for dinner, which proceeded fairly uneventfully.

***

A short while after Matt left, Carrie came up to my room. "So, what'd you think?"
"About Matt?"
"Who else? I'd like an honest opinion. I mean, I asked Mom and Dad, and they gave the mandatory positive parental response. But really, what did you think?"
"Well, he seems nice. But..." I paused. "He's kind of... odd, don't you think?"
"I know he's not exactly the prototype for the perfect boyfriend - but he's really sweet, and he's good to me..."
"Then he's good enough for me. Honestly, Carrie, since when do you really care about what anyone else thinks?"
"It's just that, I tried looking at the situation the way someone else would, and suddenly, Matt wasn't as great as I had thought. But, of course, now that I actually hear myself say all that, it does sound pretty dumb. I mean, no-one else's opinion *should* matter at all,"
"Exactly,"
"Well, I'm glad we had this talk. By the way, any news on Pepper?"
"Nope. I think we're a the friends stage, but that's about it,"
"Well, it's a start. Make sure you let me know how that all turns out,"
"Of course," I said. She patted me on the head and walked away.

***

"I can't believe I got stuck with writing an editorial about school lunches," I groaned, as Steve and I exited the school, after staying late for a school newspaper meeting.
"Hey, if you want to be with the paper, ya gotta take these things as they come. I mean, remember last year, when I got that article about the expansion of the girl's athletic program?"
"Na... remember, last year I wasn't on the staff,"
"Yeah, but everyone's allowed to read the thing..."

FREE THROW

"Ah, and yet only about twenty people actually do read it - that being the newspaper staff, and their moms,"

"Hey, just because you're just now mastering the concept of literacy, doesn't mean that everyone else hasn't been reading this thing..."

"Either way, it doesn't really mater. Whether or not anyone reads it, I'm writing about 'sloppy joes' and frozen corn. Meanwhile, you get to interview the captain of the girls' gymnastics team. Where's the fairness?"

When Steve didn't say anything, I looked at him, and found that, mentally, he had left this conversation. He was looking straight ahead - at Pepper. "Okay, man," I started, "Before this little competition we have going here, over Pepper, goes any further, we have to talk,"

"What's to talk about? We both want her - may the best man win..."

"But, you see, that's just it. If Pepper decides she'd rather be with you than me, or that she isn't interested in either of us - I'm cool with that. But I don't like the attitude - like she's a prize to be won, or like you just want her for her body. That's not right,"

"Okay, seriously man, all that's just big talk. I mean, sure I like the way she looks, but I'm there for more than that. But I do mean it when I say, 'may the best man win'. No hard feelings, whatever happens. Deal?"

"Deal,"

Pepper was sitting alone on a bench when we approached her. Steve ran up ahead, and sat up on the back of the bench, beside her. "Hey Pepper! What's happening?"

"Oh, hey Steve. Hey Mike," she added as I arrived a moment later.

"Hey, what's up?"

"Ah, nothing much. Just got out of a meeting for the school play thing,"

"Oh, that's cool," Steve said. "What play are they doing?"

"Romeo and Juliet... which is really cool, because I just love that story," she answered.

"Oh yeah, I love... uh, the pool scene,"

"The pool scene?"

"I think he means the balcony scene," I jumped in.

"Oh, right!" she laughed. "You were talking about that new version of it,"

"Right," Steve smiled. "So, what part are you planning to go for? I mean, you've got to be Juliet, right?"

FREE THROW

"Actually, I'm not leaning that way. See, the main thing I'm worried about here is memorizing all the lines. Being Juliet pretty much maximizes that problem..."

"You'd be great in that part, though..."

"Hey, you know what?" Steve interrupted. "If you're worried about getting all of those lines down, I'd be happy to help you practice..." he was halted by the sound of a car horn honking. "Damn - I mean... well, there would be my ride. I guess I'll see you guys later,"

"Yeah, later," I smiled smugly after him.

"See ya," Pepper added.

"So," I started, "That whole practicing together idea... I'd be more than willing to help you out with that. I mean, if you want help with it,"

"That'd be really cool... yeah,"

***

"So, I guess to sum it all up, Stevie boy got screwed over," Chris said, dribbling the ball from side to side.

"Pretty much," I said. He passed me the ball, and I shot and made a three-point shot. "It's weird," I went on, "Because I'm really getting this vibe - that she likes me too,"

"Why's that so weird... I mean, besides the obvious... you know, the genetic defect that is your face,"

"No, seriously, man. All of my romance knowledge comes from '90210'... and 'Dawson's Creek'. Steve's... experienced. He's had girlfriends before. He knows how to act. Plus, he's got that one thing that there's no way I can top,"

"And what's that?"

"He's in a band,"

"Okay, I'll admit that the being of one in a band, does help. But you're not looking at the big picture,"

"Which is?"

"What, do I have to spell everything out for you? You're a jock,"

"I'm not a jock,"

"Look at the facts. Last year, you started for the JV basketball team. This year, you'll be playing on the varsity team. Therefore, you're a jock,"

FREE THROW

"Jocks beat up nerds, fail science, and date cheerleaders. I don't see me doing any of those things,"

"Well, besides the cheerleader part, it seems to that you've got all the favorable jock traits - namely the sports, and you're only missing all the bad stuff. All kidding aside, I really don't see any reason why Pepper wouldn't like you, or why she'd like Steve any better. That whole deal with Alicia gave you some serious self-esteem issues, that you're just gonna have to overcome..."

"You know, I just realized that we've each been relying on the other when it comes to advice, despite the fact that clearly, neither of us knows what we're doing..."

"Hey, things may not be working out with me and Erin, but you've got a decent start there with Pepper. I mean, how much time do you guys spend practicing?"

"We're on the phone every night,"

"Like you were going out with her,"

"And we usually keep going for a while.. like, over an hour..."

"Like you were going out with her,"

"But we're practicing... that's all!"

"Are you telling me that in all that time you spend practicing, you never just stop, and actually talk?"

"Well, of course... I mean, a little bit,"

"I'm betting that all of that talking... it amounts to a lot more that you think,"

I took the ball from him, dribbled up to the hoop, and tossed in a reverse lay-up - effectively ending the conversation. I knew that speaking the lines of Romeo to Pepper, and her saying the lines of Juliet back, was good practice for her, for the play. And in a way, I knew that it would probably prove to be good practice for me too - but for another reason altogether.

Chapter 4

  Ray Penner once summed up his philosophy for life in an essay for his English class. Basically, he wrote that there's nothing wrong with having ulterior motives for what someone does, as long as they aren't the only motives. He played basketball because it was fun, he was good at it, and he wanted to win. But, he would also use flashy plays to get teachers, friends, or girls to notice, and like him. His main intentions were good and pure and all that. But, he wasn't going to turn down any of the benefits that came along with his efforts.

***

  "Okay, so what do you want to work on today?" I asked Pepper as we walked toward the auditorium after school. It was the day before Pepper's audition, and earlier in the day, we had gotten special permission from the principal to practice on stage.
  "I don't know... I think I need work on a lot of parts..."
  "Oh come on... you've done great in every part we practiced. I'm sure you're going to nail this audition."
  "Really? Because if it's not really, then please just be honest,"
  "Totally really," I smiled. "You're a natural,"
  Pepper smiled back. "Seriously, though... the whole acting thing.. na, forget it,"
  "What is it?" I asked, grinning.
  "Well... I've never told anyone this, but once I'm out of school... you promise not to laugh?"
  "Of course,"
  "Well... I'd kind of like to try... acting," She looked at me, maybe expecting me to laugh.
  "What's so bad about that?"
  "It's just that not many people can make it in that sort of business..."
  "But some have to... I mean, if *everybody* figured they couldn't make it, and didn't even try... then there wouldn't *be* any actors and actresses,"
  "I guess so. But, I mean... my parents... they'd kill me if they heard me even talking about it..."

FREE THROW

"I don't want to tell you what to do... but it's your life.. and you can't let them decide the whole thing for you,"

"I suppose that's true," She smiled. "I don't really want to make any sort of controversy, though, you know? I mean, from day one, they've been planning my future for me... they want me to be a doctor. I don't know how I can explain this to them,"

"Well, be honest... I mean, you just tell them how... umm... actually what is your reasoning?"

"I just... okay, once again, I'll have to ask you not to laugh,"

"Don't sweat it," I laughed. "Whatever you say... I'll totally support it."

"Okay, then her goes. I want to be a star," A smile came to my face as soon as she said that much, and she saw it. "Okay... that's it,"

"No... no, come on. Remember... I'm supportive guy,"

She looked me over again, and re-began. "All right... it's just always kind of been a dream of mine. It's like, if I could be a famous movie star... everything would just suddenly be okay, you know?" She stopped, and held her head. "Okay, well now I know that I sound stupid,"

"A lot of people have feelings like that... even me. I mean my whole basketball thing... part of it has always been that I want to be, like, a superstar. It's not stupid," As I finished, we arrived at the doors of the auditorium.

"Well, before I become any sort of star, I've got to get some practice in on these parts,"

"Let's go then," I said, and opened the auditorium door, and held it for her.

We both froze, though, when the sound of a million voices attacked us. Slowly, we each stepped inside. People stood, speaking her lines everywhere in the auditorium, from the stage to the highest of the balcony seats. "I don't know if it's really worth it, practicing here," Pepper said.

"Yeah, I think you're right," I answered. Neither of us spoke for a little bit.

"Hey, you want to go practice outside?"

"Are you kidding?!" I laughed. "It's been raining buckets all week,"

"Oh, come on. It's just a drizzle. A little water never hurt anybody," She was smiling, but I knew that she was serious.

"All right," I mumbled in a moment, and threw on my jacket.

FREE THROW

"Great!" she said, pulling on her own. We left our book bags just inside the doorway, to keep them dry, as we stepped out.

This was hardly the drizzle Pepper had described it as. We were both soaked within the first few seconds. "All right," I said, "So where should we start?"

"Well, I was practicing act two, scene two last night, so I should probably, like, give it a try with someone else... I'm almost certain it'll be part of the audition,"

"Okay," I said, and removed a copy of the script from my coat pocket. It was already damp, and despite any of my efforts, it too was soaked in a short while. "All right... act two, scene two..." I said, flipping the pages. Eventually, I got there, and scanned the lines. "Oh... this is familiar," I smiled.

She smiled back. "Yeah... hope I didn't catch you by surprise," We both giggled briefly, and then she spoke again, "Okay, you can stand over there a little more, and I'll be up here," With that remark, she stepped over, and stood on top of a nearby bench.

"Funny looking balcony," I put in with a smile.

"Har, har. Now come on, seriously, go stand over there,"

"Okay, okay,"

I looked down at my part, and then looked at her. "Where should I begin?"

"Umm..." She thought for a moment. "How about right after I speak my first line?"

I cleared my throat, and then read aloud, "'She speaks: O, speak again, bright angel! For thou art as glorious to this night, being o'er my head, as is a winged messenger of heaven, unto the white-upturned wondering eyes. Of mortals that fall back to gaze on him, when we bestrides the lazy-pacing clouds and sails upon the bosom of the air.' "

She called back, not needing to look at the script, "' O Romeo, Romeo! Wherefore art thou Romeo? Deny thy father and refuse thy name; or if thou wilt not, be but sworn by love, and I'll no longer be a Capulet,"

We kept going for a few more minutes. At first, the rain's assault troubled me, but then there came a point where I was too wet to feel like I was wet at all. I just listened, and read. Her voice was soon all that I could hear. "'This bud of love, buy summer's ripening breath, may prove a...' " At that, she stopped. I had closed my eyes, knowing that she was on a large

FREE THROW

block of speaking. She shrieked. I popped open my eyes, and ran toward her.

"What? What is it?" I asked.

"Look, it stopped raining!" she spoke excitedly, with a big smile on her face. We both laughed for a minute. "Well, that sort of broke the flow of things..." she started again.

"Yeah... I guess you could say that..."

"Whoops!" She slipped on the wet bench, and landed in my arms.

"You all right?" I asked, still smiling.

Her eyes bared into mine. "Yes," She said, as if in a trance. I don't know how it happened, but all of a sudden, we were about to kiss. Our lips were just a few inches apart, when I closed my eyes.

The next thing I heard was a hard banging sound. I looked up and pulled away. There was Mr. Bronson, an elderly hall monitor, notorious for doing his best to stop any displays of affection, standing just inside the glass doors of the school, hitting them with a broomstick. This induced another round of laughter for us both. "Well, I guess we should get back to work," she said between giggles.

"Yeah, that's right," I answered.

We rehearsed for a while, before Carrie arrived to pick me up. It wasn't until that ride home, that I really evaluated the situation. We were actually about to kiss. And this wasn't just a part of a game; she had actually wanted to do it. I hated that it was broken up once more. I didn't really know how to bring it up again, and I guess that she didn't either. So, we didn't speak of it again.

***

A few days later, I was back at the park, shooting around with Chris. We were both playing with more focus, fully aware that at the end of the month, it would be time for try-outs for the team. Chris hoped to play varsity, and I would accept nothing less than that from myself. Still, the conversation revolved around an entirely different topic.

"You were about to kiss her, and you let Bronson stop you?!" Chris asked in mock horror.

"It's not like I chose to stop," I paused as I fired a jump shot from just inside the three-point arc. "Bronson caught me off guard... I just looked up," The shot swished through the hoop, into Chris' waiting hands. "And the moment was over," I finished at last.

He dribbled around the three-point line for a while as he spoke. "So what? I would've flicked off Bronson and re-began 'the moment'," He released a shot from downtown, which bounced hard off the backboard. I grabbed the rebound.

"See why I'm gonna be on varsity," I smirked. "I've got the shot and the rebounding," I hit a finger roll from where I was, and then grabbed the ball again, and started dribbling around.

"Stop changing the subject, man," Chris broke in. "You messed up with Pepper... admit it,"

"Oh come on. It's not like I'm being held to any sort of time limit.... this just proved that she likes me too. Now, we can move on from here," I stood in one place as I said it, between breaths, crossing the ball over between my legs. "Hey, and what girl could resist these skills,"

"Hey, you know that reminds me of something. Know why I'll be on varsity?"

"Why's tha...." I broke off as he charged forward and stole the ball.

He laughed out loud as he dribbled back to three-point range. "It's 'cause when the other guys are thinking about their precious little girl friends, I'm all hoops, all the time!" He bounced the ball between his legs, and then began to spin it on his finger.

"Yeah," I said. "But it's not all about style, my friend. It's about substance." With that, I ran over, knocked the ball away from him, and began my ball-handling show again.

"All right, all right," He wiped some perspiration from his forehead. "But getting back to Pepper, at least promise me this much: ask her to the dance this Friday,"

"There's a dance Friday?"

"Stop playing dumb. Now come on, are you gonna ask her, or what?"

"I'll tell you what - if I make this basket, from right here," I said, standing about a free throw's distance from the basket, "Then I'll ask her. If not, then we can forget about it,"

He was hesitant, but eventually, he said, "Yeah, all right," With that, I drained my face of any emotion, and stared at the basket. Then I dribbled thrice, and focused deeply on the hoop for another few moments, just for dramatic effect. Finally, I released my 'shot'.

FREE THROW

The ball only went about a meter forward. "Oh darn," I spoke sarcastically.

"Mike!"

"Okay, listen. Are you going to the dance?"

"Yeah,"

"All right, I'll go too, and if Pepper's there, and the opportunity comes up, I'll ask her to dance,"

"To a slow song?"

"Yeah, I guess,"

"Fair enough, then," He picked up the ball, which had rolled onto the grass around the court. "But no more funny stuff," he added, before we resumed play.

***

Friday night came quickly. Before I knew it, there I was, in the high school gym, standing with Chris, Steve, and a few other friends. "So, I hear tonight's the big night," Steve said, smiling.

"Yeah, yeah, yeah," I said, and punched Chris' arm. I hadn't been particularly eager to tell people about what was going to happen.

"Aww... he's blushing," Steve put in, in a high voice. "Don't worry about tonight... I mean, after she rejects you and then hooks up with me, I won't rub it in or anything..."

"Don't be so sure of yourself. I've got a good feeling about tonight," We continued our chat for a while, until I parted, to go and buy a soda.

As I reached the machine, and grabbed a dollar from my pocket, two hands reached room behind me and covered my eyes. "Guess who?" I immediately recognized it as Pepper's voice.

"Hmm... who ever could it be?" I said sarcastically.

"Well, she just found out that she's been cast for the role of Juliet in the school play," she answered.

"Oh, then it must be Kim Schrader," I said, referring to a highly snobbish and obnoxious girl who had also been auditioning for the part.

She lowered her hands and hit my shoulder playfully. "If I wasn't so psyched right now, I'd hurt you,"

"I'm sure of it," I laughed. "So, you got the part?"

"Yep! I couldn't believe it... thanks so much for your help,"

FREE THROW

"Ah, don't mention it,"

"Oh come on, I might not have even tried out if it weren't for you,"

"Well, however you got the part, congratulations,"

"Thanks..." she stopped as her cousin tapped on her shoulder.

"Come on Pepper, everybody's over there," Alicia said pointing off to the opposite corner of the gym.

"All right," she said to Alicia, and then turned back to me. "Well, I'll catch you later,"

"Yeah, see ya," She had already turned around as I spoke the words, glaring at Alicia.

***

The moment of truth had arrived. The DJ's voice came through on his microphone, "All right, now, for the last song of the dance we're going to slow it down a little,"

"Here's your chance, man. Catch you later!" Chris said, as he quickly walked off. My other companions all either followed his lead or began dancing with their own dates. I looked around me, and all at once, it was as if every one of the fluorescent lights in the room shifted, to focus at the center of the gym. Everybody else - all of the other bodies of students, and faculty, melted away, leaving one figure. There she was: Pepper.

Slowly, I made my way towards her, pausing for a moment, to pop a breath mint into my mouth. I got closer and closer. She just stood there, and I was only a few steps away. Just close enough to see Timothy Kahn arriving beside her first. He went to Jorles High School, nearby, and was known to slip into other schools' dances with some of his friends. "Wanna dance?" he asked her, with total confidence - as slick as humanly possible.

"Sure," was her answer, and they began. I backed up, and stood against the nearest wall, staring at them in disbelief. Just when I had been so close, I had been robbed. Kahn, obnoxious as he may have acted, was handsome and suave, and I'd suggest that he was capable of attracting almost any girl he wanted. On that night, he chose Pepper.

Alicia strutted over. "Well Mike," she said, "I hate to see you this down, so I guess that I can give you one dance,"

"No... that's okay..." I began. She ignored my words and put her arms around me, as she began to move. I sighed and followed her lead.

FREE THROW

I continued to watch Pepper and Kahn as they swayed from side to side. Her arms reached over his shoulders, and held him close, as his hands rested softly on the lower back of her yellow tank top. But then, his right hand started to slide downward, ever so slightly.

Then - it happened. He grasped her posterior. She released her hold on him, stepped back, and slapped him. He held his face for a moment, and then looked at her. He said something - clearly not a flattering line, and walked away. She stood alone once more. The moment had returned.

I let go of Alicia, and ducked out of her hold. I heard her say something, but whatever it was, I ignored it, and walked back towards Pepper.

I pulled the breath mint package from my pocket again. It was empty. I refused to let that bother me, though.

When I walked up to her, she still seemed angry. I spoke the words, "Umm... I saw what happened... and... uh... I think that was really, like wrong... and umm.." I stopped, took a deep breath, and proceeded to rattle out, "Wanna dance?"

For a moment, nothing happened. Then, without saying a word, she put her arms around me, as she had with Kahn before. I planted my hands over her waistline. We began to move.

"I can't believe he tried to cop a feel," she muttered. I hadn't really thought she'd bring it up again, and wasn't sure how to respond. Luckily, I didn't have to right away. She continued, "I mean, it's like, just because he's 'Mr. Cool', he thinks he can do whatever he wants. And then he had the nerve to act like I was the one being a jerk,"

She stopped, and I was sure that she expected me to say something. I started, not really sure what my point would be, "Yeah, the world's full of slime like that. People who think that they own everybody else," I paused, trying to think of what I'd say next. She took over instead, though.

"I just wish that there were more guys like you," I didn't know if she was looking for an answer to that; if so then I certainly wasn't prepared for it. But, maybe it was just something she let slip out - something kind of embarrassing - because neither of us said anything for the rest of the song.

Chapter 5

Ray Penner always said that his least favorite part of basketball was trying out for the team. He hated the idea that if he played badly for a couple of hours, it could prevent him for making the team. Of course, as his coach told him, playing bad for just a couple hours could cost his team a couple of games. It was a mute point either way for Penner, though. He always played well.

***

Try-outs were a two-day affair. Each day was pretty much the same: it started with a free shooting period, where notes would be taken on players' individual habits. Then the coaches would watch us do lay-ups. This was followed by running set plays, and then some defense monitoring. After that, depending on the position a player intended to play, there would be both rebounding or ball handling and three-point shooting drills. Finally, everybody would be asked to shoot ten free throws.

Deciding whether or not someone made the team was totally up to Mr. Resont, the gym teacher who coached varsity. The day after try-outs were over, he'd post his picks for the team. For me, it seemed like the longest wait of my life.

***

Chris and I walked into the gym together, for that first day of try-outs. The room virtually overflowed with people. There must have been nearly one hundred guys in there, all fighting over rebounds, trying to make steals; putting up the kind of shots that they felt, if they made, would land them on the varsity team. Mr. Resont strolled over to us.

"Hey Mike," he said plainly to me, and then looked at Chris, and extended his hand. "I'm Coach Resont. If you're any good, you'll probably be seeing a whole lot of me this year," He then walked away. That had always been his way, from what I'd heard; during try-outs he acted cold and hard, to get students to respect him. Once the practices started, he's just like anyone of the guys on the team.

FREE THROW

We started out at the least crowded basket we could find. It was a struggle to get any shots off; no-one was passing, and everybody went up for every rebound. I only managed to get off two shots - one was off a feed from Chris (he was trying to show off his passing skills), which I hit from around the free throw line.

As for the other shot, just after I released it from outside the perimeter, it was batted away from its destination, by someone behind me. I spun around, to see that it was a smiling Travis Ribalow who made the play.

"Hey Travis, glad you decided to come," I said.

"Yeah, I figured, why not give it a try?" he explained.

Shortly after that, all of the official drills began. Everything really went pretty well, until it came time to shoot free throws.

I was always a good foul shooter, so I hadn't been too worried about this part. Coach Resont bounced me the ball, and I dribbled it three or four times, before releasing my shot. The ball bounced off the back of the rim, and then slid to the ground, never passing through the hoop.

But I wasn't too concerned. I got the ball for a second time, and bounced it a few times again. All leading up to a shot that simply careened off the front of the rim. This sort of thing - the misses - continued as I was off on the third and fourth tries as well. Finally, I banked in the fifth. Then I missed the sixth, but swished the seventh. The eighth and ninth missed, though.

I was down to my last shot. Despite having missed the majority, swishing the last one would make me not look quite so bad. It would display my ability to stand up under pressure. So I took the ball that final time, and took my time dribbling, and then lining up with the basket. Finally, I shot what I thought was the perfect free throw.

If I had put just a little extra force in, my prediction would've proven correct. However, though my shot was right on line, it was an air ball.

***

I had been angry with myself when exiting the gym, and decided to pass on the ride home with Chris that I had previously arranged. I borrowed a ball from Coach Resont, and went outside to the old hoops in back of the

FREE THROW

building. I wasn't long into my practicing that I spotted Mr. Nicholes, walking towards me, with a rusty, metal folding chair in hand.

He was known as one of the kinder faculty members. I recalled the last time I had seen him; about a month before the school year had began, with his incredible shot at the park.

I stopped shooting as he got closer. I watched him as he unfolded the chair, and placed it directly underneath the basket. "Sit down there," he said, and I obeyed, not really sure what was going on. He continued, "I saw your shooting today at try-outs - not so hot. So, I figured you'd want to be improving, and if that's what you want, then I know how you can do it,"

"I'm listening," I replied.

"All right, what you're gonna do is shoot the ball up, so it goes straight through the hoop, and then drops right down. Understand?"

"Yeah, I think so," I really did understand his directions - but not what the purpose of it was.

"Then get to it," he said, and I began. The first few times I couldn't get it through at all, and then I struggled in getting it to come back down. Mr. Nicholes watched, without saying a word. Finally, I made one. "Now you've got the idea," he re-began, "So let's see you make ten straight,"

"You've got to be kidding me - it took me that long to make one and."

"Hey, this method works. You ever heard of Dana Barros?"

"Yeah... he's a basketball player... with the Celtics,"

"That's right. You'd say that he's a pretty good shooter, wouldn't you?" I nodded. "I know for a fact that he used this exercise. Now, if you don't trust me, and don't want to do this, I'll scram..."

"No, I'm sorry. I'll keep trying," And with that I fired up the ball once more, and made it again. I got up to four in a row, before missing.

"That's all right, just keep working at it. You'll get it," Mr. Nicholes said as he handed me the rebound. It took close to twenty minutes, but eventually, he proved right; I was able to do it. "Stand up," he said at that point. He picked up the chair, and placed it about a foot back. "Now, sit down again and don't get up until you make ten in a row," As it turned out, we continued like this for quite a while; he'd keep moving the chair back, little by little, and making me shoot. By the end, I was getting the ten in a row pretty quickly.

FREE THROW

Finally, he grabbed the chair, pulled it over to the side, and sat down on it himself. "Now," he said, "Step back a few steps, and keep your eyes on the basket" I did as he said. "Stop!" he said in a moment, and then proceeded to say, "Shoot!"

I did and swished the shot. In a moment, I realized that there I was... standing at the free throw line. I drained nine more shots, to achieve the goal Mr. Nicholes had been leading toward.

"Hey, Mr. Nicholes, thanks a lot," I said as he began to walk away, confident that he had done his job.

"No problem," he said without turning back to me, as he strolled into the school.

***

The next day, at try-outs, I made every shot I took. This performance more than compensated for my poor play the day before, and at the end, Coach Resont accosted me.

"That was some shooting today, Mike!"

"Thanks..." I started.

"Good enough for me to say you're on varsity,"

"Th....thanks," I had been fairly confident about making the team. Still, in that moment when it had actually came to pass, it was a surprise. It was also accompanied by a great feeling of both relief and joy. "Thank you Mr. Resont," I finished.

"Hey, call me 'Coach'," he said with a smile as he started to walk away.

I was thrilled, and knew that I had spotted one other guy who in the same situation - knowing that he was on the team already. Shawn Vetter, the team leader from the previous year, was a senior that year, and had grown to be 6'5" and able to dunk with ease. He would have to be starting center - or possibly the power forward, if Travis slipped in. Either way, I was sure that this would be a great team, and I was determined to do whatever was necessary.

***

FREE THROW

Just about everyone who tried out, rushed to the gym at the start of school on the following day, to check whether or not they had made the team. Even though I already was aware of my placement, I stopped by. Most of the faces that passed me wore frustration and grief, but I wouldn't let them get to me. It was my moment.

As soon as I stepped into the gym, Chris, who had come to school early to check the roster, raced toward me, and said excitedly, "I'm on the team! I'm on the team!"

"All right!" I said as we exchanged high fives. Travis was next to run up to me, with the same news.

We left the gym so we wouldn't be so tightly packed in, and then stood in the hall to talk. Erin passed by us, and after overhearing what Chris was saying, asked him, "You made the varsity basketball team?"

"Uh... yeah," he stuttered out.

"Congratulations," she smiled.

"Thanks," he replied, still a bit surprised that she was talking to him.

"Your welcome," she said as she started to walk away.

I waited until she was out of earshot to say, "What's up with that?"

"I don't know," Chris began, "One minute she says I'm bugging her or something... now she's all friendly... hey, this is a great day!"

"Wait, do you like that girl?" Travis asked. Chris nodded, and Travis went on, "But, she's, like, a senior. Do you really think you've got a shot with her?"

"Before, I would've asked the same question," Chris said, "But now... who knows?"

"Hey... I told you that talking to her would lead to good things," I put in.

We stopped talking as Shawn Vetter approached us. "You guys make the cut?" he asked.

"Yeah," I answered. I thought about asking him if he had, but I realized that everyone already knew the answer to that question.

"Cool," he said, and started giving us all high fives. "Welcome aboard,"

***

"Trick or treat," Chris and I said simultaneously.

FREE THROW

"Ah... well, you two are taller than most of the kids I've been seeing tonight," said the middle-aged, balding man, as he tossed a handful of tiny, generic candies into each of our bags.

Chris and I did our fake laughs and thanked him before going. "You know, I have to say, this Halloween thing isn't a bad gig," Chris said. "I mean, here we are, walking around, wearing jackets with the hoods up, and people are just giving us candy. I can't *believe* I gave this when I was a kid, because I thought it was 'babyish.'"

"Ah, another wasted youth," I said.

"There's just one thing missing," he said, while pulling a carton of eggs from his bag, "But, oh look, it's not missing any more!"

"Come on man, egging houses? That's kinda low. And besides, why would you want to egg this guy's house?"

"Did you see what he gave us?" He pulled one of the candies out of his bag, and read the label aloud, "Grimbles. What the heck 'Grimble'? The least he could've done was give us some generic chocolate,"

"Lis..." I stopped as two blond boys and a blond girl ran past me - none of them looking as though they could've been any older than six. "Hey, uh should we follow them?"

"What?"

"I mean, those were a bunch of really little kids, running outside at night, without parental supervision. I mean, shouldn't we make sure it's all okay... that they're not lost or anything,"

"What office are you running for? Seriously - it's Halloween - the night of free candy and vandalism with impunity. And you want to go be a good Samaritan, and baby-sit those kids?"

"What can I say - I have a conscience. Listen, I just want to make sure they're okay. With kids that little, we can catch up with them pretty quick, check the situation, and if all is good, then we can go back to trick or treating. We'll only have lost, like, five minutes,"

"Yeah, but suppose they do need help? You can consider our Halloween festivities over,"

"That's, like, the point - if they need help, we have to give it to them - that's the whole point of catching up with them,"

"Oh," He stopped, apparently considering.

"Look, if you don't want to go, then we can just split up - I'll attend to the kids, and we can meet up some place later,"

FREE THROW

"I'm definitely not splitting up... do you know how pathetic a high school student looks, trick or treating *alone*? If you've gotta do this, I'm there with you,"
"That's the spirit. Let's go catch up with 'em." We began jogging in the direction we had seen the kids go. In a few minutes, we caught up with them, getting candy from an old woman in her home.
"All right, let's go see what's up," I said.
"Wait, *first* let's go see that old woman. I saw what she was giving out - M&Ms! That's name brand chocolate. We have to stop,"
"We can do it in a minute. Come on, let's go check on the kids,"
Chris sighed deeply, looked at me, and said in an exasperated tone, "Fine,"
"Mark, I'm tired," the girl, who was dressed up as some sort of fairy, said as we approached.
"We'll just stay out for a little longer," the boy in a tiger suit answered. "I just want to hit a few more houses,"
"Hey," I started, "Are you kids supposed to be out here alone?"
"No," the girl started.
"Shut up," that same boy said, "Yeah, we're just out her trick or treating by ourselves,"
"Why is it that I'm not believing you, young man?" Chris said, using a deep voice, and a touch of sarcasm.
"We ran away from our sister," the girl said, "'Cause we didn't want to go in so early. But now I'm tired, and I think we're lost..."
"We're fine!" the boy said to his sister, and then turned to us. "Thanks for trying to help us, but we're okay,"
"Umm... I'd like to believe you," I said, "But I'm just a little worried. I mean, it's not safe out here for kids like you to out on your own... especially if you're lost. So, where do you kids live?"
"Fisher Street," the other boy, in zombie make up, answered.
"Okay," I started, "That's not too far aw..."
"What'd you say your sister's name was?" Chris broke in.
"Erin," the girl answered.
"Whoa," I forgot about the kids for a moment, and turned to Chris, "Are we talking about *Erin* Erin?"
"Do you know her?" the girl asked.
"Yeah, I think so," Chris answered, and nodded to me.

FREE THROW

"Okay, kids," I began, "Uh, hey Chris, what're we gonna do?"

"Me?! I don't know! Um... where did you guys see Erin last?"

"I don't know... somewhere," the boy in the tiger suit said.

"All right," Chris said, "How about if we split up... I'll find Erin - you stay nearby with the kids,"

"Not a bad plan. All right, go for it," He gave me a thumbs-up, turned, and started to walk away. "Oh, Chris," I stopped him.

"Yeah?"

"Don't stop... not even for name-brand chocolate," I smiled. He glared back.

We stood for a while in silence. Then the zombie boy asked, "Hey, can we go to a couple more houses?"

"Na... I think we'd better stay right here," I answered.

"But, come on... we can just stop by a couple houses, right here in the neighborhood. We don't have to go too far..."

"I'll tell you what..." I sighed, "You can go down to the end of the street, but then come back here, all right? I'll wait here for Chris and Erin,"

"Okay!" they all said at once, and ran up to the doorstep of the next house. I watched after them for a little while, and then sat down on the sidewalk and just waited.

***

Panic didn't really set in until about fifteen minutes later. That's when it suddenly donned on me that the kids should've been back long ago. I stood up, and looked around. There were a decent number of kids out; but the ones I was looking for were nowhere to be seen. I looked to my right, and saw Erin and Chris coming in the distance. They didn't seem to notice me, so I ducked behind some cars, parked along the curb, and hurried off before they could see me. The blame had been passed onto my shoulders. I had let them go off on their own, without giving a thought to the consequences of my actions.

I hoped that they had decided to disobey my instructions - and gone further than I had told them to. But I feared the worst - that bullies had beaten them up and taken their candy, or even worse yet, that someone had abducted them.

FREE THROW

I sped to the last house on the street. A young woman was dropping candies into kids' bags. When she was done, I asked her, "Have you seen three blond kids going around without any parents, or anyone? One was... uh... dressed like a tiger or something, and there was girl..."

"Yes, honey, about ten minutes ago. I thought it was weird that they'd have no-one looking after them. But when I asked 'em about it, they said they were fine."

"Umm.. did you see which way they went?"

"I think they turned at the corner over there. Umm.. are they lost, or in trouble or something? I could call the police for you..."

"No need for that," I laughed nervously, "Thanks for your help," I finished as I turned and walked away.

While I walked, I kept checking my watch. Minutes flew by. Every so often, I'd stop at another house, to find out whether or not anyone had seen the kids. Most of the people couldn't remember, after having seen so many kids that evening. As more time went on, I stopped less frequently, not wanting to lose any time in catching up with them.

I hadn't realized how long or far I had gone until I was standing in front of Steve's house. I decided to stop there.

"Hey man, what's going?" Steve asked when he saw me.

"Hey, I'm looking for these three kids that I was supposed to be watching. Two boys, one girl, all pretty short... a tiger, a fairy and some kind of monster, I think. Have you seen them?"

"No man. At least, I don't remember seeing them. Why were you baby-sitting a bunch of kids, anyway?"

"Long story. I don't really have time to explain it now," I glanced at my watch. "Geez... I gotta get back, and tell them what happened,"

"Who is 'them'?"

"I promise I'll tell you everything later. But for now, I've got to go,"

"See ya," Steve said as I left. I ran back toward the meeting place. About a block away from my destination, I stopped. All three kids, and Pepper, were rounding a corner, as I came to it.

"Hey, it's Mike!" shouted the girl.

"Oh... my... God," I said as I tried to catch my breath. "I can't believe it! I finally found you guys!"

"Is Erin mad? Is she gonna tell Mom and Dad?" the kid in the tiger suit asked me.

FREE THROW

"I... I don't know," I was still gasping for breath. I suddenly remembered Pepper, and tried to hide my tiredness. "I mean, I haven't talked to her yet. I've been looking for you three for the last forty-five minutes. Where did you go?" I said as calmly as I could manage.

"Well, we just went to a few more houses..." started the zombie kid.

"But then we got lost!" the girl interrupted. "And Mark said he knew how to get back, but he just got us really really lost!" The boy in the tiger suit glared at her, and she stuck her tongue out at him in retaliation.

"So, hey Pepper," I said, trying to be casual.

"Hey... umm are you okay?" she asked.

"Yeah," I laughed, "It's just been a really long night,"

"Were you... uh... baby-sitting?"

"Well, kind of. You see a friend of mine was taking them around trick or treating, and they ran away from her. Then my buddy Chris and I found them, and while Chris was trying to find our other friend, they got away from me too,"

"A-ha. Well, I guess that really would kind of mess up your evening," she grinned.

"Yeah, you could say that," I smiled back, "So... uh, how did you find them?"

"Actually, they found me," she smiled. "They were walking along, and when they saw me, they said they were lost. So, like the good citizen I am, I started walking with them, planning to take them home. That's when we ran into you,"

"Well, I'm sure glad I found you," I stopped, and laughed, "I mean... you know, met up with you,"

"Yeah, of course," It was a horribly awkward moment. Even if she hadn't seen any double meaning to my comment, she had to have caught on after my back talk.

"So, anyway," I went on, "We'd better go meet up with my friends... and get these kids home,"

"Yeah, absolutely," she said.

"Hmm... so what were you doing out here anyway?" I asked, as we walked.

"Ah, just walking around," she answered.

"Just walking around? Pretty odd night for a moonlight stroll..."

FREE THROW

"Hey!" the kid in the tiger suit turned around, and said, "Are you two boyfriend and girlfriend?"

"Um..." Pepper started, but then trailed off. I didn't want to say anything that would make it seem like I was revolted by the idea or anything, but I did have to say something.

In a moment, the perfect line came to me. "Are you kidding? A girl this pretty... with me? No way," We exchanged winks. It was perfect. But then the little girl moved back and walked next to me.

"I'll be your girlfriend," she said, in what, under other circumstances, I would have considered an incredibly cute way. Goodbye to potential romantic situation.

We continued to walk, until we reached the meeting spot again. There, Chris and Erin sat out on one of the front porches, talking.

"There you are!" he said. "Where have you been?! We were waiting for, like, fifteen minutes," As he spoke, Erin checked on the kids.

"Don't you ever do that again!" she scolded them. "You had me worried, and now," she stopped, and looked at her watch, "Damn it! It's after nine," She turned to Chris, I. "I have to be getting these kids home," she said, standing up, and walking toward the street, where Pepper, and I stood. "Thanks for everything," she said directly to Chris, and then started off with the kids.

"Well, I suppose it's a little late for me too," Pepper said. "I guess I'll see you guys later," she finished and walked off by herself.

"Bye," I said slowly. Chris and I just stood there for a while.

"So... sorry for making you wait," I said as we started to walk home.

"Don't mention it," he said, happily. "I just got to spend twenty minutes talking to Erin Devron... it was definitely worth it."

"Well, in that case, you're welcome,"

"Yeah," Chris laughed. "So how about Pepper... what was going on there?"

"Ah... she found the kids, after I lost them again, and then we walked back together. Not much to tell,"

"I'll bet you liked that little walk, though. Eh?" Chris said, and nudged me.

"Yeah... it was pretty cool," I said.

FREE THROW

"Meanwhile, I think I might've scored some major popularity points with Erin tonight. I mean, she was worried about the kids and all, but I got her to laugh and all... so that's a step,"

"Indeed," I smiled. "So, are you ever going to make your move?"

"I'll tell you this much... me *ever* making my move became a lot more likely tonight,"

We didn't say much more during our walk. I guess we both had other things on our minds- namely Pepper and Erin. If nothing else, through all of the hardships, and troubles, we each had gotten to spend some quality time with our respective favorite people.

"See you later," I said when we got to my house.

"Yeah. Later," he said, and walked away.

Chapter 6

Ray Penner was in his own world when he played basketball. He hated hearing his teammates moan about not having any free time to hang out with their friends, because of practices and games. Penner would tell them to leave the team if they didn't want to play. No-one ever did, though.

***

I started to miss practicing with Pepper almost as soon as we stopped. It got all the worse as November rolled around. Between my basketball practices and Pepper's play rehearsals, it was impossible to be able to spend time with her outside of school, even if I could have made an excuse to do so.

We still did talk on the phone occasionally, though. She no longer asked to work on memorizing lines; she seemed pretty sick of the whole thing whenever I brought it up. She did seem to like hearing about basketball, though. We usually talked pretty late at night, so maybe it was just a sedative for her. Either way, I would enjoy it.

The basketball practices weren't quite as much fun. Coach had us working hard almost every day, in preparation for our first game, on the twentieth. He said that with the talent he saw in us, he expected one of the best teams the school had ever had. For all my effort, I could only hope he was right.

Travis was clearly a project; a player who had a long way to come, before meeting his full potential. Coach selected him to play varsity because of the old basketball adage that 'you can't teach height', figuring that he could make anyone that tall into a star.

Travis first displayed his shortcomings during the shooting drills. No matter where he shot from, he couldn't seem to do any better than just grazing the backboard. This naturally discouraged Coach, and the rest of the team.

Travis shocked us all, though, when we began scrimmages. He was pretty slow coming up on defense - that was what we all noticed first, causing us more turmoil. But that's when it happened. Shawn, who was on the opposing team, shot a long jumper, and Travis swatted it down.

FREE THROW

Someone else on that other team fired a three. Travis blocked him too. Nearing the end of practice, he had already accumulated fifteen blocks by my count. His defining moment was still yet to come, though. Shawn went up, holding the ball over his head, and was about to score, with a powerful dunk. To the shock of everyone there, Travis' sixteenth block came right there - annihilating Shawn's attempt.

The center position wasn't the only one that deserved attention though. Brad Davies and Chris were both very capable players, lobbying for playing time at the point guard position. Chris was probably the best 'pure' point guard, as the so-called experts like to term it - meaning that he tended to look to pass before taking a shot for himself. Brad was more well-rounded, though, in my somewhat biased opinion, he was a bit of a ball hog.

It seemed pretty clear that I would start at shooting guard. Shawn was the best player on the team, period. The Highman brothers, my friend Greg and his sibling, George, would be sharing time at the small forward position. Again, because of my being able to see everything from inside, I can't be completely impartial. But the team really seemed to be shaping up, as one with a lot of talent, that I felt confident would win a lot of games.

It was a week and a day before the first game, that Coach formally announced the starting five. Brad beat out Chris at point guard. I was starting shooting guard. Greg was chosen to start over his brother, because of his quickness advantage. Shawn was moved to the power forward slot, to make room for Travis at center.

***

"Hey Mike!" I turned, to find Pepper coming from behind me at my locker.

"Oh, hey!" I answered, trying to control the enthusiasm I felt just by seeing her, but probably not doing the best job at it. "What's up?"

"Well, I just wanted to let you know that I will be at your first game tonight, so you'd better play well."

"Actually, I was planning on just losing this game, but since you're going to be there, I guess I could oblige, and make a few shots," I joked. It was a pretty corny thing to say, of course, but I just couldn't seem to help it.

FREE THROW

"Oh good," Pepper smile.
"Hey Pepper! Mike," Steve greeted us as he arrived from behind us.
"Hi," Pepper smiled.
"Hey," I answered, less enthusiastically.
"So, I couldn't help overhearing that you'll be attending the big game," Steve said, shifting all of his attention to Pepper after all of the formalities were out of the way. "I was just wondering if you might be interested having an escort for tonight's festivities - namely, me,"
"Well, I wouldn't want to impose on you..." Pepper started.
"Who's imposing? We'll have a great time. What do say we meet outside the school tonight, around 7:30,"
"Okay," Pepper smiled. "Sounds like fun,"

***

Coach hadn't hidden the fact that we had a very strong team that year. After advertising the game during each of his gym classes, and putting up promotional flyers all throughout the school, a huge crowd filled the gymnasium for our first game, against Nilesboro.

During the pre-game shoot around, I wasn't focused on basketball at all. Between shots, I scanned the crowd in search of Pepper. I rationalized the situation - thinking that if I played well enough, it wouldn't matter that Steve was with her that night - she'd have to be thinking of me.

I felt a tap on my shoulder as I lined up for a three-point shot. Alicia had left the rest of the cheerleaders, and was standing beside me. "Mike," she started, "This is a really important game for the whole school. You know that, right?"

"Uh... yeah, I guess,"

"Okay, so as much as I know that you're still obsessed with me," she said, rolling her eyes, "You really have to pay attention to just basketball tonight, and not let me distract you,"

"Don't worry about it," I answered, in as calm and cold a tone as I could manage. I then drained my shot. Alicia pretended not to notice, as she rejoined the other cheerleaders.

***

FREE THROW

"Mike," Travis whispered to me, "I'm really worried about..."

"Look," I broke in, "You have nothing to be worried about. I know this is your first organized basketball game. But don't sweat it. Just get rebounds, and block shots. That's what you're here for,"

"That's not really what I'm worried about," he said, hesitantly.

"What is it then?" Travis didn't say a word - he just gestured toward the sidelines. I followed the path of his gesture with my eyes. It led straight to Karen, waving one of her pompoms in the air, like all of the other cheerleaders.

"See what I mean?" Travis began. "What if I get fouled, and have to shoot free throws? Or what if I have a wide open shot. I'll look dumb if I don't take it,"

"Look, you're not going to get the ball much on offense. And if you have an open shot, just don't take it. You owe that much to the team,"

"But, wait... I just thought of something. I mean, why should I assume that I'll miss everything? If I can make, like, a three-pointer or something, I'll look like a hero,"

"All right, back over to the bench!" Coach called out.

"Look man, don't forget what has happened in the past. I've seen you shoot. I'm not saying this to be mean, but you're *not* a shooter," I doubt that he heard a word I was saying, as we both jogged to the bench, and the crowd became louder in anticipation of the game starting in a moment. Coach began giving us his pre-game speech, the instant we had all arrived at the bench. It was too late to give any more advice. All that was left was the game.

***

The public address system sounded scratchy at best, as both teams' starting line-ups were announced. Shawn received the loudest ovation. Travis was an attention grabber - for his tremendous height. However, any aura of invincibility that his height may have provided, disappeared as he tripped over himself, jogging onto the court.

"Did she notice? Did she notice?" he whispered to me.

"What?"

"Karen - did she notice?"

FREE THROW

"Yeah, I think everyone in the building noticed. But look, that doesn't matter. You can't spend the whole game trying to impress her..."

"No!" he interrupted, "You're wrong! That's exactly what I have to do - especially now!"

"Travis!" I yelled after him, when he turned and walked to center court for the tip off. He ignored me.

***

Travis controlled the opening tip, knocking it to Greg. The defense immediately swarmed toward Shawn. Not seeing an open man, besides Travis, Greg handed it off to the center, right outside the three-point line.

Travis hesitated, and for a moment, I thought he had come to his senses. However, after that moment, he released the shot.

The ball careened hard, off of the upper right corner of the backboard, out of bounds. If he wasn't before, Travis had surely then become little more than a joke for virtually everyone in the gymnasium. I glared at him, when I was sure he would notice. He hung his head as he ran back on defense.

Probably assuming that Travis' ineptitude extended to his defense, Nilesboro's point guard threw the ball inside, to his center. The center tried a hook shot. Travis blocked him. The guy I was guarding recovered the ball, and shot a long jumper over me, which missed. Travis snagged the rebound.

Brad got the ball, and passed ahead to me, as I ran to half court. Shawn sprinted ahead of me, and when I reached the three-point line, he was already waiting, beside the basket. I lobbed him the ball, for the alley-oop dunk. The crowd's cheering reached its loudest point of the evening at that moment.

We moved straight ahead from there. We had eight points before our opponents made their first basket. That occurred when Travis missed a dunk attempt, leading to Nilesboro scoring off a lay-up at the other end. Following that play, I was fouled on a three-point shot and made all of the free throws. Then Brad made a jumper, and Shawn got a dunk and a lay-up. Finally, I hit two foul shots, before Nilesboro broke our second run with a three-pointer.

FREE THROW

Things were far from perfect, though. After Travis' initial displays, it was agreed silently that he wouldn't touch the ball again on offense. After several possessions, he began to notice, and call, "I'm open! I'm open!" when we had the ball. It was hard to hide that we were freezing him out.

At the end of the first quarter, we were ahead, 25-12. Before Coach could say a word, Travis shouted above the crowd, "Why are you guys keeping the ball from me?!"

"'Cause we didn't know what you were playing!" Greg yelled back, "But it wasn't basketball!"

"All right, so I blew a couple shots..."

"Travis," Coach broke in, "You're here for defense and rebounding. We want to be able to get the ball to you, but we have to know that you'll be willing to pass it, or only shoot if you know that you can make it,"

Travis looked to me, and I simply nodded. He looked to Shawn, and he did the same. Travis went through most of the team like this, before nodding himself, and saying, "All right,"

The score was 54-25 at half time. Travis was back in the game, the way he was supposed to be. As we walked toward the locker room, I heard Pepper's voice call my name.

"Hey Pepper," I answered. "And Steve," I added when he came beside her. They stood over me, up on the bleachers, and hanging over the railing as we talked.

"Hey Mike. Good game you have going there," Steve smiled, as he nestled closer to Pepper. She didn't seem to notice.

"Umm... thanks... I've been a little off my game, though. I mean, I barely made that ninth straight free throw..."

"You know," Steve cut me off, "I was just telling Pepper about my band, in which I play lead guitar and do back up vocals," He turned to Pepper, "Hey, did I tell you yet that we're talking about putting out our own CD next summer?"

"Umm... great," Pepper said. I worried that our competition was becoming too obvious. I wasn't about to give up, though.

"So, do you guys remember that last play, where I got the ball, and...."

"Hey, Weaver!" George Highman called out. "Coach says to get your butt in the locker room, now!"

FREE THROW

"Oh, umm... well, I'll see you guys later, all right?" I said quickly to Steve and Pepper.

"Yeah, see you later," Pepper smiled.

"Yeah, later," Steve said as he licked his lips, behind Pepper.

***

Nilesboro started to make a comeback in the third quarter, making the score 64-50. We were never in any serious danger of losing, though. With only nine seconds remaining in the game, we were ahead, 85-63. That's when I got fouled, going to the basket.

As I made my way to the line, Shawn whispered into my ear, "Miss the last one," and winked as he positioned himself next to the basket. I swished the first shot, and then prepared to set Shawn up for the play on the second.

My intention was to shoot the ball too hard, so that it would bounce off the backboard to Shawn for his dunk. However, after nailing the backboard, the ball caught an edge of the rim, knocking it to the other side of the rim. Back and forth it went for longer than I'd ever seen a shot go, before finally dropping into the basket.

Shawn looked a little disappointed about the turn of events. He compensated, though, by intercepting a long Nilesboro pass, dribbling back down to the basket and dunking hard at the buzzer. We had won the game, 89-62.

On my way off of the court, Karen stopped me. "Hey, can I talk to you for a sec?" she asked.

"Yeah, sure. What's up?"

"It's... uh... about Travis," she paused, and then continued, "I don't want to say anything if I'm wrong, but I've been getting the impression that he, you know, *like* likes me. I mean, was it me... that made him do those things at the beginning of the game?"

I sighed. "Look, he really wouldn't want for me to say anything... but, yeah... he really likes you," Karen covered her face with one of her pompoms. "But," I went on, "You know, don't blame yourself for anything he did tonight. It's not your fault,"

FREE THROW

"Oh, no. I don't really care about that... well, I mean of course I do, because Travis is a good friend and all, and I want the team to do well. God, I sound like a rambling moron."

"Okay, slow down Karen," I said, "Just tell me what you're trying to say,"

"I'm trying to say that I really like Travis in that really good guy friend way, but not like *that*. And I don't know what I'm supposed to do about this,"

"I could talk to Travis..."

"No," she interrupted. "I don't want to drag you into this too. It's not right,"

"Okay. But if you change your mind, just say so,"

"Yeah," she smiled, "And thanks Mike,"

***

As I pulled on my T-shirt, Travis talked to Chris and I in the locker room. "After that first quarter, I think the game went really well for me. I mean, I had seven blocks, and a ton of rebounds. And I know I saw Karen smiling after I stuffed that little guy... number ten,"

"Look, no offense," Chris started, "But isn't thinking about what Karen thought, what got you in trouble in the first place?"

"Hey," I broke in. "I think Travis' romantic ventures are his own business. He knows how to keep his personal life separate from his basketball. And I'm sure... you know, if he were to get any signs from Karen that she didn't like him, that he'd just move on... right?"

"All except that last part," Travis began. "I mean, I've never felt this way about somebody before. There's just something about her..." as he droned on about her, I decided to just ignore him, before I ended up saying something that I shouldn't.

As he continued talking, I was handed the stat sheet from the game. My eyes flew directly to one line - free throws. I had made all fourteen that I had taken. For some reason, that just made me really happy for that moment. Happy enough to forget the rest of the world.

Chapter 7

The Boy Scouts' motto is the same as Ray Penner's was: "Always be prepared," More than anything else, he meant this mentally. In life, and on the basketball court, things often come about unexpectedly. Ray Penner wouldn't let any surprises hurt him in either respect.

***

Pepper and I ran into each other in the parking lot, walking toward school the following Monday. "So... nice game," was the first thing she said.

"Thanks. Did you have a good time with Steve?"

"Yeah, we had fun. This'll probably sound dumb, but it was the first time I ever went to a basketball game, so Steve kind of walked me through it,"

"*Steve* walked you through a basketball game?"

"Yeah. Oh, and congrats on making all of your touchdowns," she said. I couldn't help laughing. "What is it?" she asked, smiling. "Did I sat something wrong?"

"No," I said between giggles. It's just that I'm guessing Steve didn't tell you all of the right terms. I made all of my *free throws*. Touchdowns are a football thing. Steve doesn't really know much about sports, you see,"

"Oh... that's weird,"

"Why's that?"

"Well he was telling me about how he taught you how to play basketball. He even said that he'd be playing on the varsity team if he wasn't so busy with his band and all,"

"Gee," I smiled, "Steve must have seemed pretty impressive,"

"Well, yeah, kind of. I mean, he's... well, I thought he was good at, and knew about all of those different things. But actually, he seemed sort of arrogant, like he was trying to show off, or win me over or something," She paused. "Don't get me wrong, he's a really fun guy and all... just a little... odd,"

"Trust me, I understand totally. I've been friends with the guy for years, and I've thought exactly the same things at times," We both smiled.

FREE THROW

***

"So, you taught me how to play basketball?" I asked Steve, before homeroom officially began.

"Yeah, she seemed to like that one. I scored some big points there," Steve smiled.

"Well, I burst that bubble for her when we talked a few minutes ago. Seems like you'll have some explaining to do,"

"Hey, it's your word against mine, buddy boy. And I'll be sitting next to her for this whole homeroom period. I like those odds," He stopped, and then went on to say, "Hi Pepper,"

I turned to find that Pepper had arrived. "Hi Steve. Hey again, Mike," she said.

"Hey," I answered, as the bell rang.

"All right, everybody get to your seats," the teacher called out. Steve waved mockingly as I walked away.

"So, good game the other night, Mike," Alicia said when I arrived at my desk.

"Oh, thanks. Umm... good job with the cheering and all,"

"Well, look at mister 'I'm better than everyone else'," she fired back, using an offended tone.

"What?"

"Cheerleading isn't just some sideshow... it's as much a sport as basketball. So you can get over your little ego trip,"

"I didn't mean any disrespect or anything. I was just saying..."

"Mr. Weaver!" the teacher cut me off, "The no talking during roll call rule applies to everyone. Your athletic achievements do not set you above anyone else in this room!"

"I'm sorr..."

"I said for you to be quiet, Mr. Weaver! One more outburst and you'll be sent to the principal's office,"

I simply nodded in response that time. Alicia shot me a triumphant smile, and then turned away.

***

FREE THROW

"So how goes it with Erin?" I said, while dribbling the ball back and forth between my legs.

"Oh, it goes," Chris answered. "I'd say we're making remarkable progress... you know, in a kind of subtle sense,"

"What does that mean?"

"There was an exchange of 'hi's and waves in the hall today. But it was more about what we each knew the other was thinking and *didn't* say,"

"Okay," I said slowly. "I'll just take your word on that one,"

"Hey... just you wait and see... by graduation time, we'll be engaging in full conversations... oh yeah, I can see it now,"

"Gee, just in time for her to go off to college, and forget that you exist,"

"I'm telling you, I'm opening up a whole new world to her, and when she sees that, she'll wait to be with me,"

"Are you really so sure? I mean, I want this to work out, but she's coming around pretty slowly... if at all. I don't know if you can ever convince her to go out with you,"

"Hence the extremely slow progression of things. Now, if you don't mind, we're out here, in this not so pleasant weather - we'd might as well play some ball," he said as a gust of wind blew the majority of his hair to one side.

"Okay, man," I said. I bounced the ball a few times, and then fired a long two pointer. "Ooh, nothing but net!" I called out as the shot fell in.

Chris grabbed the ball. "I'm telling you, I've got to get some more playing time in these games. I mean, I was only in there for, like, ten minutes,"

"Hey - Brad's the starter - I doubt it was anything personal,"

"Personal or not, I'm on this team to play - not sit on the bench,"

***

Chris got his wish. Before our second game, visiting Springfield, Brad sprained a finger during the practice, paving the way for Chris to start.

The year before, Springfield had been a tough team. However, the graduation of virtually all of the team's top players made them easy opponents for us this time around. We led by nineteen points at half time.

FREE THROW

It was early in the third quarter that I apparently upset the wrong guy. When a Springfield guard ran against me, in a one on one fast break, I gave him a hard foul as he took his shot. I did it purely as a strategic move for the game; not as a personal attack. However, the guard didn't take it that way. He retaliated by giving me a hard foul whenever I received the ball on offense. I didn't mind, though, as I continued my streak - making every free throw that I took. Meanwhile, the other guy just got deeper and deeper into foul trouble.

Very late in the game, when victory was already virtually sealed, my luck took a turn for the worse. Chris, Travis and I ran from one side of the court to the other, in a three on two fast break. I had noticed that from time to time, Travis' attention veered away from the game - to Karen on the sidelines. As he trailed about a yard behind me on that play, I noticed that same thing.

Chris dribbled toward the basket, luring in both defenders, and then tossed the ball out to me for the open three-pointer. I took aim, and then, a moment after I had left the ground for the shot, Travis, not looking where he was going, crashed into me. We both fell out of bounds.

Travis was sprawled at the feet of most of the cheerleaders, including Karen. I, however, had knocked over, and landed on top of Alicia.

"Get off me!" she screamed, and scrambled to her feet.

"I - I'm sorry..." I began, flustered. I stopped as she slapped me across the face.

"I know that you have this fairly unhealthy crush thing on me, but this lame attempt to get on top of me, is just..." she stopped and slapped me again.

Travis, perhaps even more embarrassed than me, kept apologizing to all of the cheerleaders. Meanwhile, a referee, probably feeling extremely out of his element, held back Alicia. I just held my face and watched the scene in disbelief.

"Hey, are you all right man?" Chris asked.

"Uh... yeah. Just kind of... shaken up,"

"Yeah, well the Jolly Green Giant just cost me an assist. That's one less assist that'll be taken into consideration when Coach is deciding how to split up the playing time,"

FREE THROW

"Don't sweat it... you're having a good game... I'm sure Coach is noticing. Travis and I are the only ones who have anything to worry about on this one,"

"Well everyone saw that it was Travis' fault... you don't have any problems," he stopped. "Oh... I guess you've got that one... the red head on the sidelines looks pretty pissed,"

"I would use the words, 'out to kill'... but 'pretty pissed' sums it up,"

"Hey, sorry, man," Travis jogged up and said to me.

"It's all right, but you've got to keep your head in the game, all right? There's only a couple minutes left. Just stay focused," I answered.

"Right," he said, and jogged away from us.

"You see that?" Chris said, "He didn't even apologize for screwing up my assist,"

"Relax man. It isn't worth the aggravation,"

***

The rest of the game went on with little of importance. In the end, we won with a score of 70-45. Shawn was not happy, though.

"Where is your head at?!" he scolded Travis in the locker room. "We've got a shot at having a successful team here... a team that people have to worry about! And then you go and pull a stunt like that - making the team a big joke!"

"I'm sorry," Travis said softly.

"Look," Shawn started more calmly, "I don't want to create any bad blood here, but you have to stay focused, all right? You're an important part of this team,"

"All right. It won't happen again," Travis said, and they slapped palms.

Alicia wasn't as forgiving as Shawn. Boarding the buses that would take us back to our school, she didn't seem happy at all when she caught sight of me.

***

FREE THROW

Alicia glared at me as I sat down next to her in homeroom. I tried to ignore her at first. But as I glanced over at her several times, to see her glare not breaking, I had to say something.

"All right, what is it?!" I paused and continued, just as Alicia was about to answer. "Wait, I know what it is. It's because of that little spill I had at the game..."

"Little spill?" she broke in, "You could've seriously hurt me with that stunt... jumping on top of me like that..."

"Let's clear a few things up," I interrupted her, "I didn't jump on you... I fell. Travis didn't see me in his path, and I didn't see him coming..."

"You didn't see him? How do you miss an eight-foot tall gorilla, running towards you?"

"I was focused on the game... on my shot! Travis ramming into me was an accident. My falling on you was a result of the accident. God, what makes you so permanently pissed off at me?"

"Maybe it's the fact that you're a loser. A worthless slime ball, who thinks that he belongs with me. Just because I seem to be the only one around her that notices it, doesn't mean it's not true,"

"What evidence do you have? If you want to call me a loser... that's your prerogative. But I don't have any feelings for you... at least not positive ones,"

"Sure," she said sarcastically.

"Get over yourself, Alicia. I know I have,"

After that comment, she seemed to lose her smugness. No snide comeback ensued. "What- are you out of insults?" I asked.

"Shut up," she said softly.

I was surprised by her sudden loss of energy, and apparently humble attitude. "Um... are you okay?" I asked cautiously.

"What do you care?" she asked, more angry than anything else at that point.

"I - I'm sorry if I said something wrong..."

"Just..." she said loudly, and then lowered her voice. "Just drop it," I looked at her, but she looked away. Alicia had puzzled me before, but at that moment, I had no idea about what to think.

Steve entered the room and immediately accosted me. "So, I made a big play in the Pepper department..."

"You like Pepper?" Alicia entered the conversation suddenly.

FREE THROW

"No!" I said quickly, not wanting Alicia to have any chance at interfering with my pursuit of Pepper.

"Not you... I know that you're still dedicated to me," she said - her spunk returned. She focused on Steve, "So, is it true? Are you holding out for Pepper?"

"That's not really any of your business, Curly Sue," he said, holding a strand of her curly red hair.

She turned her head to release the hair from his hand. "Keep your hands off me, monkey boy,"

"Ooh, monkey boy... that hurts, especially since I know that you are an authority on monkeys... you know, having owned all of those flying ones back in the Wizard of Oz,"

"Real cute. But actually, I just meant that you're a big, hairy, ugly, stupid primate, who appears to have missed a few crucial steps in the way of evolution,"

"Touché," Steve smiled. Alicia smiled back, mockingly. The bell rang, causing the teacher to end all discussion. Alicia's sudden mood swing had me even more confused than before.

Chapter 8

There are few big moments in a person's life. A lot people thought that Ray Penner had more of these moments than most. But, if you asked Penner himself, he'd say that he had about the same number of big moments as anybody. Sure, making an important shot could be a thrill. But Penner defined his really big moments as things that few people even know happened. Finding out something incredible, or doing something that was a great personal achievement were the sort of things that he thought of as "big". Sometimes even let downs could be big moments, because they were often what truly defined people.

***

As we were shooting around at the start of practice, Coach told the whole team to sit down on the bleachers. "All right," he began, "As you all know, our next game will be at Jorles on Friday night. This is going to be the toughest game we've had yet, and we'll be practicing a little differently today.

"Jorles' star player is Timothy Kahn. They've got some other good players out there, but he's the go to guy. So, we're scratching the usual man to man defense and going to a box and one," I knew who Kahn was. He had been the one I had played against at the park months earlier, and who had danced with Pepper before I did at the dance.

Coach went on, "For those of you who aren't familiar with this defensive concept, it's pretty simple. We play a regular zone style of defense except we'll have one guy sticking to Kahn. Shawn, he's all yours," Shawn nodded, and Coach continued, "If we can limit him to about fifteen points, we should get the win. So, to start out today, we'll have a scrimmage. Shawn and Mike, you are the captains. I want to see both teams using the box and one, with the captains sticking each other. Any questions?" no-one had any, so Shawn and I picked up sides and started to play.

The practice went well, in that it accomplished the goal of learning the tough defense. Shawn made seven shots, and I only got four attempts, three of which I converted into baskets.

FREE THROW

***

Each team put forth a different defensive strategy to start the game. We had our box and one of course, which held Kahn to only two points in the first quarter. Meanwhile, Jorles double teamed both Shawn and I, and left their center under the basket for shot blocking. We were ahead, 12-5 going into the second quarter; Shawn pulled off one short jumper and I hit three free throws. The others picked up the remaining scoring load.

The second quarter was a turning point, though. Kahn adjusted to the box and one, and poured in fourteen points in the quarter. Brad stepped up for us, to hit a pair of threes at the end of the quarter, but Shawn went scoreless, and I was limited to scoring with foul shots, draining each of my two attempts. Greg was the only other one of us to score, with his lay-up. The score was 29-22 in their favor, at the half.

In the locker room, Shawn was clearly upset. Coach wasn't too happy either. "In the first quarter, things were fine for us. But we're clearly slipping. We're dropping the box and one. Now, it's time to focus on everyone but Kahn. Let him get his ten points in the quarter, but don't leave anyone out there to help him," He paused, and turned to Shawn, "It's time for you to become the enforcer. You don't have any fouls yet, so show the guys some muscle. Make it so they're scared to get in your way, or challenge your defense," He then looked to me, "Mike, you haven't missed a free throw yet; keep slashing to basket. Get the field goal if you can, but either way, get to the line,"

"All right," I answered, and Shawn just nodded. At the start of the third quarter, Shawn waved off Chris, who was guarding their point guard. The scrawny player had been their best defender; something Shawn was about to put an end to.

As the guard tried to dribble past him, Shawn grabbed his jersey, and flung him to the ground. The guy didn't seem hurt, but was clearly shaken, and missed both of the free throws he tried.

On the other side, Shawn dunked the ball hard, then bent down and growled at the guy who at one of the guys who had been guarding him. The Jorles defense began to break down.

It was still a close contest, though. Going into the fourth period, we led: 54-53. Both of our teams' defense deteriorated further, leading to more threes. They were ahead by two with thirty seconds remaining.

FREE THROW

That's when I went up with the ball, and managed to bump into one of the Jorles players, while laying in the shot. I made the free throw, giving us a one-point lead. On the other end, their players moved around quickly, struggling for the last shot, which could bring victory. Finally, their point guard faked a three. Shawn, Brad and Greg all went up for the block, and ended up falling over each other on the way down.

Kahn cut free from me, and the ball was shoved inside to him. He fired a short jumper. It seemed that the game was all theirs. That's when Travis came up, out of nowhere, and swatted the shot all the way back to half court. All of the players from our bench leapt to their feet, as the rest of us rejoiced on the court. We had won.

However, luck, as well as hometown referee, was clearly on Jorles' side. The referee stopped our celebration, announcing that Travis had goal-tended the shot. We took a one-point loss.

It was discouraging to come so close to beating the best team in the league - only to fall short on a technicality. Still, we took things in stride; it was arguable that we should have won, and either way, we could handle having one loss on our record. The bus ride back home held the same atmosphere as it would usually have had after a win.

***

Between the game against Jorles, and the middle of the month, we had four straight wins. My free throw percentage was still perfect, and Shawn's scoring average of 38.5 was good enough to be tops in the league.

However, basketball was set aside for one Saturday night. It was opening night for the school's performance of Romeo and Juliet, and I wasn't about to miss Pepper's big moment.

Chris and I arrived later than we had intended. "I told you we should've left earlier," he said, glancing at his watch. "It's just three minutes before the show begins."

"It's not my fault that you didn't come pick me up until so late..."

"Well, if you want to get technical about it, that's my mom's fault... but that's not really where I was going with the blame placement... I was angling more towards you... so, uh... yeah. That's pretty much it."

"Whatever," I said as we came upon the auditorium. I pulled my wallet from my back pocket, and removed a crisp five-dollar bill.

FREE THROW

"It's $2.05 per person," the woman sitting outside the auditorium doors said.

"Here ya go... uh, that'll be for both of us," I said.

"Okay," She handed us each our ticket. "Now let me dig out your change," she said, as she began rummaging through the moneybox for the exact change.

"You're paying for me?" Chris asked. "Gee, that's really super nice,"

"It's just to save time," I turned back to the woman, "I'll tell you what... keep the change,"

"Hey, wait," Chris broke in, "If that money was for both of our tickets, in theory, that change is just as much mine as it is yours. So, please pass along that change here, ma'am,"

"Chris, we don't have time for this!"

"I always have time to pick up a free buck... college is expensive these days. The way I see it, this is just ninety cents less, that I'll actually have to earn somehow. Thank you," he said, as the woman dropped several coins into his hand.

"All right, let's hurry now," I said, pushing the auditorium doors open,"

"Holy crap," Chris said, looking past me.

"What?" I asked, and turned around to see what he had been talking about.

The auditorium was filled. There wasn't an open seat in sight - much less two together. It also appeared that we were even more lately than I had suspected, as the principal already stood on stage, greeting the audience.

Seconds after the principal concluded his remarks, Steve's voice yelled out, "Hey Mike!"

I looked around, to see where he was. However, just as I began looking, the auditorium was flooded by darkness - the only light to be seen being up on stage.

"Where is he?" Chris asked.

"Shhh!" someone said.

"I don't know," I said.

On stage, a group of people began to speak in unison, saying, "Two households, both alike in dignity,"

"Steve?! Where are you?" I called out.

"Shhh!"

FREE THROW

"Are you still at the door you came in on?!" Steve yelled back.

"In fair Verona, where we lay our scene," the performers spoke louder.

"Yeah!" Chris answered.

"Shhh!"

"Then go up the stairs, to the right upper level..."

"Right facing the doors, or the stage?!" I asked.

"From ancient grudge break new mutiny," the people on stage said, becoming a touch louder, and visibly annoyed by the distraction that we were creating.

"Facing the doors!" Steve yelled.

"Shhh!"

"Hey," I said hesitantly, "Maybe we shouldn't be yelling back and forth during the middle of the play,"

Chris glanced up at the stage, and then turned back to me, "Ah, I don't think they're noticing," He then yelled back to Steve, "All right, we're coming up!"

"When civil blood makes civil hands unclean!" the performers spoke, yelling themselves, at that point.

***

Near the start of Act I, Scene III, Pepper made her first appearance on stage.

"Go Pepper!" Chris called. He looked around, to find several people glaring at him. "Guess this isn't that type of crowd," He said, his voice lowered to a whisper.

Pepper looked puzzled on stage for a moment after Chris' comment, before returning her attention to the play.

"How now! Who calls?"

"Your mother," said another girl.

"Madam, I am here," Pepper said. "What is your will?"

"Man, she's hot," Steve said softly.

"Yeah," I answered, in agreement.

***

FREE THROW

Intermission came after the end of the second act. As Chris, Steve and I arrived on the ground floor, the principal, a teacher, and Alicia accosted us. "Are these the boys you said were doing all of the shouting during the show?" the principal asked Alicia.

"Yes, they are," Alicia answered.

"Wait a second, what are you guys talking about?" Steve asked.

"Remember when Mike and I walked in," Chris started, "And you were tel..."

Steve hit him in the chest to stop him. "I think that whatever or whoever you're looking for, you've got the wrong guys," he said, keeping his cool.

"I don't think so," Alicia said. "I saw those two come in right before the play started," she pointed at Chris and I, "And I recognized their voices calling back and forth. I'm sure it was them,"

The teacher joined in the conversation next, "I'm the director of this play, and we worked long and hard... way too long and hard to let you come in and ruin it..."

"And that's the last thing we would want to do," Steve said smoothly. "I think that there's just been some sort of mistake,"

The principal turned to me, "Michael, you're a varsity athlete... a part of this school. Now, I suggest that you tell us the truth. The only punishment you'll receive now is having to leave the play. If we find out you've lied... we're talking about a number of detentions... maybe even getting cut from the basketball team,"

I swallowed hard, and just stared back at the principal for a moment. "I think that his silence should be taken as an admission of guilt," Alicia said.

"Shut up," Chris said.

"Ooh," Alicia started, "That really hurt,"

"Enough you two," the principal said. "Now, tell us the truth,"

"Umm..." I began. I looked at Steve, who was subtly shaking his head. Chris just looked at me. Alicia smiled. "Uh... yeah, we did all the yelling," I said at last. "We didn't want to disrupt the play... that was never our intention. We just..."

"I don't want any excuses," the teacher said. "Get out of here,"

"Look, we paid to get in," Steve said, still calm, "And our reasons for shouting really weren't just to disrupt things... it was... practical,"

FREE THROW

"Hey," Pepper said, coming from behind us. "What's going on?"

"These are the people who were shouting at the start of the play... and probably were the same ones who hollered when you came out," the teacher explained.

"Yes, so they'll be leaving now," Alicia said brightly.

"Wait... you're kicking them out?" Pepper asked.

"Yes," the teacher said, "So you don't have to worry any more about their disruptions,"

"Wait, these guys are my friends... I don't think they meant any harm... I'm sure they'll behave for the rest of the play..." Pepper said.

"Absolutely," Chris slipped in, "All further disruptions will be due to us, only in the way that they're not,"

"What?" the principal asked, confused.

"He's being impudent, sir," Alicia said. "He's trying to insult you, with tricky wording..."

"Oh, will you shut up?!" Chris fired back.

"I don't like the tone of this exchange," the teacher said, "I think I'll have to ask you all to leave," Alicia smiled. "That includes you, Alicia," she finished.

"What? But... but..."

"No buts," the teacher went on. "Get. Get," she began to push us all towards the door.

"Wait," Pepper said, backing up along with us, as we were herded out of the auditorium, and then toward the exit of the building altogether. "I mean..."

The next thing I heard was a loud clatter and a scream. "I'm sorry. I'm sorry," a boy said over and over again. Pepper was on the floor, and a large bowl was broken on the ground. The French Onion dip that it had contained, covered Pepper.

"Ew..." Pepper began.

"I'm sorry," the boy went on, "I didn't see her coming... she just backed into me..."

"And what were you doing with... that?" I asked.

"It's dip..." he started nervously.

"We know what you are. Now what was in the bowl?" Chris said, and grinned.

83

FREE THROW

We all looked at him, and Alicia said what I think we all were thinking. "Could you have made a more lame comment?" Chris looked from one of us to another, continuing to grin, until he had seen that on one was amused.

"Okay...so I can't make a joke?" he paused to see no-one changing their expressions. "Okay... just checking," he finished meekly.

"So what's the deal with the dip?" I asked.

"Ew..." Pepper said again, looking at the backs of her arms.

The boy had only gotten more nervous. "It... I was carrying the dip over there... for the cast party. But then she backed into me. I didn't see her coming... I swear. I'm sorry..."

"Well..." the teacher started, turning to Pepper, and asking hesitantly, "How bad is it?"

Pepper tried to stand, and slipped back down, on the dip that had trailed onto the floor below her. "Ow... and ew."

"Oh my gosh," Alicia said, "It's all over you... and in your hair and everything. Gross,"

"It is?" Pepper said, her voice beginning to crack.

"Well, hey... it's not that..." Steve said, kneeling beside her.

"That's right," I said, not about to let Steve do all of the consoling. I knelt down on her other side. "It's just a little... gunk. I'm sure you can wash it all right out."

"But," the teacher began, "We can't put you back on stage with that... stuff..."

"It's dip... French Onion dip... it's really good," the boy put in.

"All over you," the teacher continued, ignoring the boy's interjection. "Or have you go out their soaking wet after you wash it all off,"

"But... the play's only half over..." Pepper tried.

"I'll go back stage right away, and tell Cynthia to get ready," the teacher said.

"Cynthia? M-my understudy?" Pepper stuttered.

"Who else? Just go get cleaned up, and be ready for the next show, tomorrow night," the teacher said to Pepper. She then refocused her attention on the rest of us. "You can all leave before we start the next act. And don't even *think* about coming back tomorrow night," With that, she stormed off.

"Oh... my... God," Pepper said.

FREE THROW

"I'm really sorry," the boy repeated.

"Just a tip," Chris said, coming up to him, "Those two guys... very devoted to that little lady. When they're done consoling her... if I were you, I'd be out of here," The boy listened, and hurried away.

"Here, I'll help you up," Steve said, offering his hand to her. She held his hand and worked her way to her feet, as I supported her back.

"Gross," I said to myself, looking at my hands, covered with dip, after Pepper had gotten on her feet.

"It is?" Pepper asked, her voice cracking again.

"No... not you... it's just... that stuff..."

"Look, I appreciate you guys being here," Pepper started, and paused as a tear rolled down her cheek. "But... but I really just want to be alone right now,"

"Pepper..." Steve began, but stopped as she ran off to the bathroom. He waited until she was gone, to speak again. "Man, that was some nasty crap,"

"Hmm... real nice comment about the girl you like. Maybe I should tell her you said that," Alicia said.

"Were you born this bi-" Steve started.

"Hey, let's not say something we're going to regret later," I broke in.

"Na... I don't think he would've regretted saying that," Chris put in.

"Why don't you go find your own conversation," Alicia said to Chris. "You know, one where everybody's at your intellectual level. Hey... I think I saw a few four year olds sitting up front, back in the auditorium..."

"Yeah, and I think that *you*... um... can shut up!" Chris paused before finishing, "I'll be going now... see y'all later, outside,"

As he left, Alicia said, "Well, that's one less moron to deal with. Now, if you two will excuse me, I'll go console Pepper,"

"I think that your face is the last thing that anyone who's already upset needs to see," Steve smirked.

"Very funny," Alicia said sarcastically. I grabbed her shoulder to stop her as she continued toward the bathroom.

"I think she wants to be alone," I said. "And I don't like the idea of you going in there and making her feel worse,"

"Hm... Pepper's two white knights. That's really cute. But you can take your greasy paw off of my arm now, and go away,"

FREE THROW

"Hey," Steve broke in, "I've got stuff to do, and don't really fancy the idea of staying here all night, debating with the Wicked Witch of the East. So, if you and Chris want a ride home, we should be going right about now,"

"Just a second," I said, "You can go, get the car revved up and everything. I'll meet you outside in a minute,"

"Okay," Steve said, and left.

"A-ha, I knew it," Alicia said. "You just wanted to get me alone to profess your love..."

"No," I said coldly. "Look, I'm worried about you Alicia,"

"You're worried about me? This oughta be good,"

"Alicia, I'm serious. A couple weeks ago in homeroom... we were arguing, and you almost broke into tears."

"Don't flatter yourself... you could never make me cry,"

"All right, then what was it?"

"It... it was... it was none of your business! Now, I'm going to go check on Pepper... alone. See ya!"

"Alicia, wait," I called out. She didn't listen. I still didn't know what to think about her, and decided to give up for that night. Pepper was the one I was really worried about, anyway. Alicia would probably be nice to her though, I reasoned, since they were cousins and all. So, I left, and rode home with Chris and Steve.

***

"Hello?" I said, answering the phone.

"Hey, Mike?" I recognized Pepper's voice.

"Yeah. Hey, Pepper, are you okay?"

"Yeah," she laughed. "I just kind of freaked after having that stuff all over me and not being able to finish the play and all."

"So, did the second show go off all right?"

"Yeah, it went great... I'm sorry you couldn't be there to see it,"

"Well, that teacher was probably waiting for me with a shotgun..."

"Yeah," she laughed. "So I guess it's just as well that you didn't show,"

FREE THROW

I laughed too, and said, "Oh, and I'm sorry if Alicia bugged you or anything the other night in the bathroom. I tried to stop her from coming in."

"Oh, don't worry about that. She helped me get that stuff out of my hair... and she was really nice,"

"Alicia?"

"Yes," she giggled, "When you're not around she can actually be somewhat nice,"

"Wow. I never realized..."

"Well don't take it the wrong way... actually, I'm not sure what the right way to take that is... but, take it that way,"

"Umm... okay," We both laughed. "So really," I went on, "You're all okay now?"

"Yeah, really. And I'm sorry that I shouted at you and Steve and Chris the other night... like I said, I just got really upset about... everything. And I didn't want you guys to see me like that,"

"I totally understand. I'm just glad to hear you're okay,"

"Never been better," she laughed.

We talked for a while after that, mostly about insignificant things. Most of all, after our conversation, I couldn't help being in good spirits after this news. If nothing else, it all made me realize how much I cared about Pepper.

After all of this, I was sure that I would be asking her to the Winter Formal that year, hopefully with more luck than I had had with Alicia the year before. Of course the problem remained of how I would do it. I mean, you can't just go up to someone who has been your friend, and that you love, and just ask her out. At least I couldn't - not without turning into a stammering idiot. I had to find a way, though.

***

Coach canceled practice on the next Tuesday, because he had some other things to attend to. Unfortunately, I missed the announcement and went anyway.

I walked into the gym that day - only to find that no-one else from the team was present. I was about to leave, to see if I could find out for sure if

FREE THROW

the practice had been canceled from someone, when I heard a sound all basketball players have a trained ear for. Swish!

I looked to the opposite end of the gym. There was Mr. Nicholes, calmly shooting. He had a rack next to him, with about ten or eleven balls. One by one, he tossed each one in from three-point range. Once he had fired the last one, I approached him. "Not bad for a janitor," I said.

He turned around, startled. "Oh, hey." He paused and then walked over to a broom, leaning against the nearest wall. "Well, I guess I'd better get back to work,"

"Na... hold on for a second," I said. "I hope you don't mind my asking, but... how'd you get so good at basketball?" I laughed, knowing that that had probably sounded kind of dumb. I continued then, "I mean, I remember that time at the park... and how you helped me with my shooting. And now this... you're great man,"

"I *was* great is more accurate," he sighed, and then wiped his forehead. "Not too many people know this... but, well, I'm not exactly just your everyday janitor,"

"No kidding..."

"Really kid. You ever heard of Ray Penner?"

"Of cour..." I stopped short, as I suddenly was hit by the realization of what he was getting at. I took a long, hard look at him, and remembered that old picture of Ray Penner, from the newspaper article. With the addition of a bald spot, a few gray hairs, and some extra pounds to the young Penner - there he was - standing before me. "Oh my God," I said slowly. "You're him... you're Ray Penner,"

"Guilty as charged. From high school hoops star to high school janitor," he smiled. "That's the story of my life,"

"But why... why are you a janitor? I mean..."

"I can't play ball any more... not competitively anyway. It's my back," He gestured to it as he spoke. "The damn thing blew out on me in my sec..."

"Second college game," I finished his sentence. "I know the story. But what I want to know is why you never cashed in on your fame and all. Even if you can't play any more... you're still a big name."

"Thirty years ago, maybe," He looked down. "Ya see kid, you're one of the only people from your generation who still knows my name. Heck...

FREE THROW

I'll bet most of the guys that *I* went to high school with couldn't recognize... or even remember me today,"

"Maybe not now... but that's because you disappeared. No-one expects to see you any more. If you had taken advantage of your name back then..."

"That's another part of the problem. It hurts. For so long, everybody... I mean *everybody*, that I knew or spoke to, associated me with basketball. Then, one day... I just couldn't play anymore. Suddenly, it just hurt to listen to the voices of the people who I had let down. And back then... to me, it seemed like I had let the whole world down."

"You were already in college, though. You could have finished... gotten a diploma. Then you could have gotten a better job, and lived past basketball,"

"That's the final piece of the problem, kid. Even though I couldn't play basketball, it was still the only thing I wanted to do. Every person is something... one thing. I was... and am a basketball player. A person can't change what they are,"

"But now you're a janitor..."

"Being a janitor pays the bills," he said sternly. "In my head, though, I'm still running pick and roll plays, and hitting the game winning shots. Even if that's not real any more - it's still a part of me,"

"Who knows about all this? Does Coach?"

"Yep. If it weren't for him, I'd probably be dead right about now," He began to laugh. "He was even coach here back when I used to play. He got me this job... telling people that I was his long lost, second cousin, or some garbage like that. And I've been working here ever since... keeping a low profile. That's the whole story,"

I paused, to let everything sink in. Then, I extended my hand to him. "Well, Mr. Penner," I said, "It's great to meet you." He shook his head and smiled. Then, he grabbed his broom and walked away. I thought I might've offended him. Things proved different, though.

Before, he had helped me with my shooting. After that day, whenever there wasn't practice, we would meet up in the gym and shoot around after school. I became sort of his protégé - I title I wore quite proudly.

***

FREE THROW

The situation with Pepper was getting harder and harder to handle. Whenever I was near her, I couldn't help looking - even staring at her. I think that she caught me a few times, too. The Winter Formal was only a couple of weeks away by that time; I had to make my move if I was ever going to. But still, I lacked the confidence.

Fortunately, it wasn't the same situation with basketball at all. In our next game, I managed my highest assist total of the year to that point with seven, my rebounding numbers were picking up, and I stayed perfect with free throws. The team held a record of 7-1.

Our next game was at home, against Cartrial, and we expected to dominate. Cartrial had yet to win a game that year, largely due to the fact that they had few offensive threats; their top scorer was a senior named Bob Wiggins, who managed only 11.7 points per game. Plus, their defense and rebounding play was weak. However, an article in the newspaper, printed one day prior to it, raised the level of this game.

When I entered the locker room for practice, I saw everyone reading a fragment of a newspaper. I strolled over to my own locker, to find the same clipping attached to it by a small piece of masking tape. It was a brief interview with Wiggins, regarding his thoughts on playing against us. The comments were not those of respect for a strong opponent, as was usually the case in these situations.

One line about said it all. "Just look at who's leading them: a dumb nigger, and a guy who can't even dunk," He also criticized some of the other team members, but no statements really were quite as bold as those.

In a minute, Shawn stood up from the bench where he had been sitting and reading, and said quite simply, "We're gonna kick this team's butt."

***

It was a home game for us, and one could tell by the audience's reaction. When Bob Wiggins' name was announced, I heard one of the loudest chorus of 'boo's that I have ever encountered. It became clear that he was not at all penitent about his words. On his elbow pad he had drawn in a southern cross, with markers.

As he walked out, onto the court, his coach followed and forced him to remove it. He laughed it off, though, as his teammates gave him high

FREE THROW

fives and smiles. This made us aware that it wasn't him alone causing trouble; the whole team was supporting him. When our starting five moved toward center court, the first blow of the night was fired - literally.

When everybody was setting up for the tip off, Brad walked over and slapped Wiggins in the face. The tall, handsome guard from Cartrial reeled back, not nearly as cool and cocky as he had been just moments before.

However, Brad would have to pay, as one of the referees jogged over and handed him a technical. "Ah, to hell with it," Brad fired back at the official. "You know he deserved it. You should eject him!" This caused him to receive a second technical, leaving him benched for the whole game. No foul shots were awarded due to the special circumstances, and the game proceeded as planned.

Despite the consequences, I think anyone on our team would gladly have done the same. The opposing team was smart, though; Wiggins shook off the blow, and none of his teammates retaliated for him. They knew that they couldn't afford to lose any of their starters.

Coach decided to try out Chris at point guard, as Brad's replacement, and then the game began. As was always the case, Travis took the tip-off, this time knocking it to Shawn. Ordinarily, a quick pass to the point guard would ensue, but this was different. Shawn dribbled past all of the defenders, and hit a thunderous dunk.

The crowd went wild, and continued their cheers when I stole the ball and nailed a short jumper. Travis blocked their first shot next; getting it into Chris' possession he dribbled all the way down court, and then waited for Shawn. When our power forward arrived at the scene, a simple hand-off was converted into an easy lay-up.

We continued to trounce them. By the end of the first, the score was up to 32-10, in our favor. By half time, it was 55-17, with Shawn having thirty-two points, and me pouring in twenty-one. Wiggins had managed four, off one three throw, and a three that Travis goal-tended.

The scene in the locker room at half time was completely upbeat. Coach approached Shawn and I aside from everyone else, for a moment. "All right, we all know this one's turning into a blow out. Still, I know this is important for the two of you guys... we've gotta send a message to that punk. So, if you guys want, I'll let the two of you stay in the game for as long as you'd like,"

"I'm in," I answered.

FREE THROW

"Yeah, I'll be out there for the whole game if you'll let me," Shawn said with a smile.

"Great," Coach said. He patted Shawn's shoulder. "Now, you two get ready for the second half... we can't let up now!"

***

It wasn't until the start of the fourth when things took another turn. Two minutes into it, we had an incredible 112-30 point lead, yet Coach called our first time out of the game.

"Yo, what's the deal Coach?" Shawn said, running over.

Coach wore a big smile as he spoke the words, "Shawn, I've just been informed that you're just two points away from breaking the school's record of fifty-seven points in a game,"

"All right, man," Travis began, as we all began to congratulate him.

"But wait, there's more," Coach continued. "Mike," he looked toward me, "You're just six away from beating the record yourself," I couldn't believe it, and apparently, neither could the rest of the team. And yet, there was still one more announcement.

"And finally" Coach went on, "Travis, with your twenty-two blocks, you've tied the record already. Now come on people... let's go out there and make some history!"

We obeyed this command when the game re-began. As soon as I touched the ball, I fired a three. One of the opposing players gave blocking it their best try, but he only ended up fouling me, as the shot fell through the hoop.

I swished the free throw. Then, it was, as Coach termed it, time to 'make some history'. Cartrial inbounded the ball to their point guard. He bounced the ball once. He tried to dribble it a second time. Before the ball could hit the ground, I had picked it off. Feeling more confident than I think that I ever had before, in anything, I dribbled back to three-point range.

I wouldn't be able to break the record that easily, though. Maybe it was just a pride thing - not wanting to be embarrassed as much. Either way, the opposing point guard gave me a hard foul as I took my shot. It didn't go in, and I would have to earn my fifty-sixth, fifty-seventh, and fifty-eighth points from the line.

FREE THROW

I swished the first two free throws flat out, without really thinking about it. I knew that just one more foul shot would not only maintain my perfect percentage, but also get that last necessary point. The public address system suddenly boomed out both my and Shawn's point totals, and then named the record. I winked at Shawn, and then bounced the ball thrice. All that was left was the shot. It barely even rippled the net going down, as everyone from our bench, and the crowd rose, and cheered. Running back on defense, I spied Pepper smiling at me. I smiled back.

However, I didn't hold the smile, or the record for long. Shawn grabbed the rebound off of Cartrial's miss on the other end, and then dribbled the full length of the quarter, to our three-point line. He fired the long jump shot. *Good!*

Our opponents managed to score on their next possession, but we came back, and off a pass from Chris, I tossed up a lay-up. *Good!*

Travis rebounded the next Cartrial miss on the other end, and flung the outlet pass way down to Shawn, who went up for the dunk. *Good!*

Things continued on like this, until there was just over a minute left, with me holding a 69-68 lead over Shawn. That's when he took a jumper from just inside the perimeter. He missed the shot, but was fouled. He stepped up to the line.

Now, Shawn was a spectacular player - probably more talented at that time than I ever was or ever will be as a player. But his free throw shooting just wasn't up to par with mine. He hit one of two to tie it up between us. On the opposite end, a Cartrial player missed a three, and Chris grabbed the board. It was he, Shawn, and I, racing up court by ourselves, with Wiggins as the only one even close to us.

"Pass it to me!" Shawn said, slightly ahead.

"No! Me!" I said, lagging just inches behind. Chris stopped dribbling when he reached paint, and shouted, "Jump for it!" As he threw the ball straight up in the air. Wiggins was catching up. I knew that Shawn had the edge in leaping ability, but I managed to outsmart him.

As it was what came naturally to him, as a former center, Shawn tapped the ball behind him, toward the basket. Wiggins, by that point, stood directly under the hoop, in hopes of interception. However, I caught the ball in air, and slammed it down.

FREE THROW

I'm not sure what was best about that moment - moving ahead of Shawn, pulling off the first dunk of my life, or the thing that happened right after the ball went through the hoop.

I was usually a pretty reserved, quiet guy on the court. But that time, I couldn't resist hissing, "In your face!" at Wiggins, after having done what he said I couldn't, and with him right beneath me to boot.

Finally, Cartrial's point guard decided to bring the ball up slowly as the game neared its end. It was with only about five seconds remaining that he shot his three-pointer. Travis swatted it back to break a record of his own. There was one problem though, at least for me. The ball went straight to Shawn.

With time enough for the just one step, Shawn lunged forward, and fired the ball from a little past the half court line. *Swish!* At the buzzer, Shawn had beaten me by one point. But with that effort, I knew that he deserved it, as we high fived.

***

The story from the game received a large article in the sports section of the paper the next day. Perhaps one paragraph summed things up best. "The game broke so many records: Vetter and Weaver each took turns setting new scoring records, it was the widest margin of victory in state history, Travis Ribalow swatted a record 23 shots, and I'm pretty sure Brad Davies' early ejection was a sort of record of it's own - two technicals before the opening tip!"

That wasn't the only praise the team received. During the morning announcements in school, the principal made a rare mention of an athletic event, as he continued in showering us with flattery. I was actually somewhat embarrassed by the attention, but considering what we had done, I wasn't about to shy away from compliments.

***

I was changing for gym class when Mr. Nicholes entered the locker room. He immediately came toward me, and said, "Follow me," Naturally, I obeyed.

FREE THROW

He led me down the hall, into the janitors' supply room. It was a dusty place, with ragged old brooms, and dust cloths lying here and there. Cobwebs stuck to bottles of polish and cleanser, leading one to think that this was the one room the janitors didn't attend to. However, the overall shabby look of the place only accentuated the presence of one object.

Sitting on a dull oak table near the center of the room, was a shiny brass trophy, with the words, "Ray Penner High School Athlete of the Year" carved into the base. I looked at it, and then at Mr. Nicholes.

"You see," he began, "During the summer between my graduation and start of college, Coach approached me about starting this annual award thing. Since I'd been such a big name guy, he wanted for me to present a trophy like this to whoever was considered to have been the school's best athlete at the end of each year. Of course, before I got that far, there was the injury and all. So, I held onto the trophy, and decided that someday, I'd give it to whoever broke my scoring record," he paused to clear his throat. "Anyway, I had a little trouble deciding between you and Shawn... but, you did do it first. And so, it's yours," At that point, he lifted the trophy, and held it out for me to take.

"I'm not sure I can accept this..."

"Na... come on. I've held onto this old piece of metal for years now. Way too long. Here - it's yours now,"

Neither of us did anything for a moment. Then, I lifted the trophy at last. "Thank you," was all I could say.

***

"So what has you in such high spirits today?" Karen asked as I sat down with her in the cafeteria later that day, across from her at the table.

"Nothing important," I said, knowing that it would be hard to explain, and for her to understand. "So, what's up?"

"Not much," Karen said, and sighed.

"Okay, from that response, I guess I should be asking what's wrong..."

"It's nothing," she laughed. "It's just that, you know, the Winter Formal is only a few weeks away," I turned my head, to see tickets for the event being sold - probably the sight that prompted Karen's bring up the subject.

FREE THROW

"Don't I know it," I went on. "I'm planning to ask Pepper tomorrow night."

"You're actually going through with it?" Karen smiled. I gave her a look. "Oh... no, no, no," she went on, " I didn't mean it like that. Actually, I respect you for having the courage to ask her. But, um... does that mean, that you're, like, totally over Alicia?"

"Totally. After all the aggravation she's given me... I know that you're close with her, but it's really just gotten out of hand. Besides... I feel this really strong connection with Pepper. It's incredible," I paused. "So, by your dramatic sigh, I'm guessing you don't have any plans for the big night yet,"

"No," she whined.

"Well, look at it this way... at least you're not going with that same guy you did last year... the one with the eyebrow ring,"

"Yeah," she laughed. "But at least I *had* a date last year,"

"Oh come on. If you really want to go, you could probably ask, like, any guy, and he'd say yes,"

"Yeah right..."

"No, really," As I spoke, I saw Travis coming to the table out of the corner of my eye, inspiring an idea. "I'll tell you what... ask the next guy you see,"

"What?" she said with a laugh.

"Seriously... the next guy who comes by here... just ask him to go to the Formal with you,"

"I don't think so..."

"Come on... what's the worst that could happen?" I urged her, as I was Travis coming closer.

She looked at me for a moment. "Okay... you win. I'll ask the next guy I see."

Just as she spoke the words, Travis stopped, to talk to a teacher. "Damn it," I muttered.

"What?"

"Oh, nothing," I said, hoping that he would still be the first guy her eyes fell upon.

"Hey Chris," she said suddenly. I looked behind me, to see that Chris had arrived.

"Listen..." Karen began.

FREE THROW

I cut her off, "You know, you don't really have to do this,"

"Don't be silly," she said, and then turned back to Chris. "I know that this is kind of out of the blue, but, how would you feel about going to the Winter Formal with me?"

"Whoa... uh... me?" he asked, suddenly nervous. Karen nodded. "Well... I'm flattered. But... uh..."

"Don't worry about it, if you want to say no," Karen said. "It would just prove my point... that guys don't really flip over me,"

"Well, it's not that... because I'd love to go to the Formal with you. It's just..." He looked to me for help, but I could only shrug. I was glad that he had thought of Travis above all else, but he couldn't just reject her. "You know what... okay. I'll go with you," he said at last.

"Great," Karen said, just as Travis sat down next to her.

"What's great?" he asked.

"Chris and I are going to the Winter Formal together," she said.

"Oh... um... that's good," Travis responded, his true feelings evident in his voice and on his face.

"Yeah," Karen began, and then began making plans for the Formal.

***

"Well, what was I supposed to do?!" Chris asked.

"I don't know... maybe you could've said no," I said, before shooting a three-pointer that was off target, at the park.

"Yeah, but how could I say no?" Chris said as he grabbed the rebound from my shot. "I mean, I couldn't just turn her down after that whole 'guys don't flip over me' thing,"

"I know. It's just... Travis..."

"Tell me about it," Chris said as he made a lay-up. "The guy looked like he was ready to step on me at any moment,"

"Come on, man. Be serious,"

"The sad thing is, I *was* being serious," I gave him a look as he finished his sentence. "Okay, new topic," he said. "What's the game plan for Pepper... are you going to ask her or what?"

"Yes," I said definitively. "I'm sick of being too scared to at least try. I'm going to call her up tomorrow night, and get this whole thing over with,"

FREE THROW

"You've got guts... I'll give you that. I mean, at least for someone who's asking a girl out over the phone because he's too chicken to ask her straight up - face to face,"

"That's not it at all. I just think that the mood will be better that way, you know?"

"Uh-huh,"

"And night... it's so much more of a romantic time than day, right?"

"Uh-huh,"

"And, you know, a phone conversation is just a lot more... intimate than just regular talking,"

"Uh-huh,"

"And it's better this way... because we'll have privacy and all... with the whole no-one else being there thing,"

"Uh-huh,"

"And say she turns me down... it'll be way less awkward this way, than if I we were face to face when she broke my heart,"

"Uh-huh,"

"And this will definitely prevent Steve from interrupting me and all,"

"Uh-huh,"

"And all considered... you know, if anything, *she'll* probably be more at ease if I do this over the phone, you know? She won't have to worry so much about looking sympathetic... or hiding her enthusiasm,"

"Uh-huh,"

"And... I'm way too chicken to even think about doing this face to face,"

"Uh-huh," Chris smiled, and patted me on the back. "At least you're man enough to admit it,"

***

"Well, tonight's the night," I said, as Steve and I walked toward the school.

"What's that supposed to mean?"

"Look, I just had that awesome game... which has made both my attractiveness, and my confidence soar. The Winter Formal is just a couple weeks away, and it's time to make my move. I'm going to call Pepper tonight, and get this whole thing over with,"

FREE THROW

"Hold on... you can't do that,"
"Why?"
"Because I'm going to ask her to the Formal today,"
"What?!"
"You heard me. I'm asking her today. And she's the type of girl, who, even if she doesn't like a guy, she'd still probably go to a dance with him."
"All right," I started, and then hesitated, before saying, "Then I'll ask her first - right this morning."
"You'll have to beat me to it, then."
"Then I will."
We continued our walk to the school, each of us quickening our pace with every step. At last, we were actually running down the halls, to Pepper's locker. Everything had worn down to literally being a race for Pepper.
Coach stopped us. "Hey guys, this is a hall, not the gym!" he turned his attention solely to me, "You should be saving your energy for today's practice."
"Sorry Coach, we're just in a bit of a hurry,"
"Just slow it down guys. I'll see you later," As Coach walked away, I turned to Steve.
"All right, there's a more rational way of handling this, without all the running around."
"What do you have in mind?"
I removed a quarter from my pocket. "Heads, I get to ask her first. Tails, she's all yours."
"Sounds fair enough."
"Hey guys," Chris said, as he came towards us.
"Hey man," I said, "Perfect timing. You can do the honors," I handed him the quarter.
"The honors?" Chris said, looking at the coin. "What, is this some sort of bizarre religious ritual or something?"
"Just flip the coin, dude," Steve said, unenthusiastically.
"All right, I'm on it," Chris said. The coin spun in the air for a moment, before he caught it and laid it down on his forearm - head side up.
"Yeah!" I said.
"Okay, you win," Steve began. "You can ask her to the Winter Formal first."

FREE THROW

***

I was at my locker, before homeroom, at the same time that Pepper was at hers. But she wasn't there alone. Steve was talking to her.

Between the surrounding noise, and their being pretty far away from me, I couldn't hear what was being said. And I wasn't a lip reader. Still, when I watched what was happening, I just sort of knew what was going on. I mean, I didn't know the exact words being used, or the exact ramifications of what was being said. But I knew that Steve was asking Pepper to the Formal, or to the movies, or just out - in general. I didn't break in - just out of some shred of respect for Steve, I guess. I continued to watch, though.

Steve started out smiling as he spoke. He stayed calm with every word that left his mouth. When it came to Pepper's turn to respond, she played with the end of her hair with her fingers, and looked around. She spoke carefully - hesitantly - almost nervously. By the time she was done, Steve's face had fallen. What remained was a mere shell of his original, cool self.

"She's all yours," Steve said, as he passed by me, on his way into homeroom. I grabbed his arm to stop him.

"What did you do?"

"What do you think?" his tone became harsher.

"I think you asked her to the Winter Formal. And I think you did it after we had decided that *I* was going to ask first,"

"I didn't ask her to the Formal. I asked her to be my girlfriend..."

"You knew what I meant..."

"Who cares anyway? She said no. She said she doesn't like me like that. She said she's really into some other guy. Doesn't affect you. She's all yours,"

We just looked at each other for a minute. Then he turned and started to walk away. "Wait," I said. He stopped and faced me again. "Look... I know you cared about her... so, I'm sorry,"

"Save your sympathy," he said sharply. "I don't need it,"

***

FREE THROW

The fact that Pepper had rejected Steve didn't do much for my confidence. I stuck to my plan, though, of calling her that night.

My parents had made plans to go out to dinner, and my sister was going to go out with Matt. So, I waited until I was home alone to pick up the phone, and make the call. The moment I heard the dial tone, I was overcome with this unbelievable terror. For months Pepper had been the only one that I had thought of. At that moment, I realized how much this was more than just a crush. I really did feel that I loved her.

I had had Pepper's phone number memorized for a long time, but I still struggled to punch in the digits, with my finger trembling, and my mind racing.

The phone rang once. I thought about hanging up right then. It was the type of call that, once made, I could never go back on - it would change everything. The phone rang a second time. She'll pick up soon, I thought to myself. It was my last chance to turn back. It rang thrice. Then a fourth time. Then five.

Finally, Pepper's father's voice responded, "Hello,"

"Hey, may I please speak to Pepper?"

"We're not home right now. If you'd like for us to get back to you, please leave your name and number..."

It was the machine. In my nervousness, I hadn't even known that it was an answering machine. Soon, I heard the beep. "Um... hi," I started. What could I say? I couldn't just leave a message. I hadn't really thought of what to do in this situation. I had to say something, though. "Pepper, umm... this is Mike Weaver, and I really need to talk to you about someth..."

"Hey Mike!" Pepper's voice entered.

"Oh... uh... hi..." was all that I could manage.

"Sorry about the machine. My folks are out, and I was busy with some stuff when you called. So what's up?"

"Oh, nothing," I lied.

"Come on, I know there's something... you said you needed to talk to me."

At that point, I was totally off of my game. "Well, umm.... you see... I just kind of wanted to know if... well, you know if you're not doing anything... I mean..." I stopped. I had sounded like a rambling idiot. I closed my eyes, took a deep breath and then rattled out, "I really like you... have

101

FREE THROW

liked you... as more than just friends. So, I was wondering if you'd go with me to the Winter Formal?"

She didn't say anything at first. Questions raced through my head. Was she thinking it over? Or was she just thinking of the best way to say no? Or to say yes?

At last, she spoke. "I'm sorry, but..." I hung up. I knew what she was saying. People never say, 'I'm sorry, but, I like you too," It's a language thing. Those words just don't go together. I didn't want to listen to reasons or excuses. I didn't want to talk. I hung up, and then left the phone off the hook. There was nothing left to say.

Chapter 9

Ray Penner said that his favorite game that he played in, came midway through his senior year. His team had trailed all game long. Penner wasn't at his best, and had been put on the bench, because the win seemed out of reach. But right then, his team staged a comeback. By the time only five seconds remained in the game, they were only down by one. Penner came back onto the court, and made the game winning shot. He loved the idea of coming out of complete despair, and going on to the exhilaration of victory.

***

The next day, I was careful about avoiding any chance of having to talk to Pepper. I didn't want to listen to her feel bad for me. Either way, I was miserable. I didn't even tell most of my friends what had happened. They would only try to cheer me up, and I really didn't feel like being happy. It was like I was supposed to be depressed after what had happened.

I told Chris everything over a game of horse that afternoon. "Man, on a scale of one to ten, that... that just really sucks."

"Yeah, but what can I do?" I asked rhetorically.

"You should at least talk to her. Maybe there's just a good reason why she can't make the Formal,"

"Right now, I just want to keep some distance." Chris gave me a look. "All right, so I wish I didn't have to keep my distance. I wish I could see her and talk to her all the time. I just can't, though... you know that," I paused. "It's just like you can't make the jumper from that spot over there. That's why you're stalling... you don't want the 'H-O',"

"Hey, I can make it," he said as he bounced the ball to over where I had signaled. "Seriously, though, I just thought maybe we could double date to the Formal,"

"I can't believe this. Chris Brady has a date for the Winter Formal... and I'm still getting the shaft,"

"You bet," he smiled, and released his shot, which bounced off the side of the rim.

FREE THROW

"Man... who would go with a guy shoots like that?" I said, grabbing the rebound and dribbling around.

"Hey... b-ball's got nothing to do with it. It's all about style," he smiled.

"Yeah... style that's gonna lead to Travis ringing your neck,"

"I choose not to think about that side of things."

"A-ha... I think that's called denial," After speaking the words, I shot a three-pointer that rattled in and out.

"Hey, Travis will get over it. It's not like I'm actually going to make a move on her," He bounced the ball back and forth behind his back. "This isn't gonna get any more screwed up than it already is,"

"So, what happens when you see Erin there?"

"Nothing. I will be purely an Erin spectator for the evening,"

"Ever think about letting her know how you feel?"

"We've been over this. She's not only out of my league... she's playing a whole different sport. And besides... I see the way you are, after the whole thing with Pepper..."

"Hey, we're different people, man, and so are Pepper and Erin,"

"Yeah, but I see how you are now... I can't take that kind of rejection," He popped in a short jump shot as he said it.

"I'll get over it," I said, walking over to take the shot, "It'll just take some time," As I made the basket, I muttered to myself, "Just a long, long time,"

***

"Well, I think I have to agree with your friend on this one," Carrie said, while writing something on a sheet of loose-leaf paper. "You seem to really like this girl; you should talk to her,"

"I wish it was that easy," I said, pacing around her room, stepping over the shirts, crumpled pieces of paper, and whatever else was lying around on the floor. "I just don't want to screw this up... I mean anymore than I already have,"

"Look, to be quite honest, I think you've let what happened with Alicia last year scar you far too much. Don't meet Pepper at her locker with flowers or anything... just give her a call... let her know you're serious,"

"So, how's the novel coming?" I changed the subject.

FREE THROW

"Not too bad... I have a plot going now,"
"Oh... what's it about?"
"It's kind of 1984-like,"
"Huh?"
"You know, the book by George Orwell," she studied my puzzled expression, "Honestly, Mike, if you stopped spending all your time playing basketball and obsessing over girls you can't have, and actually cracked a book once in a while, it'd do you some good,"
"Hey, I'm *not* obsessing over just any girl. Much less, one I can't have."
"If you're so sure of that, why don't you go talk to her," I had no response. She went on, "You should listen to me... I mean, hey, *I* have a date for the Winter Formal,"
"Yeah, but you're still going out with that Matt guy,"
"What's so bad about Matt?"
"The guy is such a nerd. He reads Star Trek books, and when I asked him what type of music he liked, he said *soundtracks*," I laughed.
"Yeah, but he's really sweet, and he cares about me. That's more than you have," she said indignantly.
I left the room. I was miserable about the whole Pepper thing, and I knew what I had to do to do. I felt some how betrayed, by her rejecting me. It was like I didn't want to hear her side. Still, I knew that the others were right.

***

I went about a week longer, avoiding Pepper. Then, she accosted me at last on Friday, the last day of school before the Formal, and the rest of Christmas vacation. I was at my locker, putting away some things, when I felt a tap on my shoulder. There she was.
"Hey Mike," she said.
"Hey," I replied, and then started to walk past her.
"We have to talk,"
"Yeah? About what?" I hadn't really known how bitter I was about the whole ordeal, until that moment.
"I have plans for he night of the Winter Formal. That's the only reason I can't go with you. Damn it, you hung up too soon..."

FREE THROW

"If that's the whole deal, then why did you hesitate when you answered me? Huh? And why didn't you come talk to me..."

"How the hell was I supposed to?!" her voice was cracking as she shouted it. People began looking our way.

"I'm sorry I was yelling at y-"

"Well you should be!" she took a deep breath, and ran her hand through her hair before going on in her regular tone of voice, "I wanted to talk to you ever since you asked me to go to the stupid dance. I don't know why I hesitated. I don't know if it was that I didn't want you to think I was blowing you off or if I just wasn't sure... wasn't sure that it was real. I mean, I had been thinking about you saying those words for so long. And after you started avoiding me, for a little while, I thought that maybe I was wrong about you all along... about liking you," she was cut off by the bell, starting the next class period. "Look, I have to go. But we really do need to talk. Face to face. Here," She handed me an envelope and then walked away.

***

I stepped out of my dad's car, and started walking towards Pepper's house at about eight o' clock on New Year's Eve. I was a bit nervous, entering the house. It was Pepper's parents' party. I suppose I was something of a special guest.

Pepper was nowhere in sight. An old woman walked toward me soon after. "Why, hello," she said.

"Hello," I said back.

A slightly younger woman, probably in her sixties, came nearby. "Dorothy," the first woman started, "I thought that James and Margaret had a daughter... Paprika or something like that,"

"Yes, that's quite right," the second woman replied, and then turned to me. "Who are you, young man?"

"I'm Mike... Mike Weaver," I said, adding, "I'm a friend of Pepper's,"

"Oh," they both seemed to say at the same time, as they simultaneously lost interest and walked away.

I stood in that same spot for a few minutes. Then I sat on a couch. Then I stood, drank some punch, and returned to the couch. Still, I saw no

FREE THROW

sign of Pepper. And so, I sat, until about 9:30, when I first saw Pepper, looking around - I was hoping - for me.

I walked to her side, and said, "Hello,"

"There you are," she said, with a sigh of relief. "Follow me,"

I followed Pepper past a large number of people, all of whom we had to stop and say hi to. Then she led me down a hallway, up a staircase, and finally into her bedroom. That's when I first really looked at her. She had on this little black dress, that just made her look more beautiful I had ever seen her appear before. I didn't hide the fact, saying, "You look really great tonight,"

"Thanks," she said, walking towards her bed. She sat down, and signaled for me to come next to her.

"Look, I'm really sorry about everything," I said, "I've been really... I... I've been a jerk,"

"No, don't say that," she said with a smile. "The truth of it all is, that ever since we met, back at Karen's party, I've had, like the biggest crush on you. I've even thought at times that maybe it was..." she looked at me and giggled, "No, it's stupid... I can't say it,"

"No," I laughed. "Go on,"

"Well, I... I thought maybe it was love," I had this sudden burst of happiness. " I mean, do you remember those times when we almost kissed?"

"Yeah, of course..."

"Well, those were so great for me... but when you never said anything afterward... I just assumed you weren't interested,"

"I thought the same thing... only, you know, about you,"

She started laughing. I guess it was about the irony of it all - it was sort of funny. "Well, anyway," she started again, "If you're not too put off from me, would you want to... start going out?"

I smiled. "Of course," We talked for a long time after that, all leading to that one moment I had been waiting for so long. I doubt that I'll ever forget that moment when our lips first touched.

***

By the time Pepper and I rejoined the part, the television was on, tuned to some station, showing the ball drop in Times Square. All of the adults were already chanting in unison, "Three, two, one... happy New Year!"

Indeed it was.

Chapter 10

Ray Penner once said that the key to winning in basketball was perseverance. His idea was that no team could win against him. He thought that no matter how out of control things got, or how much he was losing by, eventually, if he could ride things out, everything would work itself out - at least for the most part.

***

It can be so weird when you finally get something that you've wanted for such a long time. I had surrendered so much of my time to just thinking about Pepper. At that time, I could give my imagination a rest. I had the real thing.

I rolled out of bed at about noon on January first, still recovering from the party. The very thought of her brought a smile to my face. Before I met Pepper, I had never really believed in love - not the way they portrayed it in the movies or on TV anyway. But the way I felt just that moment went unparalleled by anything I'd experienced before - especially since I knew that she felt the same way. If it weren't love, then I would settle for it anyway, for the rest of my life.

***

Chris left for a family vacation the day after the Winter Formal, and came back on the second day of January. Hence, we had a lot of catching up to do.

"So you're going out with her now?!" Chris said, shocked after I told him the whole story of the New Year's Eve party.

What seemed revolutionary to him was commonplace to me by then. I just said, "Yeah," as I put in a short jumper. As usual, the park was vacant, except for us.

We went on, discussing he matter in the same way, until finally, I said, "Look Chris... yes, we're going out. Yes, Pepper actually likes me back," I released a hook shot from the top of the key. As it swished through the net, I continued, "And yes, I am the greatest basketball player of all time," I paused. "But, on an entirely different note, how'd the big date go with Karen?"

"Not so hot," he answered curtly. I waited for him to say more, but instead he entered his fancy dribbling routine, and didn't speak another word.

"*Not so hot*? What's that supposed to mean?" I asked at last.

"Look, let's just say that any... tension with Travis, resulting from us going to that stupid dance... it'll be multiplied by, like, infinity, if he ever heard what happened,"

"What did you do?"

He stopped dribbling, and glared at me. What makes you automatically assume that whatever happened is directly my fault?" I just looked at him, and he went on, "Okay, so what happened was entirely my fault... not the whole evening sucking, but the big, huge, sucking climax... that was all me,"

"Look, you're gonna have to fill me in, because I have no clue what you're talking about,"

"Okay," he said, and took a deep breath. "It all started out really awkward, 'cause, I mean, we're friends, but not really tight friends, you know? So..." he trailed off. "I'm sorry, but I can't tell you this... it's way too embarrassing,"

"Oh, come on Chris," I said. "We've been best friends for years. I know all of your embarrassing stories."

"But this one is, like, all of those embarrassing stories added together and put to the power of nine million."

"All right, I'll put it to you this way. I either get the story from you - from your perspective, and with your explanations, or I'll go talk to Karen."

"Don't go talk to Karen!" he cut me off suddenly.

"Okay, then tell me what happened,"

Chris was at last resigned to his fate, and re-began the telling of his story. "Okay... so, like I was telling you, it was really awkward. We didn't really have anything to talk about. And I wasn't sure if I should ask her to dance, or whatever, because she said that we were only going as friends. Of course, I didn't really know for sure at that point, if we really were there, just as friends, or if she had ulterior motives,"

"Okay... that doesn't sound too bad," I said.

FREE THROW

"Right... but we're no where near that sucking climax I told you about,"

"Well, don't let me stop you,"

"All right," he said, "So, eventually, we did dance... and it was a slow song. A really slow song. And a really long slow song,"

"Okay,"

"And dancing right in front of me, were Erin and some guy,"

"Well, that's good... right? I mean, non-awkwardness with Karen and a chance to scope out Erin... kind of a two for one,"

"Yeah... I guess you could say that. Except, after the first minute or two of the slow song... things went bad," He paused and looked at me. "I got a little... excited... watching Erin and all. And I kind of started imagining that I was dancing with her instead of Karen,"

"Okay,"

"Not okay," Chris said. "Because then I... I... I copped a feel, man!"

"What?!"

"I didn't plan it or anything."

"What... you involuntarily moved your hand down to her buttocks, and then accidentally squeezed?"

"I'm telling you, it wasn't like that."

"Look, I don't really care about what you decide to do... romantically. But Travis... he's going to flip,"

"Which is why he can't find out."

"I have news for you," I said, "He's friends with Karen, and this isn't the sort of thing that stays a secret for very long," Neither of us said anything for a few moments. "All right," I said after a while, "What'd she do after... that?"

"Well, I'll tell you this much... she didn't like it. She kind of looked at me after I did it, and then said she had to go to the bathroom... so, you know we stopped dancing,"

"And then what?"

"And then nothing! She stayed in the girls room for he rest of the dance, as far as I know, and then hitched a ride home with someone else,"

"So you haven't even talked to her yet?"

"No... I left for vacation the next day... you know that,"

"Yeah, but that means that she still thinks you're just a creepy pervert. I mean, at least your explanation kind of helps,"

111

FREE THROW

"Well, gee, thanks for all the support. You're a real pal,"

"Look, I'm sorry man. But this is serious. I mean, if you don't talk to her.."

"But I don't know if talking to her is the best route," he cut me off.

"You can't just run away from this."

"I'm not *just* running away from this. The fact is, that I really don't see how talking will help all that much... and it will likely be awkward and painful."

"It'll help because you and Karen won't have to be permanently awkward. And I really don't see how it could be all that painful... talking with one of your friends."

"No. When I said painful there, I meant more that I was lucky to escape without her physically hurting me *then*. Going back... explaining the *reasoning* behind copping a feel... now that's going to be painful... I don't care who the girl is," he said. I laughed, and he soon joined in. "See... you're laughing. That's good... you've gotta be loose. I'll tell you... I started thinking Pepper was taking all the fun out of you," He stopped and lined up to take a shot.

I blocked him, and took the ball. "I don't know about me, but your game is definitely taking a hit because of this whole Karen thing,"

"Oh, so that's the way it is," Chris said, en route to the start of an impromptu game of one on one.

***

Before school, I ran into Karen outside of the building. "Hey, Karen, wait up," I called.

"Oh, hey Mike," she said. "What's up?"

"Not much..." I stopped as I spotted Chris out of the corner of my eye. "But... umm... yeah, I guess there is something,"

She followed my gaze - over to him. He stopped suddenly when he saw her, and just stood there, at the edge of the parking lot, looking at her. "This is going to be bad," Karen said. "Umm... I'll see you later," With that, she started off away from Chris, towards the school.

"Wait!" I said, as I ran up alongside her. "I - I heard what happened... and you really can't just run away from this."

"Yes I can! And that's exactly what I'm doing."

FREE THROW

"But when a friend makes a mistake, you can't just..."

"Chris isn't my friend," Karen said, matter-of-factly. "I thought he was. That's why I asked him to go to the ball with me. But if you think that I can talk to... after that.... then you must have heard the story wrong,"

"I know that what he did was wrong. I *don't* think that it was unforgivable..."

"Then either you heard a different story, or you're not my friend either. It might sound like nothing to you... like a joke or something. But to me, it was serious. It's like he attacked me... I don't care if it sounds like it was something small... he attacked me! And I've spent all this time... trying to decide on what I should do... how I should handle this. I decided that Chris isn't my friend, Travis - he's my friend. He had feelings for me - but he knew how to control them. I don't want anything to do with someone that could make me feel this way," By the time she had finished, her eyes were watery, and her voice was quivering.

I put a hand on her shoulder, to try to console her. She pulled away, though, and walked off on her own. Moments later, Chris arrived. "Hey, I've decided that you're right, and I should definitely do the talking thing. So did Karen say where she was going?" He looked at me, hopefully, and totally unaware of what had just been said.

***

Walking toward the school the next day, I couldn't help but notice Chris struggling to get off the bus as he carried one of the biggest bouquets of flowers I've ever seen, in one arm, and managing his book bag with the other.

"Hey," I said. He nearly lost control of the flowers, but then regained it, and looked over the bouquet, at me.

"Hi... how's it going?" he said at last.

"Um... fine, I guess. Did some florist have a going out of business sale or something?"

"Oh, no. This," he said, lifting the flowers, "Is a peace offering for Karen... and about five years of my allowance, down the drain..."

"Look, it's a nice gesture, but I think you'll need more than that to get any kind of forgiveness out of her,"

FREE THROW

"I know. But there's nothing else I can do. I tried, like, a zillion times, yesterday, to just talk to her, but she kept walking away. I tried calling her, but she kept hanging up on me. And then I wrote her this note - saying I was sorry, and explaining things - and she just ripped it up, without even reading it. This is my absolute, last resort here,"

Just then, Karen walked past us. "Wait!" Chris called. She stopped, and turned to face him. "Karen... we have to talk," he began as he walked toward her. The flowers having blocked his face, it wasn't until then that she realized who had stopped her. "These are for you..." he went on.

"I guess I probably should try to talk to you," Karen said, "And tell you that what you did was wrong. And you don't get out of it by just saying that you're sorry... or.... or getting me presents. Why can't you understand that?"

"Look, all that I want is for things to go back to the way they were. I did a horrible thing. But it wasn't..."

"Is he bothering you?" Travis cut Chris off, coldly, as he arrived at Karen's side.

"What - is he your bodyguard?" Chris asked.

"Maybe I am," Travis said, and pushed Chris, who was already off-balance, sending him to the ground, with the flowers on top of him.

"You didn't have to do that," Karen said.

"Sorry," Travis began, and then said with a loss of confidence, to Chris, "Stay away from her,"

"Come on," Karen said, and they walked away.

***

As I passed by Travis, on the way to my gym locker before practice that day, I intentionally bumped into him. "I'm sorry sir," I smiled.

"Oh, hey Mike," Travis smiled. "Sorry I was so harsh before..."

"Na.... don't mention it. You've gotta do things for your woman..."

"You said it," Travis grinned. "And... uh... incidentally, anything you may hear, or have heard, that I've said about you.... that can be totally disregarded,"

"What?"

"Well... you know... I've just been working to be, like, totally supportive of Karen and everything she says. And... she was saying some....

unflattering things about you, after you supported Chris. So I kind of had to too,"

"Well, what were you guys saying?"

"Nothing... it's not important, you know... because I was only doing it to get closer to Karen. I mean, I've even been getting closer than Alicia... and they were, like, best friends..."

"Wait a second... what do you mean?"

"Oh, well, Alicia just came up to her... and actually, she started to say something about you..."

"Like an insult or something?"

"No... just, like... 'Hey, guess what? Mike...' and then Karen, like, snapped at her... saying she didn't care about whatever Mike did, or something like that... and, well, you get the picture,"

"So you're still cool with me... and Chris?"

"No, I didn't say that. I'm cool with you... but very not cool with Chris. I mean Karen has a right to be mad at him, and he totally betrayed me,"

"Look... what he did... it didn't even have anything to do with Karen or you. Erin was dancing right there... it was more about her than anything,"

"What?"

"It's hard to explain... but I'm serious... it's not the way it seems,"

Just then, Chris arrived. "Hey guys," he said, and began working on opening his lock. He stopped after a moment, though, and turned to Travis. "Okay, look, I'm sorry about what I did. It was a mistake, all right? But I most certainly had no intention of hurting Karen, or killing our friendship..."

"Then I guess you're having a lot of accidents these days, if you did both without trying," With that Travis stormed out.

"Okay," Chris said, "Now, I didn't even ask him to apologize for shoving me down before..."

"Look, right now, no-one is that inclined to give you any sort of sympathy... or forgiveness..."

"All right, hold on!" Chris interrupted me. "Don't you start pulling that holier than thou crap on me. Listen, I made a mistake. But it's not like it was that big..."

"How can you say..."

FREE THROW

"How can I say that?! Easily. I'm getting all of this heat... you'd think I hit her ... or raped her or something. I *didn't*! Why is it that I'm the only one who can remember that?!" As he finished, he sat down, his head in his hands.

"I'm sorry man... but..."

"But what?! Everybody else is against me, so you have to be too?!"

"You know that's not what I mean. Look, you screwed up... big time. I don't know if you really deserve all of this heat you're getting, but it's not like you can really change that now."

Chris looked at me for a moment, before going on. "I know that I can't change the way people feel, because I've kinda already tried that, like, a zillion times. But I can ask for your support. And since we're supposed to be best friends, I think that's pretty reasonable,"

"You're right," I said. "From now on, I'm behind you," We clasped hands, and then left the locker room for practice.

***

"Wait up!" Karen's voice halted Chris and I, as we were on our way out of the school after practice. She was still wearing her cheerleaders uniform from her practice that apparently had also just ended.

We stopped, and as Karen caught up to us, Chris said, "Well, I guess I'll be... elsewhere," He began to walk away, but Karen grabbed his arm to stop him.

"Wait," she said, "I want to talk to you,"

"Okay," Chris said, surprised. "Shoot,"

"That whole... thing at the dance, had me really freaked out, you know? But I've been thinking it over, and even though it *did* really offend me, I think that I might've been a little too hard on you. I'm not saying that all is forgiven... but, I want to end this whole grudge thing, and just be friends,"

"You have no idea how much of a relief it is to hear you say that," Chris said. "But still, I feel compelled to keep apologizing,"

"Really, it's okay," Karen smiled. "It's over now. But... just don't... you know... do anything like that again, please,"

"No sweat. I mean, it's like I was trying to explain to you before..."

116

FREE THROW

"Hey, Karen," Alicia's voice cut him off. "As soon as you're done talking to dumb and dumber over there, I'd appreciate you getting ready to leave, if you want a ride home,"

"Gee," Karen said to us, "I've got such great friends," Chris laughed nervously. Karen went on, "You can finish telling me what you were saying tomorrow, okay?"

"Yeah, great," Chris said.

***

Pepper and I walked to the cafeteria for lunch together the next day. "So I'll meet you at the mall at seven, right outside the theater?" she asked, finalizing our plans for the coming Saturday night.

"Exactly," I said. "Sorry we can't do anything earlier than that, but my mom's making me come on the family trip to my aunt's house that afternoon,"

"It's okay. I'm sure you'll be worth the wait," she said, and kissed me on the cheek.

When we reached our table in the cafeteria, Steve and Karen were already present. "Hey," I said.

"Hey," Karen answered. Steve didn't say anything.

"Hi, Steve," I said, somewhat bluntly. He had been out of school for the first few days back from the vacation, but I could tell immediately that he had received the news about Pepper and I - or else our holding hands when we arrived had tipped him off. I pulled away from her when I noticed this, in an effort to minimize the awkwardness of the situation.

"Oh, right," Pepper said.

Steve looked up, and said unenthusiastically, "Hi," before returning his full attention to his food. We sat down, only to be met by more silence.

Soon after, Chris showed up. "Hey," he said.

"Oh, hey Chris!" Karen smiled.

"Hi," Pepper and I said at the same time.

"So," Pepper went on, "I take it the war is over with you two?"

"Yeah," Karen said, "I mean, I'm still kind of offended that he would do that to me, but he explained about Erin and all, to me earlier. And actually, I decided that what he had done wasn't so major after all... boy, I'm rambling, aren't I?" She broke off with a laugh.

FREE THROW

"That's totally okay, though," I said. "I think we're all glad to have some return to normalcy," I stopped as my eyes came to rest on Steve. "Okay, let's just talk about this," I said directly to him.

He looked up from his food again. He waited a few moments before saying anything, looking back and forth, between Pepper and I. When he spoke, there was no joke in his voice. "Okay," he said at last, "I just have to say a few things. No interruptions, please, because it's all I can do to say this once," I nodded and he went on, "Pepper, I care about you a lot. And Mike, you're one of my closest friends. I don't want to be mad at either one of you... and when I really think it over, there's really not any reason to be pissed off at anyone," He paused before finishing, "It might be weird or chauvinistic for me to say this... but it's what's on my mind. Mike... she's all yours. But treat her right, okay? We've had our little competition, and now it's over. I won't try to screw you guys up or anything. But, promise me that you'll treat her right... so that I *can* be all right with his,"

"You've got it," I said, almost solemnly.

There was another patch of silence that followed. That is, until Travis arrived. He glared at Chris as he passed him and sat down beside Karen.

Karen noticed this, and said quickly, "It's okay, now, Travis, Chris and I have pretty much worked things out,"

"Oh... umm great," Travis said.

Apparently not aware that Travis still had his feelings for her, Karen was visibly surprised by his curt, unenthusiastic response to the news. "Uh... so, did anyone see that Heat - Knicks game the other day?" Chris started, trying to change the subject.

"Wait," Karen said. "Is there something going on... that I don't know about,"

"No," Chris, Travis, Steve, Pepper and I all said at once.

"Well... that's reassuring," Karen said and laughed nervously.

"Actually, there is something," Travis said. We all turned our eyes to him. After all that time, we all saw Travis' secret on the verge of coming out. "Karen... I... for a while now... I've," he looked Karen in the eye and went on, "I'm just really surprised... and happy that everything has worked out,"

As Travis feigned happiness, we all looked at Karen, for her response. "Oh. Great!" She said with a smile. She had believed him.

FREE THROW

However, sitting there, I couldn't help wondering for how much longer that secret could be kept.

Chapter 11

 By the time Ray Penner played in the city championship game in his senior year, a number of his critics claimed that he was a ball hog, and that he totally carried his team. Today, Penner will admit that that was at least to some degree true. He wasn't worried about what anyone said about him, though. Like all players, Ray Penner always dreamed of just making one big shot, to win his team a championship. In that championship game, he had a chance to live up to his aspirations. The game was tied with only seconds remaining. Penner faked out his defender, leaving him with a wide open shot. However, he noticed that one of his teammates was also open, right under the basket. So, he gave up the game winning shot, in order to get the game winning assist. Things didn't work out the way he had planned. But, in a way, the way that things did happen was even better.

***

 Pepper and I had made plans to have our first date on that coming Saturday night. We were going to meet at the Tarris Mall, at about seven. Then we'd hang out at the mall, just talking or whatever, until eight, when we'd go and see some chick flick she had mentioned before.
 However, my parents had also made plans, for the whole family. We were visiting my aunt for the afternoon. Nonetheless, my mom did promise I'd be back home in time for my date, so I went along with everything pretty agreeably.
 All was going fine - that is, until the drive home. I had heard this weird ticking type sound coming from the front of the car on the drive to my aunt's house. On the ride back, it was louder, and accompanied by smoke rising from under the hood.
 Needless to say, we had to stop. My dad popped open the hood - an action that was followed by a series of sparks flying up.

***

 I almost knocked over an old woman, running past her to get to Pepper. The whole ordeal with the car had left me forty-five minutes late

FREE THROW

for our date. She was still waiting on the bench, right inside the mall. Her head was down, so her hair covered her face, and I was sure that she was crying. "I'm sorry, Pepper. I mean, it wasn't really my fault... you see, the car broke down on the way..."

She looked up. No tears. No stains on her face from having just stopped crying. Actually, she was smiling. "It's okay," she said. "I knew you'd come,"

"Oh, thank God. I said as I flopped down onto the bench beside her. "I just thought that you might get the wrong idea... like I didn't care, or was standing you up or something..."

"That's what I was afraid of... I'll admit it. But, well, I know we haven't known each other that long, but I feel like I know you... and I knew you wouldn't do that,"

I just smiled back. I don't know how someone can really respond to that. She didn't say anything either for a little while. I guess it was just a hard statement to follow, in general.

Finally, I broke the silence. "So, I guess we can still catch that movie if we go now,"

"Yeah, great," she said, as she rose to her feet. I put out my right hand, and she clasped a hold of it. It was so weird. We were actually holding hands, while we walked. We were a couple.

She tried to stop me, but I paid for both of our tickets and the popcorn. Then, right when were about to enter the theater, she stopped. "Actually, would you mind if we skipped the movie?"

"Well, what did you have in mind?" I asked.

"It's just that... this is our first date... I mean, what're we doing going in there, and staring at a bunch of overpaid Hollywood stars for two hours. I'd just assume sit down somewhere, like in the food court or something, share a tub of popcorn, and talk,"

"That sounds really nice," I said with a smile, and we walked away from the movie, to the center of the mall.

We found a deserted table amidst the busy and crowded place. I set the tub of popcorn on the table, and we sat down across from each other. "So, once again, I'm really sorry I was so late," I said.

"Don't worry about it. Really," she smiled. "I mean, it probably sounds kind of dumb, but that's what I like about you," She saw my puzzled expression and went on, "You see, when I just had a crush on you,

FREE THROW

I thought all sorts of things about you. How nice you were, how sweet you were... you know, that kind of stuff. Well, you see... I always think that sort of stuff about guys I like. Then, once I start going out with them, or just get to know them better, they turn out to be such jerks," She popped a piece of popcorn in her mouth. "You're not like that. You're the only case, where the reality lives up to the fantasy. I've been stood up for dates before, and while I waited for them, I always kept thinking that they were on their way. With other guys, they just forget, or decide they don't want to go out. You came, though. That's what separates you from the rest,"

She stopped and giggled for a second, "I hope I'm not freaking you out or something... I mean, if that came off as kind of heavy..."

"No... no. I think I can really understand. I mean, look at me. You're the first girlfriend I've ever had. The only time I ever felt even close to as strongly about someone, as I do with you, it was Alicia. And, well... you know how that worked out. She was just a dream, you know? You're my reality,"

She laughed for a second, "You know, Alicia told me I shouldn't waste my time with you,"

"I'm glad you didn't listen,"

"So am I," she said with a smile, as she put her hand out on the table. I clasped it with my hand, and we both smiled.

We spent the next few hours just sitting there, talking, and eating popcorn. Then we came down to the last kernel in the bucket. "You take it," she said.

"No, please. It's all yours," I said.

"Tell you what," she said with a smirked, "We'll share it," With that, she threw that last one into her mouth. Then, she pulled me toward her and we kissed. Allow me to say this much - a piece of popcorn has never tasted better than it did to me at that moment.

***

The buzzer sounded, ending another Lankford victory. I had had sixteen points, including my six-for-six free throw shooting. I waved up to Pepper in the stands, and then headed to the locker room, trailing the other guys.

FREE THROW

"Hey, wait up!" a voice called from above me. I looked around, but couldn't see whoever had said it. So, I continued my walking out of the gym.

"Wait! Weaver!" the voice called. This time, I saw whom it belonged to. It was a short girl, with long brown hair, who I'd seen around school before, but never spoken to.

"Me?" I called back.

"Yeah!" she said. "Hold up a sec!" she was up on the fifth or sixth bleacher, and was pushing her way through the crowd to get to me. "Get out of my way!" she said to one man, and "Move it!" to another, as she maneuvered past him. Finally, she reached the railing, and jumped over it, to the ground beside me.

"Um... hi," I said.

"Hey, I'm Kelly Jayne," she said, as she grabbed a hold of my hand and started shaking it.

"Um... okay..."

"And you are?"

"Mike... Mike Weaver... I thought you knew that,"

"Hell no," she said, releasing my hand. "I only knew your last name from your jersey." I didn't say anything, so she went on, "Anyway, I've seen you hanging around with Chris Brady, and I wanted you to tell him to meet me outside, by the flagpole, once he's all done changing and all. Can you handle that?"

"Yeah... but, um... could you tell me what this is about?"

"No," she said plainly. And with that, she walked away.

***

When I told Chris about what Kelly had said, he decided that he would meet up with her, and asked only that I tagged along, to back him up in case anything happened.

Kelly was already waiting by the flagpole in front of the school when we got outside. "Hey," she said to Chris. "Glad you could make it," Then she turned to me and said, "You can go now,"

I started to walk off, but Chris stopped me. "No," he said, "If you've got something to say to me, you can say it with both of us here," I was glad he said it, just because I was too curious to leave.

124

FREE THROW

"Fine," she said. "I'm getting a little bored with my current romantic situation. I want some spice. And I saw you at the Winter Formal, suddenly grabbing *Karen Miller's* ass. That's the sort of thing you don't see too often," I could tell Chris was embarrassed, but she went on, "I liked it, though. I can barely remember the last time Phil did that to me... and I'm no Ka..."

"Wait, who's Phil?" Chris broke in.

"Phil Ramms... you know, big linebacker on the football team. He's a junior like me. Anyway, I've been getting really sick of him, and you seem like a suitable replacement... so how 'bout it?"

"Um... Phil," Chris started, "Is he... uh... here?"

"Yeah, but I've got some friends of mine keeping him away for now, so we can talk. So what do you think?"

"Uh... um..." he started. That's when Kelly reached over and grabbed his - bottom. He fell silent, and just looked at her.

"I've found that to be a pretty effective cure for the stutters," she explained naturally. "So..."

"What are you doing?!" a voice boomed from behind me. Chris and I both spun around, and saw Phil Ramms. I stepped back. The guy was easily 6'2" and over 300 pounds. He shoved Chris, hard. He moved in closer, but Kelly stopped him.

"Come on," she pleaded, "You know you can't play football next year... your *senior* year... if you get in any fights between now and then. Just cool off..."

"Shut up!" he yelled at her, as he shoved her down. He turned back to Chris. "You trying to pick up my girl?! Huh?!" He pushed Chris with each word.

"Didn't any one ever tell you not to hit girls?" Chris fired back. He had courage, and a certain degree of honor I guess you could say. But sometimes, he didn't have the best discretion. He followed is words with a solid punch to Phil's cheek.

The linebacker shook off the blow. Chris winced and held his knuckles. "Let's get out of here," he said, and we ran. Phil chased after us.

"Run! Run!" I could hear Kelly shout after us. It's not like we needed the encouragement. If anything, though, we were lucky to have an incredible speed advantage over our nemesis. We ran all the way to the parking lot, where we jumped into Chris' mom's car, and yelled for her to

FREE THROW

get driving. Phil stood outside, shouting expletives after us. He couldn't do anything then, though. We were safe at last.

Kelly ran up alongside the car, and Chris rolled down the window. "My number is 555-2172," she yelled. "Call me!"

Chris grabbed a pen from the dashboard, and scribbled then number down on his hand. "You couldn't possibly, actually be considering calling her after all this," I said.

"I don't know, I kind of like, like her,"

"*Like* like her, or the more rational, platonic liking her, and you're now going to be keeping a safe distance from her,"

"Um, I think I like, *like* like her.

"What happened?" Chris' mom broke in.

"Uh... it's a long story," Chris said. "Nothing too big, though. I'll tell you about it later," Chris never had talked much to his parents about things like that, and he wasn't about to change his ways. There was silence for the rest of the ride.

***

Saturday afternoon, Chris and I went to the park as usual, to play some basketball. Only, that time, we weren't the only ones playing.

Carrie had started taking on a few baby-sitting jobs, not too long before that day. And, though she had already made plans to spend the day with Matt, she didn't turn down the last minute request from some wealthy employers, to watch their kids on that Saturday afternoon.

So she brought these two little boys, each about five or six years old, to the park, and sent them off to go play basketball with Chris and I; while she made out with Matt on a bench nearby. I wasn't too fond of the situation, but it's not like I could really tell the kids to go away.

Chris and I pretty much tried to ignore their presence, in terms of what we talked about. "So, I called Kelly," Chris said after we had shot around for a little while.

"What'd she say?"

"Well, let's just say... she's interested. And I think I am too,"

"So, are you going to ask her out or what?"

FREE THROW

"Actually, she already kind of did... but I told her I'd get back to her. I want to let a little suspense build... maybe it'll give me the upper hand with the relationship or something,"

"Sounds like a plan,"

"Well, hey, when it comes to relationships, I am the man. We both knew that it was only a matter of time before everything would work out,"

"Whatever," I said. I looked over at Carrie. She was still kissing Matt - I wondered if she had any idea where those kids were, or what they were doing.

"George has been hogging the ball!" one of the boys complained.

"No, we're just taking turns... Jordan gets three shots, then I do," said the other one.

"No! You said we each get two shots, you big liar!" said Jordan, as he stuck out his tongue at his brother.

"Come on, guys, just play fair. I picked up the ball and handed it to Jordan. "From now on, each of you gets two shots, then gives it to the other one. I'll be watching - so no cheating," I said.

"Okay," they both mumbled, and Chris and I went behind the basket and continued our conversation as we watched them play.

"So... you and Kelly... this could be interesting," I said.

"Yeah, but the timing sucks. I mean, our first weekend as a couple, and I'll be out of town for that tournament,"

"Ah, so you'll have to wait a week to hang out with her. It's not that big. Besides, this tournament is a pretty big deal. We're the number two team in the league!"

"Yeah, but Kelly is pretty tempting..."

"You'll get over it. I mean... it's just one weekend,"

***

Every January, near the beginning of the month, McDonnel High School held an invitational tournament, with the top three local schools and their own team playing. For the first time in the tournament's existence, Lankford was invited to play.

I climbed on the bus at 6:07 on Saturday morning, one of the last few to arrive for our trip. Everyone was tired, but you could tell no-one would mind anything about this trip. If we were to win our first game that

FREE THROW

afternoon, we'd be staying the whole weekend, for the game on Sunday and the banquet to follow. If we lost, we'd be headed for home early the next morning.

For the first hour or so of the journey, most of the guys, including myself, drifted in and out of sleep. But by the time we pulled into the lot in front of the Marriott hotel where we were staying, everyone was up and lively.

Chris and I would be sharing a room right next door to that of Greg and George. As we left the room after setting our luggage down, Alicia and Karen arrived at their room - right across the hall from ours. Upon sight of us, Alicia dropped her suitcases, and signaled for Karen to follow her lead. Reluctantly, she did, though she clearly didn't know what Alicia was up to.

And so, the four of us stood there in the hall, just waiting - none of us knowing what was going on, except for Alicia. At last Chris broke the silence. "What?"

"Neanderthals," Alicia said in clearly condescending tone.

"What?" I wondered aloud, as she bent to lift her bags again.

"Neanderthal - it means, primitive and ape-like. Any gentleman would be happy to help carry our bags for us... clearly, you're far from being gentlemen,"

"What bull...." Chris started, before I cut him off.

"Keep cool man," I said, and then turned to Alicia. "All you had to do was ask," And with that, I opened their door and carried in Alicia's bags. Far more reluctant was Chris, but eventually he acquiesced and did the same for Karen.

"Uh... you don't have to do that..." she began.

"Oh, but I *want* to," Chris said, glaring at Alicia.

***

Our first game was against Stone Hill. We hadn't played them before, but had certainly heard about them. Stone Hill was known as a school that tried to recruit all of the good players from anywhere nearby, to come and get their education there, so that they could help the team. That year, they weren't particularly rich in talent, but had one - or actually two - special weapons.

FREE THROW

Their starting center, Adam Sczerbiak stood 7'5". The starting power forward, Derrick Presomp was a solid 7'2". Together, they dominated on rebounding and were strong defensive stoppers. That's what had carried the team to third place in our league. However, their height could also be a disadvantage. They were both awfully slow, and had trouble defending fast breaks, and handling the ball much on their own.

It was for speed's sake that coach decided not to start Travis, moving every one over one position, and starting Chris at point guard.

As would be expected, Sczerbiak won the tip off. With us having no-one over 6'5" on the floor, the Stone Hill players found it easy enough to get the ball inside to Presomp for an easy basket. After that was when we began to implement Coach's strategy. The plan was, for the person inbounding the ball to hurl a nearly court long outlet pass down-court each time, where we could score before their seven footers got back on defense.

It worked pretty well during that first half, putting us seven points ahead. That's when Stone Hill called a time out, and set up a new system, with their twin towers unit staying on defense the entire time.

We countered this action by putting in Travis as our own defensive stopper. Though our own offense was limited by the switches, the changes hurt Stone Hill more as they went scoreless for the remainder of the half. From that point forward, they tried various changes - none of which proved all that effective. Once our lead grew to sixteen near the end of the third period, they essentially gave up and benched Sczerbiak and Presomp.

I was fouled on a three-point shot at the buzzer, which ended the game. Going to the line, I drained all three free throws, to end up eleven for eleven from the line, with eighteen points overall. We won 72-53.

***

We soon found that our opponents in the tournament final would be the Jorles Knights - the top ranked team in our area. They had lost just one game up to that point - their successes including an 80-32 blow out in their first round match-up. We'd be hard pressed in this one, but preparation seemed to be the last thing on the team's mind that evening.

***

FREE THROW

Greg and George had a message passed along, for most of the team to meet up in their room that night. When Chris and I showed, the brothers, Brad Davies, and a couple other guys were already there, guzzling beer, and blasting rap music from someone's boom box.

"Hey there... I doubt that we're allowed to have that type of stuff here. I mean, if Coach finds out... we're pretty much no longer of the living," Chris said.

"But Coach won't find out, man!" George said. "That's why guys like Travis and Shawn weren't invited... no tattle tales allowed," He paused. "You ain't gonna tell anyone, right?"

"Na... don't worry about it," Chris said. "In fact, pass me a Miller Lite," I shot him a look, but he simply shrugged it off.

"All right, my kind of guy!" Greg laughed, handing him a beer. "And here's one for you, big guy!" he said, pressing another bottle up against my chest.

"No thanks man... I think that I'll just stay clean and sober for tonight," I answered.

"All right, suit yourself," he smiled. "More for the rest of us,"

There was knock on the door. "Hide the stuff!" George hissed. Promptly, every beverage slid into a hiding spot, and the bed covers were pulled up to conceal the rest of the alcohol. Greg opened the door.

Alicia and Karen were waiting outside. "Hey," Alicia said. "Sounds like you guys have a little party going on in here..."

"Yeah, so beat it!" Brad said and laughed.

"Na man, you crazy?" George answered. "Some chicks is all that we're missing!" He turned to Alicia and Karen, "Come on in,"

As soon as the door closed, the beers came back out. "Want one?" George asked the girls.

"Got any wine coolers?" Karen asked.

"But of course," he gestured grandly toward the bed. "Help yourself," Both girls did.

In a few hours, everyone but me was totally stoned. I was surprised that no-one came to complain about the music. I was grateful, though - even if the booze was hidden, there was no longer any hiding the fact that they had all been drinking. If I wasn't there - I mean, if some how I could have just been watching from outside - it would have been kind of funny, just

FREE THROW

seeing the way they were all acting. It was a bit less amusing, actually being there.

"Man, there's not enough room in here. Let's go some place!" Brad said.

"Yeah, guys!" George agreed.

"But where are we gonna go?" Chris put in, his speech badly slurred.

"I know... we'll go to the pool!" Alicia said.

"It's too late," Greg said. "The life guards must've already left... no way they'll let anyone in,"

"But what if we sneak in?" Karen started. "Like you said - anybody who would stop us is already asleep. We've just got to be quiet getting down there,"

"By golly, she's right!" George kind of shouted with what I think was an attempt at an English accent. I suppose he was trying to be funny, but was too out of it to realize that he wasn't.

"So it's settled... let's go to the pool!" Greg exclaimed, and everyone started moving toward the door.

"Wait," I said. "It's pointless... nobody has there swimming stuff or anything..."

"Oh shut up," Alicia said. "I can't even swim... it's just a cooler place to hang out,"

"Weaver's just scared of getting caught," George laughed as he opened the door. It was settled - they were going to the pool. I didn't really want to, myself, but I ended up following along anyway.

To my surprise, at the start, we actually managed to get along pretty steadily, and normally - without drawing any attention. That is, until we got on the elevator. "All right, I guess the only logical place for a pool would be on the top floor," George said as he pressed the appropriate button.

"What are you talking about?" I said, as I pressed the button to stop the elevator, and then redirected us to the ground floor.

"No, I was right!" he yelled, and stopped the elevator again. He sent it back up from there.

Karen stepped up. "Seven's my favorite number," she declared, stopped the elevator once more, and pressed that button. To give you a hint of how out of it they were, it should be noted that we were already on the seventh floor. Things continued like that for a while, until finally we had

FREE THROW

a vote on which floor to go to. My choice won by a show of hands - though just barely.

It didn't take long to find the pool after that. We ignored the sign, saying that the pool was closed until the next morning, and went in.

We goofed around for a while - just talking mostly. Then George took things a step further. He lifted up Alicia, and carried her toward the water. "Now, I'm going to throw you in!" he yelled, and laughed loudly.

"No!" she giggled. That's when it happened. He set her down on the ground - but right on the edge of the pool. Her senses were pretty dull by that point, and she couldn't keep her balance. Hence, she fell in.

Alicia bumped her head on the way down, but wasn't completely unconscious. Her clothes weighed her down, though, and as she had said earlier, she couldn't swim. Soon, she was completely under water.

Some of the guys were actually laughing - I don't think they really knew how to act. "What should we do?" Chris asked.

"Uh..." I thought for a moment. Should we get security, or see if we could find a lifeguard? Ultimately, I knew there wasn't time to waste. "Watch my stuff," I said as I flung off my shirt and sneakers.

I remembered something from my old swimming classes that I took when I was much younger - that you should never jump in after somebody, because they'd only hold you down, so you'd drown too. But I knew that she was pretty light, and besides, I had to do something.

When I dove in, the chlorine in the water stung my eyes, so that I couldn't keep them open. I swam blindly for a while, reaching all over, in my attempts to find her. When I came up for air, I looked down, trying to see her. It wasn't easy. I had a sudden pang of fear. This was quickly becoming an actual life and death situation. She may not have been my favorite person at the time, but that had to remain an afterthought.

Finally, I did see something. Alicia's red hair stood out anywhere - that included under water. She seemed to have floated or rolled even further from the side of the pool. But when I saw what looked like a big red ball, I held my breath and swam right to her.

I slid my arms under her, and with all my strength, lifted her up, and kicked as hard as I could, to get to the surface. To keep her head above water, I had to keep my own mostly under. I kicked frantically at the water, but we moved slowly to the side. Alicia was completely unconscious.

FREE THROW

"Gimme a hand!" I screamed when I got within a foot of land. I was having trouble getting air by then, but I refused to give up on her. Chris reached out, pulling at us while I kicked. Soon, I was holding the side of the pool, while Chris and Greg worked together to drag Alicia out of the pool. The others all just seemed to be in shock, as they stood there watching.

As I climbed up and out of the water, Chris put his ear down to Alicia's mouth. "She's not breathing, man!" He seemed on the verge of tears. I was probably already crying, but didn't notice.

I bent down toward her, to find that Chris had been right. "All right, Chris, start pumping on her chest," I ordered. As he started to press down, I blew into her mouth. I really didn't know anything about CPR and all that stuff, and just tried to do it the way I'd seen it on TV.

We were at it for minutes that seemed like days. I was starting to lose hope. But then she coughed. I now know that it wasn't the medically correct thing to do, and for my own sake, I probably shouldn't have, but I issued her one more breath. This time she opened her eyes, and saw me. She probably would have complained if she could have. However, she entered a series of coughs, each time spitting out more water. She looked straight up at me, but didn't say a word.

***

A short while after, it became clear that the incident had sucked all of the life from our party. We all just went back to our rooms, Chris and I helping Alicia along. By the time I was all settled in my room, it was already 3:30 in the morning. Coach wanted to meet us all in the hotel lobby at 9:00 or breakfast as a team, and an early shoot around. At least half of the team would be tired and largely troubled when we showed up.

***

Chris and I made a special effort not to be late the next morning, and though tired, we managed to achieve that goal. Most of the other guys and cheerleaders had been early - but not all of them. About ten minutes after I arrived, Alicia and Karen showed up, a bit late. But their tardiness wasn't the most noticeable thing for me, concerning their arrival.

FREE THROW

Alicia was ordinarily the effervescent type. Even though I usually didn't like what she was saying, she was always talking. That day, she was silent. I kind of expected her to thank me or something. Instead, whenever we came close to making eye contact, she evaded it. In place of Alicia being grateful, I found her avoiding me.

My thinking was interrupted when Coach glanced at his watch and shouted, "Where are those two!" in reference to Greg and George. It was 9:30, and they were the only ones to not come down by that point. Finally, he called their room, and demanded their presence.

After about ten minutes, they stumbled out of the elevator, wearing the same clothes as the night before. For both of them their hair was uncombed, and parts of clothing hung out of the sides of their suitcases. George was clutching the back of his head, leaving clear evidence of his hangover.

The morning practice was more of the same. There were some guys like myself, who were very tired, and missed more shots than we should have. Then there was George, Greg, Brad, and to a somewhat lesser degree, Chris. They were constantly fumbling passes, and losing their dribble.

All of this was discussed at my table, when we stopped at Burger King for lunch later on. Greg started, "Man, Coach told me that I'm not starting today... it's such bull,"

"Man, you should've seen yourself out there... you looked more like some cheerleader who got lost, than a starter for the varsity team," Chris started.

"Shut up," he answered, holding his head again.

"Look, seriously," I began, "If you don't start looking any better, you won't see any playing time at all," I turned to Brad and George, "Same for you two. I'm not trying to be mean, but you guys are playing really sloppily out there," I couldn't think of much else to say, so I ended my lecture at that, hoping that somehow it would help.

***

After lunch, Coach gave everybody two hours of free time. Greg and George checked in at a hotel and slept for the full period. Most of the rest of us wandered around town. That included Alicia.

FREE THROW

Chris and I saw her when we entered this music store. While he stopped to look at some posters, I walked toward her. Somehow, by that time, I was at the point where I didn't just expect, but actually wanted gratitude. She didn't seem to notice me as I first walked by her, as she flipped through a row of CDs. I walked past her again, with the same result. Finally, I stood next to her, looking at the CD rack to her left.

She looked up, "Do you, like, want something?"

"No... I'm just looking at some music..."

"Oh, please. I know you just came over because of me. You think I didn't see you walking by me twice, and then stopping right here next to me? You know, if you still like me, then just come out and say it. Stop sneaking around and going behind my cousin's back..."

"Trust me, I'm over you,"

"Fine, then give me some space!" She took a step back, but I followed after her.

"Yeah, and maybe I should've given you some *space* last night at the pool,"

"Oh come on... I'm not stupid! The only reason you *saved* me was because you wanted to kiss me!"

"What?!"

"Your little mouth-to-mouth resuscitation act... it's pretty clear what that was all about. You probably copped a feel when you were bringing me out of the water too!"

A short, gray haired, man, working in the store, stepped between us, saying, "If you two wish to proceed in this discussion, I'm going to have to ask you to do it outside of this store,"

I ignored the warning, and continued shouting, "Alicia, I don't love you! Heck, I don't even like you!" I started to say something else, but stopped short when I saw that Alicia was starting to cry. She looked at me again, and then walked out of the store quickly.

I realized that I had probably gone too far. I started to go after her, to apologize, but Karen, who had apparently been standing behind Alicia the whole time, stopped me. "Look," she began, "The situation's a lot more complicated than it looks... but she really wouldn't want me to explain it. Just try to avoid her, okay?"

"Okay, but..." She left to go to Alicia, before I could finish.

"What happened?" Chris asked.

FREE THROW

I glanced at the store employee, who looked pretty upset. "Let's go," I said. "I'll tell you about it outside,"

***

When we warmed up before the game, everyone looked a lot sharper. Greg got to start after all, putting us back to our usual starting line-up.

During the shoot around, the stands began to fill up with spectators. This was the cheerleaders' cue to start their job. I couldn't help thinking about Alicia. I just wanted to talk to her - or at least simply tell her that I was sorry about yelling at her. But when I saw Karen, I remembered her instructions. I would leave Alicia alone - at least for the time being.

I wasn't the only one looking to the sidelines, though. I caught Chris stealing a few glances at Erin, though he dismissed it when I asked him about it. Travis, though, actually seemed pretty focused on the task at hand as we prepared for the game to begin.

I had enough to think about one way or the other. Jorles had stolen a victory from us earlier in the year, and though I thought that we should have had that win, I have to admit that they were definitely a tough team. In addition, I was sure to have my hands full with Timothy Kahn once more. He hadn't done much trash talking in our previous encounter, but I had a feeling that it was only because he was scouting me out in that first game. Either way, I would be guarding him this time, so there'd be plenty of opportunities for us to have words.

While I launched a three-point shot, I peered cross court, where he was warming up. As I watched, he fired, and swished, a three of his own.

***

The game opened with Travis tipping the ball to me. As I tried to hand it off to Brad, Kahn ran through and slapped the ball ahead. He then sprinted forward, grabbed the ball, dribbled up and lay in an open finger roll.

"I hope that ain't all you got, Weaver!" he hooted as he ran back on defense. "I was hoping for a challenge,"

"Don't sweat it," I fired back. When I got the ball, I shot a three, which just made over Kahn's outstretched fingers. Due to his presence, right up in my face, I couldn't get a good look at the hoop. The shot careened off the back of the rim, into Travis' hands. He slipped it over to Shawn for the dunk, and our first points of the game.

"Lucky you had the big fella to bail you out on that one," Kahn said as we headed back to the other side of the court.

"Let's see you do better," I said, hoping not only to get back at him, but also to distract him, and take him out of his game.

"No prob," he said, and then shouted to their point guard, "Gimme the ball!" His teammate complied, and Kahn shot and made a three right over me.

At the end of the first quarter, we were down 19-15. At the half, Jorles had expanded the lead all the way to 45-21. We had tried different double teams on Kahn, but he would always either find a way to score, or he'd dish off to the open man. Near the end of the second quarter, Shawn was moved onto Kahn. However, the guard was able to speed by our big guy, and their rebounding situation was aided when Shawn had to play defense out on the perimeter.

We started the second half by going back to a man to man set up, with me guarding Kahn. Slowly, we began to creep back into contention. While we were able to switch off our starters with bench players (with the exception of Shawn and I) due to our depth, their starters had played the entire first half. Usually, Jorles relied on blowing out their opponents early, and then letting their starters sit down for almost full periods at the end of games. In this contest, every starter from Jorles, except Kahn, sat for a long stretch in the third quarter. By the time they came back, were only down by five. Jorles led by seven at the end of the quarter.

Defense became less and less of an option as the fourth quarter progressed. Before long, the outcome of the game was just a question of who made more baskets, more quickly.

With just over a minute remaining, we trailed by only two points. Kahn hit a three, and on the way back to the other side of the court, he called, "Who's guarding me? Who's guarding me?"

On the opposite end, I got the ball and made a head-fake that drew Kahn up in the air. I dribbled past him and made a three of my own.

Fifteen seconds remained. Kahn fired another three, only this time, I blocked him. The ball was in my hands. Kahn probably could've caught up to me if he wanted, but he stayed down on the other side. I looked back

FREE THROW

as I dribbled past the half-court line. Travis was a few steps back, with Shawn and a Jorles forward at his side.

Wanting to kill some time, so Jorles wouldn't be able to score again, I handed off the ball to Travis, who threw it over his head. Shawn leaped upward, caught the ball in air, and slammed it down, with just four seconds remaining. The score was tied.

Kahn had a trick up his sleeve, though. He hadn't stayed back on his offensive end because he was lazy. The inbounds pass went straight cross court to him. Since he was wide open, he stood still, spinning the ball on his finger, until just one second was left. Having killed any time for us to score again, he then laid the ball in, off the glass, as the final buzzer sounded.

They had won, 103-101.

The show wasn't over, though. After the game they had both teams line up to walk along and shake hands with the other teams' players. Kahn had other ideas.

He stepped out of the line, and made his way forward to our cheerleaders. One by one, he raised their hands to his mouth, and kissed them softly. He was a handsome, smooth guy, so most of the girls didn't exactly fight him off. I noticed Travis watching every move Kahn made - especially when he came to Karen. She tried to pull her hand away from him, but he held on tight, and wouldn't let her go, forcing her hand up to his lips. Travis left the line up.

Travis grabbed Kahn's shoulder and spun him around. "What's happening big guy?" he asked. Travis shoved him - hard. Kahn wasn't about to back off though. For a moment, it looked like a major brawl was on the way.

I exited our line and held Travis back. "It's not worth it! It's not worth it!" I yelled up at him.

"Listen to him, big guy," Kahn smiled. "His game might be weak, but he's giving you some good advice... you don't want none of this,"

It took several of the guys from our team to hold Travis back after that remark. Kahn walked away, laughing.

Once Travis had calmed down, Karen approached him. "Thanks," she said, and gave him a smile.

"O-of course," Travis stuttered out.

FREE THROW

My attention was diverted, as Alicia walked past. "Hey, Alicia..." I said. She didn't stop. Karen grabbed my jersey. "Remember what I said," "But... why? What's going on?" I asked. Like Alicia, she just kept walking. "Women," I muttered. I turned to Travis, as Chris talked to him. I could tell that the big guy wasn't really listening, as he smiled and stared after Karen while she left the gymnasium.

"That was a pretty smooth move," Chris was saying, "Of course, if he'd made it as far as Erin, I would've done the same,"

"As far as *Erin*?" I asked.

"Well... I meant Erin in the sense of... any cheerleader, you know, who really didn't want to have that... done to them," Chris stuttered.

"Sure," I said. I patted them both on the back and walked away.

***

On the bus ride home, Alicia, probably unknowingly, sat down in the seat in front of Chris and I. It was late, and everyone was tired. To the best of my knowledge, by 12:30, everyone but the driver and myself was asleep. I saw that Alicia still had the headphones from her Discman on, and I could still here the faint murmur of music coming from them. Because of this, I figured that maybe she was still awake too.

"Alicia?" I whispered. No answer. "Alicia?" Again no answer. I figured that she was probably asleep, or else couldn't hear me over the sound of the music.

I had let Chris have the window seat, and as he dozed I gazed out at the scenery we were passing. When I turned my head so I was looking back into the aisle, I'm almost certain that I saw Alicia's head turning, as if she had been looking at me when I faced away from her.

I was about to tap her shoulder, but then decided that it wasn't worth it. If she wanted to talk, she would come to me. It was dark, and I was tired, so I closed my eyes, and fell asleep, listening to the sound of the faint murmuring from Alicia's Discman.

Chapter 12

Ray Penner was never the most trusting of people. That's not to say that he didn't have a lot of close friends, but he always thought that every person had some sort of deep, dark, secret. Most people would never confess to this, but Penner believed that virtually everything that anyone did was merely for the purpose of covering up that one thing, that no-one else knew about.

***

I didn't think about Alicia much at all once I got home. It seemed everyone just wanted to forget about the night when I had saved her, and so it became unimportant and unmentioned. Besides, at home the only girl I cared about was Pepper.

We sat next to each other in study hall, Monday afternoon, passing gushy love notes back and forth. That's when Kelly entered the room. "You wanted to see me Mr. Dylan?" she asked the teacher up front.

"Yes, Ms. Jayne. Did you really expect for me to accept this?" the old man asked her, handing a sheet of loose-leaf paper to her as he sat at his desk.

She looked at it. "Yeah, what's wrong with it?"

"Ms. Jayne, I asked for you to write 'I must learn to respect my teacher.' fifty times on this sheet of paper,"

"Yeah, and I did that..."

"No, Ms. Jayne, what you wrote fifty times was, 'I must learn to respect my *stupid* teacher," A couple of guys in the back of the room started to chuckle, but Mr. Dylan silenced them with a cold glare.

"Sorry, Mr. Dylan. I thought you would appreciate all of the extra work I put in. I mean, I wrote a total of fifty more words than you asked for,"

"Do the assignment over again, Ms. Jayne. This time, write it one hundred times, and don't put in any extra work. Try to learn the lesson from the exercise this time,"

"Oh, don't worry, Mr. Dylan, it's my pleasure to put in any extra effort in the name of my education,"

FREE THROW

"Ms. Jayne!"

"All right, all right. Is that all you wanted to talk about?"

"Yes. Now, go back to wherever you're supposed to be,"

"Sure thing," she smiled. As she was on her way out, I was handing a note to Pepper. Kelly reached between us, and intercepted the message. She unfolded it, and stood between Pepper and I, just reading it. Finally, she unfolded it. "That was really sweet, Mike," she said, while she messed up my hair with her hand. She then dropped the piece of paper on Pepper's desk and left.

***

The next Saturday, my parents insisted on inviting Pepper over for dinner. After the first impression that they had made so long ago, I was a little reluctant to agree. Eventually, I acquiesced, though, and did invite her, under the condition that my parents would be on their best behavior.

Just as my family and Pepper were sitting down to dinner on that Saturday evening, the phone rang. I answered, and was greeted by the voice of Rob Sperling, sports columnist for the local newspaper.

After introducing himself, he went on to explain that he thought my, "free throw shooting streak is incredible, and it's been the key to Lankford's emergence as a basketball power,"

"Uh... thank you," I stuttered out.

"So, anyway," he continued in his smooth voice, "I'm looking to do a little article on you for the Saturday paper. You up for it?"

"You bet!"

"Super. I'd be at your game on Friday night, at some point I'll run a few quick questions by you, and that's about it. Okay?"

"Great! I'll see you then,"

With that we both hung up. "Guess what?" I said as I reentered the kitchen, "That was just some guy from the newspaper. He said he wants to do an article on me, about my basketball playing and all,"

"That's great!" Pepper said.

"Yes it is!" my mom screeched as she ran over to me and kissed my cheek. The bright pink lipstick she wore was without a doubt smeared across my face.

FREE THROW

Our family had this old - ritual - of sorts, where if I did something particularly noteworthy, I could have a marshmallow with supper. It didn't really make much sense, but usually I just accepted it to humor my mother. However, it was far too embarrassing for this situation. I shook my head vigorously, pointing at Pepper. Luckily, my mom seemed to understand. "Oh, right," she whispered, and then winked.

Despite the rocky start, the rest of dinner was mostly uneventful. Ordinarily, I may have had a bad taste in my mouth because of how things had gone, but after Pepper left, I refrained from reprimanding my mother. It was kind of weird how I was worrying totally about how my girlfriend would like my family, rather than the other way around.

Aside from Pepper, though, I was thinking about that newspaper article all night. I had received some attention for my basketball before, but somehow, this was bigger.

***

The team was shooting around before the game, when Sperling met up with me. Since our last conversation, Coach had warned me to be careful about what I said during the interview. He said Sperling was notorious for contorting what people said, emphasizing the negatives, in order to spice up his stories. The idea of this sickened me - I mean, I never liked when I heard about journalists doing that sort of thing to celebrities, and there Sperling was, trying to sabotage the image of a *teenager*. It just seemed totally wrong.

He didn't look particularly like someone with a great deal of integrity, either. His hair was slick - almost dripping with gel, and he wore this crooked kind of smile. His line of questioning didn't improve my opinion much.

He started out with soft questions, like "How does if feel to be such a successful shooter?" and "What pro athlete do you respect most?" But then, he gradually got more serious - asking my opinion on various other players, from rival schools that I had competed against. It was like he was inviting me to say something derogatory. I simply gave the most complimentary statement that I could.

FREE THROW

It was easy enough to tell that Sperling was getting frustrated. He began inquiring about my teammates, trying to create dissension there. For Travis, I replied, "He's a tremendous defensive force for us,"

He jumped on what he thought was an opening. "Is that to say that Travis is a non-factor in the offense in your opinion?"

"Not at all," I smiled. "His rebounding and blocks are what open most of our fast breaks,"

"But that's staying with defense," He was almost yelling by then. The smile seemed more deranged than anything at that point. He went on, "Anyone can see that he never shoots - so wouldn't you agree that that hurts the team as a whole?"

"No, I wouldn't. Shawn and I are comfortable shouldering the bulk of the scoring load. Travis' role is primarily on defense. That's not to take away from his passing ability. It's really improved,"

"So you're saying that he wasn't good enough at the beginning. . ."

"I'm afraid not. I've found Travis' contributions to be sufficient all year long,"

We went on like this for a while. Chris passed me a ball, so I could still warm up a little, while I talked. I fired a three, that went off the glass and in.

"Ah-ha!" Sperling cried. "Did you just put that shot in off the backboard, because you weren't confident that you could swish it?!" I could tell that he was getting really desperate.

"Na... just seemed easier to bank it from this angle," I grinned. Finally, he walked away, seething. I was confident that I had won the battle of wits.

***

We won the game with relative ease. I scored twenty points, and kept my free throw streak alive, by going six for six from the line. On my way off the court, Pepper leaned over the railing and we kissed. I managed to escape Coach's watchful eye, and walk her out to her parents' car and kiss her goodnight after that, before heading to the locker room.

The next morning, I rolled over in bed, to see that my clock read "7:12". While it was rare for a Saturday, I got up at once, and ran out doors.

FREE THROW

I knew the newspaper would already be waiting on the front porch, including an important article.

I jammed some waffles into the toaster, and unfolded the paper as they cooked. Opening to the front page of the sports section, I spied my own picture at the center of the page, showing me guarding one of the opposing players from the night before.

Underneath the photo began the article. It started out pretty much as one would hope - nothing negative, mostly just going over the well-known information of my perfection at the free throw line, and the team's overall success.

However, things then shifted gears. It read as follows: "Despite his noticeable skills, Weaver is clearly far from perfect. After the game, I had a word with his girlfriend. She tagged Weaver as everything from a 'sore loser' to a 'braggart' to a 'stupid jerk'," The article continued on like this. Coach had warned me about Sperling - telling me to watch what I said. I couldn't control Pepper, though. I couldn't understand why she would say those things, even so.

I knew that it was still early, but I couldn't wait. I was angry and hurt, and had to get some answers, Hence, I called Pepper. After several rings, her tired voice answered, "Hello?"

"Hi, Pepper?"

"Yeah... Mike?"

"Yep. I'm sorry to call you so early... I guess I'm just a stupid jerk," I said in a sarcastic tone.

"What?"

"I've read the newspaper. I saw what you said to the reporter,"

"What reporter?" she said with a yawn. I couldn't believe it - what I was saying was actually boring her.

"Oh forget about it," I paused for a minute, and then continued, "And forget about us,"

***

After finishing a pick up game at the park, Chris and I sat down on a bench, hot and exhausted. "So Pepper ripped you in the newspaper?" I just nodded. He continued, "Man, now that's up there among the toughest breaks in the history of man. What are you gonna do?"

"I don't really know," I said. "I mean, I called her this morning, and told her we're through," I sighed. "But that's not what I really want. I... I just can't see why she'd say those things,"

"It doesn't sound like her to do something like thi..." he stopped abruptly. "Wait a minute - when did you say Sperling said Pepper was talking to him?"

"Some time after the game,"

"But don't you remember - you met up with her right after the game, and then walked her to her car, right?"

"Yeah, so?"

"So, when could she have given that guy a quote for the article? She was with you the whole time after the game,"

"But... well, if she didn't do it, then who did?"

"Well, that guy - Sperling, or whatever - he lives just a couple blocks away. We can go see him right now,"

"That's right. All right, let's go!"

***

I recognized Sperling's place from a couple of years ago, when he had had a big garage sale that I went to. It was a small place, with partially peeled old yellow paint covering the walls. I rang the doorbell, with Chris standing at my side. In about a minute, Sperling stood before us, on the other side of his screen door,"

"Hey boys. Great game last night. So, what can I do for you?"

"Hey Mr. Sperling," I said, "I was just wondering about a couple of things from your article,"

"Oh, sure,"

"Okay, now, you have some quotes from my girlfriend, but you say you got them after the game. Only things is, she was with me the whole time once the game ended,"

"I'm afraid not. She hung back when all of the other cheerleaders were going in to change..."

"Wait a second... she's not a cheerleader,"

"Well, she sure was last night,"

"Hold on," Chris stepped in, "What did she look like?"

"Well, she had this really curly, big, red hair, and..."

FREE THROW

"All right, I think I know who you're talking about now," I said, looking down. "She's really not my girlfriend, but she tends to do things... like this. Thank you for your time,"
"Sure thing," Sperling said as we walked away.

***

"Alicia," I said, as I saw her walk by on her way out of school Monday afternoon. "We've got to talk,"
"Sure," she answered, and then turned to her friends and said, "Be back in a minute,"
I guided Alicia to a vacant part of the parking lot for privacy, and then began, "Look, I know that you're the one who said all of those things to the reporter,"
"What? I..."
"Save it. All year long, it's been this same crap. The snide remarks, telling people things - doing everything you can to disrupt either my life, or things between Pepper and I. I... I'm just sick of it," I expected her to say something, but instead, she just looked at me." I started again. "Don't just take it... say something!"
"What do you want from me?" she said softly, looking down.
"How about an explanation?!" I shouted, as loud as she had been quiet.
She looked up at that, staring me straight in the eye. "It's really pretty simple," she smiled, and then sniffed, as if fighting back tears. "I love you,"
"What?" I said, my emotions turning from anger to disbelief.
"Oh, come on. Don't be so surprised," She really looked like she was about to cry then. "I just didn't realize it until it was too late," A tear did roll down her cheek at that point. I removed a tissue from my pocket, and offered it too her. Instead, she leaned her body into mine, and began to hug me. Reluctantly, I put my arms around her too.
"There, there," I said slowly, not really sure what else to say. I had to get to practice, but I knew that I couldn't just leave her. She didn't budge for what must have at least been a few minutes.
Then, it happened. She raised her head, and kissed me. And not just a peck - she was really laying it on. For so long, I had wished for a moment

FREE THROW

like that. I think that's why I didn't pull away at first. When I did, though, things only got worse.

The first thing that I saw upon looking up, was Pepper. I stuttered, to try to explain, but she started instead, "When the people over there said that they saw the two of you coming over here, I guess I should have assumed the worst,"

"No... this isn't what it looks like..."

"Oh, spare me. I guess you really are just a *stupid jerk*," With that, she stormed off.

***

The next day, some club was selling flowers during lunch, as a fundraiser. Naturally, I bought one for Pepper. It wasn't until after school that I was able to give it to her, though.

I saw her walking toward her bus, and called out her name. She turned and smiled when she saw me, and walked over. As soon as she arrived, I started to speak rapidly, "Look, I'm sorry... I mean it really wasn't what it looked like, but..."

"Mike, take a breath," she laughed. "Alicia called me last night and told me everything... I'm sorry I overreacted... I should have heard you out first,"

"You have no idea how relieved I am to hear you say that," We both just kind of stood there for a little bit after I said that - I think each of us expected the other to say something.

Finally, she broke the silence, "So is that flower for me, or is it just a fashion statement?"

"Oh! This," I laughed, "Is most definitely for you," I gave her the flower, and received a kiss in return.

***

Pepper and I attended a school dance together the following Saturday. There was a fairly large crowd - ordinarily something we would use to our advantage - relying on the mass of people to shield us from the eyes of the chaperones, while we made out.

FREE THROW

However, that night was different. Kelly had a recent suspension on her record, which barred her from attending. Chris hadn't known about this until about fifteen minutes before the start of the dance, and so he came anyway. Hence, the evening was spent with the three of us hanging out together - Pepper and I determined not to make him feel like a third wheel.

That feeling was kind of inevitable, though, as Pepper and I went to the dance floor without him for every slow song.

"You know, this really sucks," Chris said as we returned to him after dancing. The evening was nearing its end by that point. "I mean, I finally have a girlfriend, and I had all these pre-conceived notions about relationships. There are supposed to be late-night phone conversations, and groping in broom closets... and we've had all that. But most importantly, there are supposed to be dances."

"Look, Chris, I'm sorry tonight hasn't gone the way you planned," I said. "But it's just one night..."

"I know," he cut me off. "It's mostly just that that 'losers who made fun me' thing hasn't been so past tense tonight,"

"Well, I'm sure things will get better," Pepper said. "There's another dance in just a couple weeks... I'm sure everything will go the way you planned then,"

"But what if it doesn't?" Chris started. "Who's to say that Kelly won't be in trouble again then? I mean, one of the things that gets to me more than anything else is the fact that she didn't even tell me about it, until it was too late,"

Chris went on like that for a while - until the DJ announced that he was about to begin the last song of the dance. It was another slow one.

Pepper and I stood, and began to move. I couldn't help looking back at Chris, many times. I tried to think just about Pepper, but couldn't. Finally, I let my conscience take over. I stopped moving.

"Damn it," I muttered.

"What?" Pepper asked, startled.

"It's Chris. I can't just stay out here, dancing with you when I know he's miserable,"

"Well... what do you want to do?"

"I know this is going to sound weird, but, if you don't mind... I'd really appreciate it if you'd dance with him. I mean, he's my best friend and

FREE THROW

all, and I hate seeing him down like this. I think he'd really feel better if you'd do this,"

"Well," she smiled, "He's not as cute as you, but I suppose that I could manage," We both laughed, and then separated. She walked back over to him, and after a few words, they both came to the center of the gym and began to dance.

I leaned against a wall, and watched them for a while. Then I saw Alicia, sitting alone in a corner. I looked back at Pepper and Chris, to see them still dancing - oblivious to me. So, I made my way toward Alicia.

"Hey Alicia," I said, as I sat down on the ground beside her.

"Oh, hey," she said, visibly surprised. Also visible, was a tear in her eye.

"Are you okay?"

"Yeah... yeah," she said, wiping her eye dry. "It's just..." she trailed off.

"What?" I smiled. "What is it?"

"All of my friends... they're out there, dancing right now. And..." she trailed off again.

"All right," I said, "Do you want to dance?"

"No... you don't have to do that,"

"Do you want to dance?" I repeated.

"Sure," she smiled.

She stood up, and led the way to the dance floor. Once she had found a suitable spot, she stopped, put her arms around me and we began to move.

We were both quiet for a while. I didn't notice it at first - when she began to stare into my eyes. When I did finally notice, she was moving closer to me. Finally, she went for the kiss.

I dodged her head at he last possible moment, and dropped my arms from her sides. "Alicia! W-what.... that's not what I meant by all this!"

"It's not? Oh, God! I'm so sorry," Alicia said, covering her face with her hand. We both stood there, with an awkward silence for a while. Then she sighed before saying, "I know that I probably shouldn't even ask, but will you at least finish the dance with me?"

"Yeah," I said simply, and we began once more. I still don't know if it was really appropriate, but I went on to say, "You have no idea... for.... for how long I wouldn't have pulled away from that... even welcomed it,"

150

FREE THROW

We were both quiet again for a while. Then, she said softly, "How did I ever let you get away?"

"I learned to get over you... to just be friends. Now you just have to do the same thing,"

"Some friend I was," Alicia said after a moment.

"Come on Alicia. Stop beating yourself up. "You're beautiful, and smart, and nice. If it weren't for Pepper..." I stopped.

"What?"

"I don't want to go there... because I love Pepper. But before I met her, I cared about you a lot. You're a great person, and I hate to see you down on yourself like this... especially without a good reason,"

Alicia stopped moving. "You're a lot better friend than I ever was," she said. I was probably blushing, but she didn't seem to mind. She spread out her arms, and I came into them. We embraced until the song was over.

Chapter 13

Ray Penner served as his own measuring stick. If other people tried to judge him, he would ignore it, because he only cared about what he thought of himself. Few people are their own measuring sticks.

***

"Hello, Mrs. Harris," I said as Pepper's mom greeted me at the door.

"Hello Michael," she replied. "Come in," I did, just as Pepper came downstairs to meet me.

"Hey Mike!" she said.

"Hey Pepper," I said, and kissed her on the cheek. She sort of walked away from lips, though, pointing with her eyes toward her mother.

"Sorry," I mouthed to her, realizing my mistake.

"Pepper," her mother began, "Why don't you show Michael to the parlor. Dinner should be ready in about half an hour,"

"Okay," Pepper said, and turned to me. "Right this way," I smiled and followed her lead.

We sat down together on a leather sofa, against the wall, opposite the big screen TV which was the first thing that I noticed about the room. "Wow... now that's a big TV," were my exact words. "I mean, I saw it at New Year's, but..."

"Yeah..." Pepper said. "But... umm... don't comment on that when my folks get in here, okay?"

"Uh... yeah," I said, and then asked the obvious question. "Why?"

"It's just that... well, don't take this the wrong way... umm..." she stopped and started again. "See, my parents are really... judgmental. And I think that they kind of think that you're... you know..."

"What?"

"Well... dumb,"

"Dumb? But... why?"

"It's just ... well, a lot of things... I mean, they still remember that whole scene at the restaurant... back in the summer. And they were there for the disaster that was Romeo and Juliet. And you're interest in basketball... to them, it sort of translates into you being the stereotypical... dumb jock,"

"Pepper... I can't believe this," I said. "You don't agree with them, do you?"

"Of course not! But I also haven't been able to convince them to change their thinking,"

"So I guess that I should probably try... tonight..."

"I don't think that's such a good idea," she cut me off. "If it works that would be great, but one mis-usage of a big word, and their opinion only gets stronger,"

I sighed and turned my back to her. I remembered when Matt had come to my house for dinner. How, while I was talking to him, mentally, I was making wisecracks to myself, and passing judgments. The tables were turned - I had become the one on trial.

Pepper hugged me from behind. "Mike, I'm sorry I didn't tell you about this before, but it just never seemed right..." she said. "But tonight, just be yourself. I don't care what my parents think, if it's going to make you uncomfortable," she trailed off as she kissed my cheek.

I turned around, and kissed her passionately. "I love you," I said as our lips separated.

"I love you too..."

"But, I want your parents to approve, so tonight, I'm totally the intelligent guy,"

"Mike..." she began to protest, but I covered her mouth with my hand.

"Sorry, but this one isn't open to debate,"

"Mmm..." she let out, in a whiny way. I shook my head. She pulled away from my hand, and then slumped down into the couch, defeated. I sat down next to her and draped my arm over her shoulders as I heard Pepper's parents make their way towards the room.

***

"So, tell us Michael," Pepper's father said as he cut apart his slice of ham at the dinner table. "What are you interested in doing with your life... once you're through with school,"

FREE THROW

I was careful to finish chewing and swallowing my food before answering. "Well, I'm not quite sure, sir. There are a lot of areas I'm interested in... a lot of choices I have to make..."

"Yes, like guard, forward or center, right?" Mr. Harris interrupted and laughed aggressively. Pepper's mom giggled along.

"Dad..." Pepper said softly, but sharply.

"Sorry dear," he said as his laughter began to subside.

"Come now Pepper, it was just a little joke, to ease the tension. After all, someone like Mike probably hasn't given as much thought to his future, as you have," She turned to me. "Pepper is going to be a pediatrician,"

"But I thought you said..." I started.

"Let's just drop this all okay?" Pepper said, and smiled nervously.

"Why?" her mother said, apparently having been intrigued by the exchange. "What were you trying to say Michael?"

"Just that," I started hesitantly, "Pepper had always told me that she wanted to be an actress,"

There was a moment's hesitation - then, Pepper's father began to laugh again. Pepper's mother was less amused. "Is this true?" she questioned her daughter.

"I-it's just kind of an idea... I mean it's not really anything..." Pepper tried.

"Wait," Pepper's mother interrupted, "You're serious about this? Have you lost your mind?"

"No," Pepper said, more firmly, "I'm definitely not serious about it... it's just like, this dream... that's all..."

"Well, you'd better wake up then," her mother went on. "Because we didn't spend the last nearly sixteen years of our lives providing for you, so that you could blow it all on this... this, pipe dream."

"Mom..." Pepper began.

"Please, Pepper, don't interrupt your mother," her father interrupted her. "Now, go ahead, dear,"

"Actually, I was done," her mother said.

"Oh," Pepper's father said. "Well, then... actually, I think your mother has spoken for both of us. Acting... I'm sure it looks like a glorious profession, but..."

"Pardon me for interrupting, sir," I jumped in. They all stared at me. I swallowed and went on, "I know that you want what's best for your

155

daughter, and she seems to be trying to satisfy all of the standards that you guys set up for her..."

"I know that this is hard for you to understand," Peppers' mother cut me off. "But we're very different people from you. Our standards aren't to 'pass every course in school', and 'score thirty points tonight'..."

"And neither are mine, or my parents'. I don't know where either of you came up with the ignorant, and false idea that I'm an idiot. But forget about it! And let your daughter pursue her own ambitions... instead of yours,"

"Well I think that we can see who has been causing all of this wild dreaming," Mrs. Harris said.

"Look, with all due respect..." I began. "Actually, no, without any respect, because you certainly haven't shown me any tonight..."

"This should be good," Pepper's mom said sarcastically under her breath.

I ignored the comment, and went on, "You're out of touch with your daughter. Apparently, you know nothing about her. And you don't know enough about me to pass off any of your stupid judgments,"

"I think you've said more than your share," Peppers' mother started again. "And I've grown tired of listening. Pepper, go up to your room. And *you*," she said to me, "Are to leave my house!"

"He's right," Pepper said. "About everything,"

"Don't you start," her mother warned her.

"No!" Pepper yelled back. "I'm so tired of you trying to run my life! I do want to be an actress. I *do*. And if you want to say that Mike... is... is somehow causing me to 'dream wildly'... that's just ridiculous. He just cares about me enough to let me make my own choices - and support me no matter what," With that, she stood up, and stormed out of the kitchen - presumably to her room.

Her mother sighed. "I'll go upstairs and check on her. You make sure that *he* finds his way out,"

I glared after her as she left the room, and since she was gone, stood up to leave.

"Wait," Mr. Harris stopped me.

"What?"

He produced a small cloth from his jacket pocket, and began to clean his spectacles. "Sit down, Mike. She won't be back for a few minutes," I obeyed him, and then continued to listen to him "What you said tonight... it took courage. I respect that. It's not easy to stand up to adults.. especially ones that you were initially trying to impress,"

"Well, thank you sir," I said.

He smiled, "You know, her mother's going to be raising hell over this," He stopped and laughed. "Ah... she's a forceful woman. But not as evil or cruel as she may have appeared tonight. Anyway, I'll be on your side. It's good to see a young man who cares about my daughter as much as I do,"

"I really appreciate your saying all of this," I said, "I can see where Pepper gets her... entire personality,"

We both laughed, at the conclusion of which Peppers' father said, "Well, you'd better be going before the old ball and chain gets back down here,"

"Yeah, I guess so," I said. "Thanks for everything," Mr. Harris simply nodded in response, as I left, thinking that perhaps the evening hadn't gone so badly after all.

***

"Hey, Mike, Pepper... perfect timing," Chris said as he ran up to us in the hall.

"Why's that?" I asked.

"Okay, Kelly wants me to come sit at her table for lunch..."

"As I told you she would," I interrupted.

"Right. Whatever. The point is... her friends... they kind of scare me. I mean we're talking about your hard-core homey-G types, you know? So, I was wondering if you guys would come join me."

"Umm... don't you want to be spending time with Kelly... not talking to us?" Pepper asked.

"Ordinarily, I'd say yes. But I really don't know Kelly that well... so you guys can be, like, my support people,"

"If you're so worried about all that, why don't you just ask her to come to our table?" I asked.

"I don't think that would work too well," Chris started. "I mean, her interests are very specific... they're pretty much limited to sex, drugs, and..."

"Rock and roll?" I smiled.

"Well, actually more your rap and hip hop genres of music, but you've got the basic idea,"

"You're kidding, right?" Pepper said. "I mean... at least to some degree,"

"Not really," Chris started as Kelly ran up from behind and jumped onto his back. "Whoa!"

"Hey Chris," she said and kissed his earlobe. "Did you miss me?"

"Oh, you bet," Chris said. With that, Kelly slid her body, so that she was on Chris' front side, and gave him a long kiss on the lips. After this, she dropped back to the ground, and simply held hands as they walked the rest of the way.

"So Kelly," Chris began, "You don't mind if my friends, Mike and Pepper tag along to your lunch table, do you?"

Out of the corner of my eye, I saw Kelly rolling her eyes, before saying unenthusiastically. "I guess they can come,"

"Oh boy," Pepper said, and looked at me. I shrugged in response.

***

"So guys, this is my new boyfriend, Chris," Kelly said as we sat down at the table. "And Chris, these are the guys,"

"Hey... guys. How's it going?" Chris said. Kelly's friends said nothing at first, leaving a tremendously odd, as well as awkward silence.

"Who are they?" one of them the guys said at last, meaning Pepper and I.

"Hi, I'm Mi..." I started.

"They're some of Chris' friends," Kelly cut me off. "It's Piper and Mick, right?"

"Um... Mike," I said.

"And Pepper,"

"Whatever," Kelly said. She turned to one of the other guys at the table. "So, do you have my disc?"

"What disc?" the guy asked.

"The one I let you borrow two weeks ago... that old one, by Funkmaster Flex," she said angrily.

FREE THROW

"Whoa... that was yours? I sold it to Vinnie," the guy said, scratching his head.

"What? Why'd you do that?"

"I was a few bucks short for my weed... I needed the cash,"

"Whatever," she said, and turned to another one of the guys, "So give me back my disc, Vinnie,"

"Hey, I paid for that! I'm not giving it up for nothing,"

"Tell you what," she started, "You give me back the disc, and I won't have my boyfriend here kick your ass,"

"Whoa... wait a sec... where did I come into this?" Chris said, suddenly alert.

"Yeah Kelly, you could pull that stuff when you were dating a football player," the first guys said. "But basketball players ain't got nothing,"

"Hey, I got respect for basketball players," Vinnie said. "They've got speed and style," He turned to Chris, "You know, I'd be on the team if I had the grades,"

"Okay..." Chris started.

"Yeah, but I mean, in terms of giving a good ass-whooping," the first guy interrupted, "A basketball player just can't compare to a linebacker,"

"Oh, of course. I could take this guy down... nothing to it," Vinnie said as he gave Chris a noogie, "But I respect his athletic ability,"

"Umm... great!" Chris said, feigning amusement.

"Hey, have you got a cigarette?" a girl sitting next to me slurred out, as she stared at my forehead.

"No... sorry," I stuttered. She continued to stare at me for a moment, before turning her head, and then resting it on the table.

"These people are starting to freak me out," Pepper whispered into my ear. I nodded in agreement.

Suddenly, there was loud thud, and the table began to shake. "Sorry," Travis said, having bumped, or been bumped, into the table.

"You idiot!" one of the guys yelled, "You made me spill my soda!"

"Umm... sorry," Travis said, and turned to Pepper and I. "So, are we changing seating locations?"

"No, we're just here for Chris..." I began.

"But now we're going back to the regular table," Pepper said slowly.

FREE THROW

"Well Chris," I started. "You heard the lady. Okay if we..." I trailed off as I actually faced him. He was busy kissing Kelly; totally oblivious to everything that was being said. I turned back to Travis and Pepper. "Okay, let's go,"

"So how's your day going?" I asked Travis as we sat down.

"Huh? What?" Travis said, his attention having suddenly been called back to us. I looked behind me, to where Travis had been looking. Karen was there, having just walked into the cafeteria.

"I'm getting tired of this," Pepper said, "You've been obsessing over her for so long... just do something already,"

"But... I can't. I mean... what if she said no..." Travis said.

"Then she says no. Life goes on," Pepper said. "The fact is, after all this time, she probably already has an idea that you like her. Either she's just waiting for you to ask, or she's already dealing with the semi-awkward friendship thing. I'm right, right Mike?"

I hesitated, knowing from long ago that Pepper's hunch of Karen knowing, was actually a fact, but not wanting to betray Karen's trust. Luckily, I was bailed out of having to make any comment as Karen arrived at the table, effectively ending the conversation.

"Hey guys, what's up?" she said, while pulling out a chair to sit on.

"Nothing much," all three of us said at once.

"Okay..." Karen said slowly. "Umm... so, I see that Chris has switched tables, and seems to really like the taste of Kelly's tongue,"

"Yeah, that about sums it up," I said, "He tried to keep us over there too, but Kelly's friends are a little... um..."

"Freakish," Pepper said.

"Pretty much what I was going for," I nodded and smiled.

"I have to say, I'm not too fond of Kelly on the whole," Karen said, "She just really doesn't seem like Chris' type,"

"Well," Steve began, as he entered the conversation upon his arrival at the table, "She has a pretty face and... well you know," he said, gesturing toward his chest, "So, yeah, naturally, I doubt Chris would have any qualms about going for her,"

"But, he used to be so into Erin," Karen said, "And she's, like, totally different,"

"Well, to be fair, I don't think he ever really cared much about Erin's personality," Travis said.

FREE THROW

"Hey, one way or another, it doesn't really matter when it's love," I said, and kissed Pepper.

She broke off our kiss to say, "Doesn't really seem like love with Kelly, though. I mean, he wanted us to sit at the table with him..."

"Yeah, but her friends are pretty weird," I said. "But more importantly, never stop one of our kisses that quickly... you're killing me," With that, we continued our kiss.

Pepper and I stopped again, as I felt my leg being kicked under the table. I glanced under the table, and saw that it was Karen's foot, and decided that she would understand if we didn't pull apart right away.

"Ow!" I shouted, as I drew back from Pepper, after Karen kicked me again - hard this time. "What is it?"

Karen just nudged her head to her right. I looked over to see Alicia. With that, I pulled farther back from Pepper, and released her hand from mine. "Hey Alicia," I said, "How's it going?"

"Fine," she smiled. "And, you know, you don't have to not kiss on my account... really, it's okay,"

"Well, you know, we just wanted to avoid any awkward stuff," Pepper said. "Though, that would kind of be a mute point right about now,"

"Don't sweat it," Alicia said as she sat down.

"Oh, hey, did you get that math homework at all?" Karen asked Travis.

"Uh... yeah, pretty much..." Travis said. "Do you need any help with it?"

"Totally," Karen said. She began to search through her book bag. "Shoot! All my math stuff is in my locker,"

"Oh... that's okay," Travis said. "I have mine over here,"

"Great," Karen said, as Travis dropped a heavy blue binder on the table, between them. With that, he began to explain the assignment.

***

"So that was good, right? The whole helping her with her homework thing... right?" Travis asked us all as soon as Karen was away from the table to buy her lunch.

"It was good," Steve said, "But you have to learn to milk opportunities like that. I mean, sure it was cool, helping her during lunch

FREE THROW

and all. But, you could have just hung out with her here, and then arranged a study date outside of school some time. Study dates are the perfect chance to ask the girl out,"

"But when did you ever have a study date?" I asked. "Most of the time, the girl your pursuing is getting about two full grades higher than you in every class,"

"But *she* never knows that," Steve smiled. "The girl comes to my house, with the preconceived notion that I'm her intellectual superior. Then I start putting the moves on, and before long... well, let's just say, most girls forget about the studying,"

"Okay, I'm just going to ignore for the moment, that that whole account really offended me as a woman," Pepper started. "And say that the whole study date thing isn't such a bad idea. I mean, that might be the perfect chance to let her know how you feel,"

"But I just did all the studying stuff..." Travis began.

"Then wait till tomorrow, and do it then," Steve said.

"Really," Pepper said. "You have to get this out into the open.... just to get it over with,"

"But sometimes," Alicia started, while dabbing at her yogurt with her spoon. "It can be really hard to just 'get it over with'. I mean... maybe it's best that you do... but if you can't find the words... or whatever.... you can't just *do* something like that," She paused and looked up, at me. "Of course, sometimes you have to be careful not to wait too long,"

No-one said anything. I swallowed hard. Pepper took hold of my hand, under the table, and squeezed it.

The silence was broken when Karen returned. "Hey," she said. "What's with all the solemness?"

No-one volunteered an answer. No-one had to, as Travis blurted out, "Will you go out with me?"

"What?" Karen said, her surprise evident on her face.

"Look, Karen, I've really like you... a lot... since we first met. I know that we're friends and all, but... I can't help the way I feel about you,"

In her surprise, Karen dropped her tray. "Oh, God," she said, bent down, and began to pick up her things.

"Here, let me help," Travis said. He knelt on the ground and began to assist her.

FREE THROW

"Thanks," Karen said, as he put her milk, the last item, back on the tray.
"No problem," Travis answered. As they got back up, their heads knocked into each other, causing each to say "Ow," and resulting in Karen dropping the tray again.
They both knelt down once more. "I've got it," Karen said. "But thanks,"
"Yeah," Travis said, and sat down in his chair again. Karen stood back up a moment later, put her tray on the table and sat down.
"Gee, so much for that salad," she said, laughed nervously as she moved the bowl away from her on her tray.
"So, what do you say?" Travis asked hopefully.
"Um... you know, I forgot to get some napkins," Karen said quickly. "I think I'll go grab some now," Travis grabbed her arm to stop her. "What... what is it?" she asked and laughed nervously again.
"I know this is kind of sudden," Travis said. "But I'd really appreciate some sort of response to my question. Will you go out with me?"
We were all staring at Karen - certainly not easing the mood.
"I... I don't know what to say," Kate said. "Um... can.. would you let me think about it for a while... like, get back to you later on that?"
"Of... of course," Travis said.
There was little conversation for the rest of the period. Travis' question was a hard act to follow.

***

"So, how do you think it went?" Travis asked, while we were changing for practice that afternoon.
"Well, you certainly caught her by surprise..."
"It's like Pepper was saying, though," he cut me off. "Sometimes, you just have to get these things over with,"
"Hey guys," Chris said upon entering. "Oh, and thanks a lot for stranding me at Kelly's table today," he said to me.
"You didn't really seem to be needing us at the time," I said. "And by the way, you have lipstick on your cheek,"
"Uh... thanks," he said, wiping off his cheek with his hand. "Just spent ninth period with Kelly,"

163

FREE THROW

"You've been spending a lot of time with her lately, haven't you?" I said.

"Yeah... and it has been good," Chris said. "But still, I really have to have somebody there with me,"

"Why? I mean, you've been all over Kelly every second you've been together,"

"It might appear as such to the uninitiated," Chris began. "But it hasn't all been rosy. I mean, you were there before... her friends, are like, creatures from the Black Lagoon..."

"Exactly," I said, "So why should we be wasting our time hanging out with them while you suck face with Kelly?"

"Yeah, but whenever she goes to the bathroom, or leaves for some other reason, I'm left alone with those people,"

"Tell you what... we'll figure this out later. We've got bigger things to be concerned about," I said.

"What... what did I miss?" Chris asked.

"Travis... kind of..."

"I asked out Karen," Travis broke in.

"You know," I said to Travis, "You don't have to 'get it over with' for *everything*,"

"But why should I be hesitant about anything that has to do with Karen?" Travis said. "For so long... she's been everything to me. If it's meant to be - then she'll say yes, and we'll live happily ever after. There's no use in being afraid any more,"

"Hold on. Time out," Chris said. "Last I heard, you," he pointed to Travis, "Were incredibly nervous and scared to do anything even vaguely related to asking Karen out," He turned to me. "Meanwhile, you were pushing him to go faster than he wanted to, and telling him to ask her out already. Is today opposite day, or something... because I thought everybody stopped playing that game once they were out of elementary school,"

"I was and am fully supportive of Travis not waiting any longer," I said, "But what you did today... just springing it on her, with no prelude or romantic setting... it's just not the way I would've gone,"

"Mike... I'm not sure if how I did it was right... but asking Karen out was just something I had to do. And I really need your support now," He paused and looked to Chris. "And yours too,"

FREE THROW

"Hey, I'm totally on the bandwagon of support," Chris said, "That is, provided there's a bandwagon to be jumped on,"
"Of course there is," I said, "Win or lose, I'm on your side,"

***

"Why didn't you stop him or something?" Karen asked over the phone, after school. "You know I don't like him that way,"
"Well, that kind of would have gone against my whole telling him to ask you out thing..." I said hesitantly.
"What?!"
"Look, I had to constantly pretend that you never told me that you knew he liked you... or else, I couldn't have given him any real advice or support. You know me... I'm a romantic. Whether you said yes or no, I wanted to see him at least try,"
"Yeah, but do you know the position you've left me in now? I have no idea how to say no, without really hurting him," she said, her voice changing from angry to sympathetic - even sad.
"Well... I mean, you must have at least considered what you might do in this situation. It was kind of... inevitable, from the start,"
"But that's just it - I thought he was over it. We've gotten so much closer over the last few months... I *didn't* see this coming,"
"Look, I'm probably not the best guy to be giving you advice on this... but, I guess you should just be honest. You know... don't play games or use any of the 'I'd rather just be friends' lines..."
"But that's the truth. I'm not going to lie to him, so I can sound like I'm being honest,"
"I... I don't know what to tell you..."
"Look, just be totally honest with me about something,"
"Yeah... of course,"
"Do you think that after this is all over with, that there's any way Travis will still want to be friends with me?"
I hesitated before answering. "Travis is a good guy, and he really likes you. From knowing him... I would think that he'd want to be as close to you as possible... in whatever capacity. But..." I trailed off.
"What? But what?"

FREE THROW

"But," I paused again. "I remember when Alicia rejected me last year... and when I thought Pepper had turned me down this year. And... after that, I just wanted to be away from them. Maybe that's just me... but, who knows? Maybe rejection just does that to a guy,"

"Then what can I do?" Karen asked with a sigh.

"I don't know," I responded truthfully.

***

"So what do you think she's going to do?" Carrie asked as we pulled into the school parking lot the next morning.

"I'm not sure. I mean, I know she's going to turn him down, but I don't know how," I said.

"Well," Carrie said while she unfastened her seat-belt, "From my experience, the yes or no matters a lot more than the how and why. There's not really a right way to break someone's heart,"

We exited the car, and began to walk towards the school. Matt came up to us, and Carrie simply said, "See you later," before leaving me by myself. I soon ran into Chris and Kelly, though.

"Hey guys, how's it going?" I said.

"Hey, Mike. Not bad," Chris said.

"Oh, hi," Kelly said unenthusiastically, and grabbed a hold of Chris' hand.

"So, any news on the Karen and Travis front?" Chris asked while Kelly began to kiss his neck.

"Actually, it looks like there might be, right now," I said, looking past Chris, to where Travis and Karen were talking in front of the school.

We watched them for a moment. At least, Chris and I watched them. Kelly continued to pay more attention to Chris' neck. Finally, Chris said, "I wonder what they're saying,"

"Yeah, me too," I said.

Kelly moved away from Chris. "Do I have to do everything around here?"

"Huh?" Chris asked.

"Be back in a minute," Kelly said, and walked away from us, toward Travis and Karen. She crouched behind a bush, on the side away from them, so she could hear them without being seen.

FREE THROW

"Gee, she's got two uses. She can make out with you *and* eavesdrop on your friends," I joked.

"That sounds about right," Chris said, without any touch of humor.

"Is something wrong, man?" I asked.

"It's Kelly, he started, and then looked at me and continued with, "Na... forget it. We can talk about this later. I want to watch what's going on with Travis,"

"Yeah... okay," I said, disturbed by what he said, but not wanting to stop watching the scene being played out before me.

Karen did most of the talking. When she stopped Travis said something back, and walked away. Karen ran her fingers through her hair, and then walked off in the opposite direction.

"Boy, that seemed to go well," Chris said. "You know... except for the whole, it going well thing,"

"Yeah... I'd better go check on Travis," I said, and then thought for a moment. "Or maybe I should check on Karen."

"Well, let's hear what Kelly has to say first," Chris said, as Kelly strolled back towards us. She stopped to talk with one of her friends, and then continued towards us, completely casual. "So, what happened?" Chris asked when she arrived at last.

"Oh, Vinnie lost my Funkmaster Flex disc, but he's giving me his Sir Mixalot one, so it's going to be all right,"

"I meant about Travis... and Karen. You know, that whole discussion you just listened in on,"

"Oh, that," she said, "Well, that girl kept feeding him a bunch of lines... like, 'I like you better as a friend' and 'It's not you... it's me.'"

"Well... how did Travis react?" I asked.

"He kind of spazzed. He said that he didn't want to just be friends or something like that, and then stormed off,"

"All right, so I guess I'd better try to catch up with Travis first," I said.

"I don't know about that," Kelly said. "That chick seemed like she was gonna cry or something, every time she talked,"

"Oh, this is just great," I said, and walked off toward the school.

***

FREE THROW

"Hey, have you seen Karen?" I asked Alicia when I sat down beside her for homeroom.

"No. Why? Did she talk to Travis already?"

"Yeah... and it didn't seem to go too well," I said. I looked up, to see Pepper entering. "Hey Pepper. I waited for you by your locker.."

"Yeah, I missed the bus. My parents were being all weird... they said they wanted to talk to me, and then they said they'd talk to me about it later. Anyway, I kept me from being on time,"

"Hm... that's weird," I said.

"Yeah, but it's probably nothing," she said. "So what were you guys talking about?"

"Well," Alicia said, "Travis and Karen already... talked,"

"Not good?"

"Kind of an understatement," Steve joined the conversation. "I just ran into the big guy... seems pretty pissed off. I'd suggest we keep he and Karen separate for a while..."

"But that can't help," Alicia said, "I mean, whether he says so or not, a person can't just drop their feelings like that. Travis probably still wants to see her. And I know that Karen was really scared about this whole thing ruining their friendship..."

"I think the best way to go is to make sure they talk during lunch," Pepper jumped in. "We can all kind of mediate it..."

"Look, I'm telling you guys, if Travis is anything like me, he'll want to keep his distance from Karen," Steve said.

"I hate to say it, but I agree," I said.

"Maybe we should just see what they want to do first, then," Alicia said. "Because I know Karen will want this... and I think deep down, Travis will too,"

"I suppose it won't hurt to try," I said.

***

"Hey guys. We decided to come sit over here today," Chris said as he and Kelly arrived at our lunch table.

"Cool," I said, and they sat down. Karen, Alicia, Steve and I were already present - all waiting for Travis.

FREE THROW

"I don't know about this," Karen said after a minute or so of silence. "I mean, this might just upset him more..."

"You've got to talk this out, though," Pepper said. "None of us are going to choose between the two of you, so you guys have to work it out,"

"I don't see what the big deal is," Kelly said, " So, he liked you. You turned him down. It should be over with. He should move on, and you shouldn't care."

"But we were friends," Karen said.

"And he liked her for a really long time... and a lot," I said.

"So what?!" Kelly fired back. We all just stared at her. She turned to Chris, and said, "Your friends are weird,"

There was no time to debate the point, as Travis arrived. Everyone's stares were transferred to him as he sat down at the opposite end of the circular table, from Karen. "Uh... hi," he said.

"Hey," I said. As no-one else stepped forward, I went on, "Look, we all think that you and Karen should really just sit here and talk about what happened. You know... try to be friends again,"

There were a few seconds of silence, before Karen began, "Travis, I never wanted to hurt you..."

"Then why did you?" Travis cut her off coldly.

"You act like I *wanted* to..."

"Like you wanted to what?" Travis interrupted her again. "Like you wanted to break my heart? Cause you did an awfully good job for someone who didn't *want* to do that,"

"Let's not forget that you started this!" Karen raised her voice. "I was happy with the way things were! I like having you as my friend! You're the one who ruined that! You..."

"I'm so sorry!" Travis fired back. "Can I help it if you're the most beautiful person I've ever met?! Can I help it if every time I hear your voice, I feel like I'm in heaven? Is it my fault that everything... *everything* about you, just makes me want to scream because it's so perfect... but I know that it can never be mine..." he trailed off.

"Travis..." Karen began softly.

"I- I have to go," he said, as he stood up.

"No... wait..."

"I can't. I'm sorry. I have to go," Travis said quickly and choppily. With that, he left.

FREE THROW

"*That* was excessive," Kelly said after a few moments had passed.
"Shut up," Pepper, Steve, Alicia and I all said at once.
"I don't like your friends," Kelly said to Chris.

Chapter 14

One of the reasons Ray Penner loved basketball was that it never changed. As he told me, "People are all neurotic freaks, who say and do different things whenever they want. At least basketball is constant. There'll always be a ball - meant to be thrown into a hoop. It's as simple as that,"

***

"So, that was pretty intense today in lunch, eh?" Chris said as he bounced a basketball up and down, at the park.

"Yeah," I said, "I don't know where either of them can go from here. I mean, the things Travis said... they aren't easily forgotten," I paused as Chris shot a jumper from just inside the three-point line. It bounced off the rim and out, allowing me to grab the rebound. "You'd better start shooting better than that. The playoffs start for us in just a week,"

"Yeah, yeah, yeah," Chris said. "I hate to say it but my head is elsewhere... namely on Kelly,"

"Yeah... umm... on that topic, what is that girl's deal?"

"I don't know... but I think I'm going to end it soon,"

"End it? Like, the relationship as a whole?"

"Yeah," Chris said. "There's just something missing. I mean, the kissing, and groping and all... that's great. But... there's just nothing else to it,"

"What do you mean?" I asked as I fired a three-pointer that went off the backboard and in.

"I mean, all of our conversations are about whatever she wants to talk about. Then, when I try to bring up any sort of new topic, she blows it off. And she hates all of my friends... especially you,"

"Me?"

"Oh... yeah, she thinks you have this whole arrogant jock thing going on. I disagree with her about that too, of course," he added quickly.

"I should hope so," I said, flipping in a finger roll.

"But that's not everything,"

"Why? What else is it?"

FREE THROW

"It's Erin... I don't think I ever *really* got over her,"

"What?!"

"Look, it's not, like, something I chose. I mean, here I was, thinking all that I wanted was a girlfriend... any girl. But lately, I can't stop thinking about Erin..."

"Well, you've kind of already been down that road. Remember the whole Winter Formal incident?"

"Of course. But before that... I don't know... maybe there wasn't anything to it, but, I felt like I was getting closer to her. The way I felt... the way I feel about her... it's beyond compare... I want so badly to give this one more shot,"

"And Kelly is what's stopping you?"

"Exactly. I can't keep going out with Kelly and go after Erin,"

"Then why not just break it off with Kelly? You've said it yourself.... you're not happy with her..."

"I'm happier with Kelly than I am alone, though. She's not my dream girl. I'll admit that. But I'd rather settle for groping with her in a broom closet during ninth period, instead of just day dreaming about it during class,"

"Well," I paused, and bounced him the ball. "The ball's in your court," He released a jump shot that hit the backboard, the rim, and fell to the round, without ever making it through the hoop.

***

Karen, Pepper and I walked to the cafeteria together the next day, anticipating the worst all the way.

"He wouldn't talk to me at all in math today," Karen said. "Which kind of works out, since I have no idea what to say back... whatever he says,"

"Well, whatever happens, we're here for you," Pepper said.

"Right," I agreed, though I realized that I had made the same promise to Travis just days before.

He was already waiting for us at the table when we arrived. "Hi," he said.

FREE THROW

"Hey," Karen said softly. Travis was back at his usual spot at the table - next to Karen's normal seat. She began to sit down elsewhere, though - at the opposite end of the table from him.

"No... it's okay," Travis said. "You can sit over here," Somewhat reluctantly, Karen moved back to her regular seat. "Look, I want to apologize for what I've said and done..."

"No..." Karen said, "You don't have to..."

"I know I don't have to," Travis said. "But I want to," He stopped for a moment, perhaps collecting his thoughts. "I care a lot about you... too much to separate from you altogether. I want to be more than friends, but I'd rather be just friends than nothing at all,"

"Thanks," Karen said, and they both smiled.

"Well, looks like we might have a happy ending after all," Pepper said to me quietly.

"A civil ending anyway," I said.

After this, my attention was drawn away, to the other end of the cafeteria, where Chris was talking to Erin. They were both smiling and laughing - that is, until Kelly arrived. He said a final word to Erin, and then walked back to our table with Kelly.

As they sat down, Kelly asked Chris, "So what were you talking about with preppie girl?"

"Oh, nothing much... just making small talk," Chris said.

"I hope so," Kelly started. "Because I recall seeing you check her out a few times... back when I was still scouting you out... before I asked you out,"

"That's the past," Chris laughed nervously. "And now I'm totally with you,"

"I know," Kelly said curtly. "I was just busting," She began to kiss Chris' face, and then laughed. "Like, any guy would ever leave me for her," Chris laughed along with her, while he and I secretly exchanged a look.

***

I caught up with Karen in the hall, between classes the next day. "Hey," I said. "How's it going?"

"Well, significantly better than it was at this time yesterday," she laughed.

173

"I hear that," I said. "Has he said anything significant to you since then?"

"Not really," she said. "Though... it seemed like he was holding something back today. Like he wanted to say something, but just couldn't bring himself to do it,"

"Hmm... that's weird," I said.

"Hey guys," Travis said, coming from behind Karen and I.

"Oh, hi," I said.

"Hi," Karen said.

"Okay, look, I've been thinking about this whole deal... you know, between you and I," he said to Karen. "And, I mean, I totally understand that you don't feel the same way I do. But it's really just... not right, for you to just pass this judgment on me... without at least giving me a chance,"

"What do you mean?" Karen asked.

"I'm not going to try to force you into this... but, I was just thinking that maybe we should just go on one date... you know, like a trial run,"

"I don't know if that's such a good idea," Karen said. "I mean, it would be really awkward, and..."

"I don't see why it has to be awkward. We've been friends all year long... and, hey, if you're really worried about that, we could always double date," Travis turned to me. "Hey, Mike, how would you and Pepper feel about going out with Karen and I Saturday night?"

"Well," I started. "We were planning to go to a movie then... I guess that you two could come along,"

"That'd be perfect," Travis said. He looked back at Karen. "So what do you say?"

"Well... uh..." she began hesitantly, and then laughed. "Yeah! Why not?"

"Great!" Travis said, "So I'll see you guys later," With that, he left.

Once she was sure that he was out of hearing range, Karen covered her face with her hands. "Oh my God. What have I gotten myself into?"

"You know, I could always say that Pepper and I can't make it... so you can just call the whole thing off..."

"No," she said, "I don't want to lie to him, or disappoint him. But I also don't want to go out with him," she whined.

"Look, this whole 'trial date' thing... it's only getting his hopes up all over again. You're not helping him,"

FREE THROW

"I know. But I don't know how to just end this all without crushing him."

***

We all met up outside the theater at the mall. Even though Pepper and I were there to prevent it, there was till an awkward silence when Karen arrived at last. "So what are we going to see?" she asked to break that silence.

"Well, Pepper and I were just debating that one," I said. "I'm all for that new slasher flick..."

"And I say we catch that new Tom Cruise movie," Pepper jumped in.

"Hmm..." Karen began. "As much as I like blood and gore and guts, I can't resist Tom Cruise, so my vote's with Pepper's choice."

"I totally agree..." Travis said, "Well, you know, except for that whole part about not being able to resist Tom Cruise... you know... 'cause... I'm not like that."

"Yeah, okay... thanks for sharing," Karen smiled. Travis smiled back.

From there, we faced another awkward silence. "So," I said finally, "Let's go pick up those tickets."

"Yeah," Travis said, and went on to say, "No, this movie's on me," as Karen took out her wallet.

"Thanks," she said.

"I'm not letting you pay for me," Pepper said to me.

"Come on Pepper, I want to,"

"I feel bad Mike. You always pay..."

I cut her off with a kiss. "I just got my money's worth," I said.

She looked at me and grinned. "One of these days... when I'm less easily won over, we're going to go Dutch..."

"Fat chance," I said, and pecked her on the lips before going to the ticket counter with Travis.

"Two tickets for the chick flick," I said.

"Hey Mike," Travis said softly.

"Yeah?"

"I notice you doing all of that kissing and stuff with Pepper, and she seems to be really into it. Should I try that with Karen?"

FREE THROW

"No," I stopped and took my tickets from the clerk. "Thanks," I said, and turned back to Travis. "What I'm doing with Pepper is your standard, affectionate relationship stuff. It's really pushing it to do anything like that with Karen... you're not close enough yet. But during the movie, it's totally cool for you to put your arm over her, or hold her hand or something,"

"Okay," Travis turned to the clerk, "Oh... two for the same movie," He turned back to me, "But, have I been doing okay so far? I mean, I haven't done anything wrong, have I?"

"No, you're doing great man..."

"But, uh... tell me honestly... do you think I have any shot at winning her over?"

"I... I don't know..." I started. "I mean, I'm not sure that it's really something that you *can* do." I hurried back to the girls so that the conversation would have to end.

***

It was about fifteen minutes into the movie when Travis made his move. He yawned loudly, and stretched his arms up, over his head. Finally, when he brought his arms down, he left one draped over Karen's shoulders; the way people always do on TV.

"Hey, keep your friggin' arms down, you giant freak... we're trying to watch the movie back here!" said the guy sitting behind Travis.

"Right, sorry," Travis said.

"Shhh!" someone else called out.

Perhaps feeling that the romantic mood was totally gone, Travis brought his arm back to his side. Unfortunately, he was unable to do so without accidentally hitting Karen in the back of the head. "Ow!"

"Sorry," Travis said.

"Shhh!" someone else - perhaps the same someone else as before - called out.

Travis slouched down in his chair and just stared up at the screen from there. Karen, sitting next to me, looked at me, as if she was asking for help. I shrugged, and then turned my attention back to the movie.

***

FREE THROW

About a half hour later, Karen tapped me on the shoulder - effectively ending my kiss with Pepper. "Meet me outside in a couple minutes," she whispered.

"What? Why?" I asked, admittedly annoyed by the interruption.

"We have to talk. Just do it, please," She then turned to Travis, saying, "I have to go to the bathroom. I'll be right back," With that, she stood up, and left the theater. I made out with Pepper for a little longer, before following Karen's instructions.

"Okay, this had better be really important," I said when I reached Karen, just outside of the theater.

"I'm sorry that I had to... bother you. But, I'm really worried about Travis. He's trying so hard... I just really don't want to hurt him..."

"Look, sometimes, you just have to do stuff like this. Seriously... as someone who has faced the whole rejection thing before... it's not going to kill him. Sure, it will hurt, but he'll get over it..."

"But what about our friendship? What about when I'm sitting there at the end of math class... and there's no-one to talk to... because he won't even want to look at me,"

"Karen... listen to yourself. The way you say it makes it sound like he's rejecting you. No matter what, he's going to want to look at you... and talk to you. I mean... of course it'll be different, for a while at least, but it's not the end of the world,"

Karen sighed. "I guess you're right," she stopped, and then continued, "We'd better get back in there before Travis gets suspicious... or Pepper gets too engrossed in the plot of the movie to make out with you," she smiled.

"It'll never happen," I smiled back.

***

After the movie, we stopped by this little ice cream place in the mall and each got a cone. While we were eating, Travis took Karen aside to talk to her. I suppose that he had probably wanted privacy, but I could still hear and see what was going on, and couldn't bring myself to turn away.

Karen started off saying, "I'm sorry, but I really don't like you in the boyfriend type way,"

FREE THROW

"That's okay," Travis said, "This whole trial date thing was a long shot... I know that. But there is one more thing I wanted to ask you for,"

"Uh... sure... what is it?"

"Well, I've always had this... kind of... fantasy, about kissing you. I mean, in my fantasy, it was always in the context of us going out and all, but still... I'd really like to just kiss you. No strings attached, you know. I'm not hoping to win you over with this kiss or anything... I just want to do it," She didn't say anything after he finished. After a few seconds had passed, of them just looking at each other, Travis started again.

"Sorry... I guess it was a pretty dumb id..."

Karen stopped him by pulling his head down toward her kissing him - not just a peck on the lips, but a real kiss.

"That was really nice of her," Pepper said.

"Yeah," I agreed. "Um... Pepper, there's something I've wanted to say to you for a while. This whole Travis and Karen thing has really had me thinking about it a lot lately,"

"What is it?"

"Thank you. Thank you for going out with me. Thank you for always being there when I need you. Thank you... thank you for being you," A second or so later, Travis and Karen had stopped kissing... just as Pepper and I started.

***

"So are you going to be all right man? I mean, with the whole Karen thing?" I asked Travis as we changed before gym class.

"You know, I actually do. It kind of hurts now, but we were able to talk, like, pretty normally during math today. And that kiss... it really provided a lot of closure,"

"Well, I'm happy for you. I know it's hard to get over something like this,"

"Yeah... but I'm sure it's easier when someone like Pepper comes along... I imagine that kind of took your mind off all your problems,"

"What can I say? Sometimes, you get lucky. But you have to make it through the rough spots first,"

***

FREE THROW

We had the home court advantage for our first playoff game, against Chamber High School. Because we were seeded second in the tournament we got a bye into the second round. Chamber had blown away their first round opponents - playing much better than their being only the seventh seed suggested.

In the regular season, we had had close games every time we played, but always won. However, things didn't start well. Travis won the opening tip, but I took the first shot for us and missed. One of the Chamber guard tossed in a three-pointer, which was only the start of a 10-0 run for them.

We made rally late in the quarter, though, and were only behind by five going into the second period. Still, our closeness was largely out of luck, as Chamber's own sloppy play prevented them from capitalizing on our horrible shooting early on.

One of our biggest problems was contending with the size differentials. Their tallest players was only 6'6", but there shortest was 6'2", making for very big team. Through the first half, Shawn was the only effective scorer, with sixteen points. Travis was doing well on defense, and I had managed to make all five of my free throws. At half time, the score was 38-30 in their favor.

As had seemingly become routine for us, we played better in the second half. Coach encouraged me to go inside more often, in an effort to get fouled. The plan worked, and by the end of the third quarter I had fifteen points, with only two field goals. We were only down by two, entering the final period.

It was in the fourth quarter, when the game's action really began. Travis had already picked up a technical foul in the first quarter, for arguing with a referee on a goal tending call. Then, about midway through the final period of play, he got into a shoving match with Chamber's center, after Travis was hit with a hard foul. The Chamber center had fouled out on that play anyway, when a double technical was called our team was the only one hurt, as Travis got ejected.

Emotions ran high after that exchange. For every bounce of the ball, there was a word of trash talk spoken. Fouls became more and more frequent. I was able to keep my foul total down, though, while I continued to get fouled. Each of my free throws went in, much to the chagrin of the Chamber players.

FREE THROW

We were only down by one point with two minutes left in the game. Finally, I was goaded into a mistake. Coming out of a huddle, I waved up to Pepper in the stands, and she waved back.

Chambers' shooting guard, who had defended me all game long, continued with his trash talking. "Hey, is that your girlfriend up there?"

"Yeah, it is," I said, getting in position for the play we were about to run.

"Gee... I know you're not much of a basketball player, but couldn't you do a little better than that?"

I turned around, swinging. There were certain comments that I just couldn't walk away from. "Whoa! Whoa!" the guard called out, ducking and moving away from me. A number of the guys from our team rushed over, to hold me back.

The damage had already been done, though. I was called for a technical foul. That wasn't the end of it, though.

I pulled away from the guys, wanting to at least land one swing on my antagonist, if I was going to be called for the technical anyway. However, my teammates held fast, and I was only propelled backwards.

I hadn't known that right behind me, our cheerleaders were doing a pyramid to entertain the crowd. I also hadn't known that Alicia was on top. Regardless of those facts, I flew backwards, into the girls, knocking them all down - causing the most damage to Alicia, of course, as her scream pierced the air.

"Oh my God! Alicia!" I said, as I bent down to check on her, forgetting all about my previous altercation. "I'm sorry! I'm sorry!" I said to all of the girls, but never took my eyes off of Alicia.

Her eyes were closed, and she didn't respond to what I was saying. Some of the trainers and medical people, there to treat any possible injuries to the players, rushed out with a stretcher. As they carried her away, unconscious, I frantically asked, "Is she okay?!" over and over again, to no avail. I followed after them still asking that same question. I probably would have followed them all the way out of the gymnasium, if Coach hadn't stopped me.

"We've got a game to play," he said. "I want you to clear your head on the bench now," As he said that, he signaled for someone else to enter the game.

"But Coach... we're so close..."

FREE THROW

"I don't want you to go out there and get another technical, or start missing your shots because your head is somewhere else. Sit down on the bench,"

"Okay, I'll stay out of the game for a while, but can I please go and check on Alicia?" I pleaded.

"I'm sorry, but I need you to focus on the game," As he spoke, play resumed. "You can check on your friend later. For now, just sit down, and clear your head. Think only about basketball. Like you said... it's a close game. I might need you in there, right at the end. So for now, just sit on the bench,"

I was angry at the decision, but obeyed before I could cause any more trouble. Once on the bench, I buried my bead in a towel for a moment. I wanted to follow Coach's advice, but I couldn't help thinking about Alicia.

Watching the game did help, though. While I was out of the game, a Chamber player made the free throw off of my technical foul, leading to a span in which his team outscored us 6-4. Finally, Coach called a time out, with eighteen seconds remaining.

In our huddle, he began by addressing only one player - me. "Are you ready?" he asked. I nodded, and Coach drew out a play for us in his notebook, designed to allow me to make a three-pointer, and tie the game.

Back on the court, things worked out even better than any of us had expected. I was wide open for my shot when I fired.

The ball hit the backboard, the side of the rim, and then flew away from the basket. However, Shawn was right there. He soared up into the air, grabbed the ball and dunked it in, one-handed. Just as I thought I had let down the team, Shawn had saved the day.

However, we were still down by one, because I missed the three. So, I felt that since I had made the technical foul and missed that opportunity for an extra point, that it was my fault that we weren't already tied. I wanted to make up for that. Brad guarded their point guard tightly, while he brought the ball up court. As he did that, I ran around the Chamber guard's other side, and stole the ball without him ever even seeing me coming.

The opposing player was a bit faster than me, though, and managed to catch up with me as I headed back to our basket. As I rose for my shot, he clobbered me with a foul, to prevent the easy scoring opportunity, and make me earn my points from the line.

FREE THROW

By that point, however, I was back to being totally focused on the game. I made both shots with no problem. With eight seconds left, we had our first lead of the game. The Chamber coach called time out.

In our huddle, my thoughts slowly returned to Alicia. Going back onto the court, I wasn't sure that I was as focused as I should have been. However, the Chamber shooting guard, who had previously upset me, actually served to help me this time around.

"You'd better guard me tight," he said. "I won't fall down as easily as that cheerleader,"

I had a sudden burst of anger - but was able to convert it into energy on the court this time. I didn't answer him, but he didn't stop his antics either. As he caught the ball, he tried to provoke me further. "Come on," he said mockingly, "Do it for your girlfriend up there," He made a head fake, but I stayed solid on my defense. Finally, he made his real move, going toward the hoop.

His shot was an off balance one, because of my close defense. I made sure that he didn't score, though, as I jumped as high as I could, and blocked the shot.

Chris ended up with the loose ball. Less than three seconds remained. The Chamber players didn't want to concede the game, though. Chris dribbled at top speed, running away from the other players as they desperately tried to foul him, to stop the clock.

Chris was too quick, though. Looking more like a football player, trying to avoid being tackled, than a point guard, he wove all around, faking one way, and then going the other, until he saw that only two tenths of a second remained for he game. Knowing that there was no time left for any one to shoot, he taunted a Chamber guard, by simply handing him the ball. It was all over, and we had won our first playoff game.

***

Alicia wasn't back in school until two days after the game. I had tried calling her, but never got through. When I saw her sitting down in homeroom as I came in, I was overcome with fear. After all that time, of her acting as though she hated me, I had just given her a reason to go back to being that way.

"Alicia, I am so sorry," was the first thing I said as I approached her.

FREE THROW

She turned to face me. "Hi Mike," she said flatly. I sat down to continue the exchange.

"Really, Alicia, are you okay?"

"Yeah," she said, and smiled slightly. "It was just a minor concussion. I mean, I couldn't really remember how it happened for a while, but when Karen explained it all to me, it sounded totally accidental,"

"It was," I began. "But I still should have been more careful... it really was all my fault,"

"Really, don't sweat it. There's really not anything to worry about. Besides the bump on my head, a little dizziness here and there, and some headaches, you wouldn't even know that anything happened," After seeing my look of concern, she went on, "And it's not as bad as I guess it just sounded, either,"

"Still, I'm sorry. I never wanted to hurt you... and that all must have been really scary..."

"The only really scary part was the falling, and then the waking up in the ambulance. Otherwise, it's been okay. So please stop worrying,"

"You're sure about all this?" I asked.

"Yes," she said definitively. "Look, you might be the guy who gave me a concussion, but you're also the guy who saved my life just a couple months ago. I never thanked you for that..."

"And you don't have to,"

Alicia smiled, and went on, "Look, let's make a deal. I'll stop apologizing and thanking you for everything that's happened *for the past year*, and you'll stop stressing over what you did two nights ago,"

"Sounds like a good deal," I smiled.

"Great!" she said and smiled back. Then, after a moment, she continued, "So who are you playing tomorrow night?"

"We've got Stone Hill... that team with the two seven foot guys. Are you going to it?"

"Well, of course. I couldn't cheerlead if I didn't,"

"Wait... you're actually going to do that... so soon after... you know,"

"Yeah, why not? The dizzy spells all pretty much stopped yesterday, and I'm kind of getting used to the headaches..."

"Are you sure that I can't keep apologizing?"

"Only if you don't want me to start thanking you and all for saving my life,"

FREE THROW

I smiled, and actually laughed at he situation. "Okay,"

Chapter 15

As great a basketball player as Ray Penner was, he wasn't perfect. He may have always been able to control a game. However, when he couldn't turn to basketball any more, he gave up on his life, and became a high school janitor. People are constantly tested by problems that occur in their lives. When Penner's world fell apart, he didn't even try to piece it back together. The unfavorable big moments are what separate winners from losers in life. Things can go from perfect to completely flawed, and no-one can resurrect someone else's life for them.

***

Our second playoff game was that Friday night, against Stone Hill, at home. We would only have to win that one game, to get to the league finals. I didn't allow myself to think about anything further than that - like a state championship. After a long season, a league championship was the team's goal, and once we were that close, no-one was looking to blow the opportunity.

Like we had in our previous game against Stone Hill, we used a smaller, quicker line up to combat their strengths - the two seven-footers. However, our opponents had obviously worked hard and specifically to beat our strategy. To start the game, they were working much harder for rebounds, guarding our inbounds passes with intensity, and the two big guys showed noticeable improvement in their speed. We were down 26-17 at the end of the first quarter.

To start the second quarter, Coach turned to a more conventional line up - sending Chris, Greg, Shawn, Travis and I onto the court. Things began slightly better. However, it started to look like a lost cause as Stone Hill went on a 10-2 run at the end of the half, blocking three of our shots, and goaltending a short jumper from Shawn. We were losing, 46-29, going into the third quarter.

Our situation hadn't reached its worst point yet, though. That moment we had managed to avoid all year long, finally came to pass. On a set play, Chris passed the ball to Travis, who was in turn supposed to fake a shot, and then bounce the ball off to Shawn to score. However, as if 7'2" Derrick

FREE THROW

Presomp knew our secret, he quickly fouled Travis, as he faked the shot. The referee ruled it a shooting foul, which sent Travis to the free throw line.

"This would fall under the category of not good," Chris whispered to me.

"No kidding,"

Karen, standing near us at he sidelines, joined in. "What're you going to do? I mean, he can't shoot,"

"What am I going to do?!" Travis said, jogging over to us.

"Come on, Mike," Chris said, "You're the expert shooter here. Give him a crash course in it,"

"You can't just teach someone how to shoot... not in five minutes anyway," I answered.

"Let's go!" one of the referees called out.

"Okay, how about five *seconds*?" Travis asked, meekly.

"Look," Karen began, "Who's a really good free throw shooter?"

"What?" we all asked at once.

"Okay, something that works for me... when I have to do something really weird or hard, is to just close my eyes, pretend that I'm someone who's really good at doing that and just... do it,"

"All right, while the nice men in the white coats take Karen away," Chris began sarcastically, "We need an answer... fast,"

"No," Travis said. "I think I get what Karen's saying," He paused, thinking. "Mike's the best free throw shooter I know. So I'm going to do it... I'll just close my eyes, and do it like you,"

"Well... if you think it will work..." I started.

"You don't have to do this, Travis," Karen broke in. "I mean, if you think it will help - great. But, don't just do it... you know... because I told you to,"

"Don't worry," Travis said with a slight smile. "It's worth a try,"

"Okay," Chris burst in, "So now we're going to have the world's worst shooter take his free throws with his eyes closed. Am I the only one who thinks that this is a bad idea?"

"We'll see what happens, I guess," I said.

"Yeah... now," Travis said, as he began his march to the free throw line.

FREE THROW

"Whatever happens... it's going to be my fault now, isn't it?" Karen said. I'm not sure if it was due to a wet spot on the court or just a lack of coordination, but a few steps out of our mini-huddle, Travis slipped and fell. "Oh God!" Karen started out onto the court, to check on Travis, but a referee stopped her. "See if he's okay," she called to Chris and I as we headed back onto the court.

"You all right?" I asked Travis, as I knelt beside him.

"I'm a little bruised in the ego department," he said, "But physically, I'm cool,"

"All right, then let me try to instill you with some sanity one last time," Chris began. "Michael Jordan used to try no look free throws. The greatest player of all time would miss that shot,"

"Oh well," Travis said. "This isn't just some no look shot, anyway. It's like Karen was saying. For this shot, I *am* Mike Weaver," He walked up to the free throw line, without any further incidence. I gave a thumbs-up to Karen, to symbolize that Travis was okay.

I was at one side of the basket for the two shots. The referee passed Travis the ball, and at that moment, he closed his yes. He bounced the ball twice - somewhat clumsily. Then he lined up, with what I'll admit was remarkably similar form to what I liked to use. Then, he shot the ball.

I couldn't bear to look. I turned my head, and shut my eyes tightly. Then the sound came. *Swish*. The crowd cheered. I opened my eyes. The cheerleaders were jumping up and down. Travis had *made* the free throw.

I turned to look at him, but his eyes were still closed. The referee threw him the ball. He wasn't ready for it, though, leading to the ball simply bouncing off of his chest and away from him. I bent over, picked up the ball, and handed it to him.

He bounced the ball twice again, with slightly more control than the time before. I didn't look away this time, though I feared that his first shot was only a fluke. I was ready to grab a rebound - wherever it flew.

As Travis released his second shot, I watched to soar upward and then drop straight threw the hoop. "Yeah!" I said, as the other guys on the floor offered similar congratulations.

Travis at last opened his eyes. "I made them? I really made them?!" he asked in disbelief.

"You bet," I said, and added, "Now let's get back on defense,"

"Right," he nodded as we sped to the other side of the court.

FREE THROW

However, the ball never even reached it past the half-court line. Chris stole it off a bad pass, and then passed to Shawn, for a hard dunk. On Stone Hill's next possession, Travis had a block, and I was fouled at the other end. I drained both free throws. We were back in the game.

We were only down by eight going into the final quarter. Things looked even better when, after only two minutes of the period, Presomp fouled out, on a play that also sent me back to the free throw line.

After we took a one point lead, midway through the quarter, Stone Hill rallied, to put us back down by four, midway through the quarter, with less than a minute left. The game was far from over, though, as Brad drilled a three-point shot, with seven seconds to go. The Stone Hill coach called time out, to draw up one last play.

Coach knew three plays that Stone Hill might try, and quickly explained how to defend each in the huddle. Our chances at winning started to look bleak, but at least we had a chance, if we could stop them from scoring.

For the sake of speed, and an increased chance to steal, we put out a smaller, quicker line up than usual, playing both Brad and Chris on the court, with no true small forward. The referee blew his whistle, and the game re-began.

Their point guard worked first at killing the clock, taking five seconds before starting the play. He passed off to another player, who I was guarding. However, I was cut off by a strong pick from their power forward. As I fell to the ground, I watched the rest of the action play out in two seconds, which seemed like an eternity.

The shot was blocked by Shawn, but Stone Hill's other seven footer, Sczerbiak, recovered the ball. He jumped up for a dunk, which Travis knocked away. Tired and frustrated, the Stone Hill center responded by giving Travis a hard shove, with less then a second left. It was the break we had needed. One of the referees blew his whistle, and signaled for a technical foul. We had one free throw to tie the game with.

Since it was a technical foul, any of our players in the game could shoot. Hence, I was sent to the line. I had a chance to either bring us into overtime, or lose the game for the team, and stop us from reaching the city finals. Needless to say, there was no shortage on pressure.

"Come on, Mike," Alicia called from the sideline. Shawn patted my back as I stepped up to the line. A referee passed me the ball, and suddenly,

FREE THROW

the gymnasium fell silent. All eyes were on me. I bounced the ball twice, and then shot.

Swish. My free throw streak, and our chances for moving on in the playoffs, stayed alive.

The overtime period was a breeze. For perhaps costing his team the win, Sczerbiak was benched for quite a while. We capitalized on our momentum and the fact that both seven footers were out of the game, by starting off with an 11-0 run. Stone Hill never recovered. We won the game with a score of 97-90.

While most of the team yelled and exchanged high fives on the way off the court, and to the locker room, I noticed Travis separate for the pack, and begin to walk away. I followed after him to see what was going on. Perhaps also noticing, Chris followed me away from the rest of the team.

It turned out that Travis was headed towards the cheerleaders. He and Karen embraced. "Thank you," he said.

"What?" she asked, smiling.

"For the advice and all... that's what turned around the game... those free throws. And I owe it to you,"

"No... Travis..." she began.

"I mean it," he cut her off. "Thank you," Karen smiled, reached up and hugged Travis again.

"That's one happy guy," Chris commented.

"Hey... let him have his moment," I said. "He's earned this,"

"Hey guys," Erin said as she walked towards us.

"H-hi," Chris said.

"Great game," she said with a smile, and touched Chris' arm, before moving on.

"Okay... and there was my moment," Chris said, once she was gone. "Of course, mine didn't involve hugging..."

"Oh, come on. At least she actually spoke to you... that's something,"

"Yeah, I guess. I don't know, though. I want to just do something soon, you know? Maybe it's time to break it off with Kelly, and finally just go for it with Erin,"

"That's an awfully big step," I said. "I admire your courage, but I'd think about that before actually doing anything,"

"Trust me, all I've done is think about this, for as long as I can remember," he stopped and began to wave up toward the stands. I looked

189

FREE THROW

up, to see Kelly coming down toward us. She hopped over the guardrail, down to the floor, just as she had the first time we met.

She ran to Chris, and they kissed passionately. Chris and I exchanged a look. My attention was soon shifted elsewhere, though, to Greg and a number of other guys from the team ran up, still yelling and slapping hands.

It's as though, just at that moment, the realization of what we had accomplished donned on me. Since I had first become interested in, and involved in basketball, this had been a dream of mine. I was a major part of a team that was headed to the championship game.

I soon joined in on the antics of the rest of the team, jumping up and down, saying, "We did it! We did it!"

***

Going to the championship game gave me a feeling, unlike anything that I had ever felt before. It was a combination of excitement, happiness, a bit of nervousness, and the gratification of knowing that we were among the best. Without question, I wouldn't mess up this opportunity.

The same would go for Chris, as we had both lingered after school on several days, whether there was an official practice or not, to practice on the hoops in the gym. One of those days, a Wednesday, Pepper came to the gym too.

I hadn't been expecting to see her, but didn't pay much attention to that surprise. "Hey Mike," she said pretty quietly.

"Check this out," I interrupted, and then drove to the basket, finishing with a smooth finger roll.

"Yeah... umm..." she started again.

"Man, this championship is as good as ours!" I broke in again, as I dribbled the ball between my legs.

"Hey, I'm gonna go get a drink," Chris said, "I'll be back in a sec," He left the gym, leaving Pepper and I alone.

"All right, I was in the mood for a little one on one anyway," I proclaimed, and dribbled just past where she was standing, around the three-point line. "Come on, guard me," I said with a smile. She just stood in place, looking at me.

FREE THROW

That should have clued me in right away that I ought to have been listening to her. But my head was just too filled with thoughts of championships, and glory. She started again, "Mike..."
Instead of listening, I dribbled around her and laid the ball in off the glass. "Mike!" she shouted. A tear was rolling down her face.
"Oh... Pepper... I-I'm sorr..." I started, softly.
"No..." She stopped to wipe off her cheek. "My parents just told me today... we're moving away... off to New York... next week,"
"What? W-w-why? And why didn't you know sooner?"
"They didn't want me to put up a fuss or anything... so they waited until the last minute," Another tear escaped her eye.
"Pepper... I had no idea,"
"Yeah," she said, and started to say something else, but couldn't because her voice was cracking. She turned and left the gym. I ran after her, but as I opened the door to leave the gym myself, Chris was just coming through, and we ended up crashing into each other. Pepper was long gone by the time I sat up.

***

I tried to call Pepper, but either no-one would pick up, or it would be her mother, saying that she couldn't talk - as she always had since that night I'd came over for dinner. We had had some disagreements before, but this wasn't the same at all. If I couldn't reach her soon, she would be gone - possibly forever.
The next day, on my way into homeroom, I passed her at her locker. "Pepper? Pepper?" I said. She stopped for about a second, and then went about her business, putting things in her bag and taking some out. I think I saw her put the same object in, out, and back in her bag a couple of times, just to make it look like she was still busy, so I might go away. "Look, Pepper..."
I felt a tap on my shoulder and turned around. It was Travis. "Ready for the big game?" he asked, beaming.
"Yeah, yeah," I said, trying to get rid of him. He probably just didn't get the message, but either way, he didn't budge.
"Yeah, you'd better work on those jump shots," he continued.
"Yep Travis... I'm a little busy now..."

FREE THROW

"And you should be polishing off those free throws," he laughed.

"Shut up! Shut up! Shut up!" I had finally snapped. "Can't you see that I'm busy here!"

"Hey man, I'm sor..." he began.

Chris jumped in, "Hey, what's going on!"

I began, "This big idiot..."

"I am not an idiot!" Travis broke in.

"Why are you guys shouting... what's up?" Shawn said as he joined the crowd.

"Nothing's up..." Chris said, trying to cool us all down.

"Hey, if Mike has something he wants to say to me, he can go on and say it!" Travis said.

"Look, you're not the one I came over to have a conversation with!" I took a deep breath. "Now, if you guys can excuse me, I need to have a word with my girl friend," I pointed behind me, and then turned to speak with her. She was gone.

"You're girlfriend's a locker?" Travis said sarcastically.

I looked back toward Travis. I pulled my fist back, and was about to punch him. However, as I swung forward, Shawn grabbed me by the wrist, and held on. "Don't do it Weaver," he said calmly.

I pulled away from his grasp and walked away quickly.

***

My entire life was beginning to fall apart, just as quickly as I had put it together. Time wasn't on my side, either. I had one week until the biggest game of my life, and I would have to make amends with my teammates before that time. More importantly than all of that to me, though, was the fact that Pepper would be heading out some time during that same week. I had to act quickly in both respects.

Before practice on that day, I stepped up to the locker room door to listen to what was going on. There was essentially the same amount of chatter as ever. I came to the conclusion that this could mean that the whole incident from earlier in the day had simply blown over, and everything was back to normal.

However, as I entered, the room soon descended into silence. Those who were involved with the altercation stopped speaking first. Others just

FREE THROW

followed their lead. I felt like there were a million eyes, burning through me as I started to turn the combination on my lock. Minutes passed without a word being spoken, before I turned to face everyone.

"Look guys... I'm sorry," I paused to find the words. "I'm having some problems right now, but from now on, I won't take any of it out on you, and I'll definitely keep it off the court,"

Silence again. At last, Chris came up and put his hand up for the high five. "Forgiven and forgotten," In a little bit, all of the other guys exchanged high fives with me. I was a part of the team again.

"Now," Shawn started, "We've got a championship to win,"

"Yeah!" everyone chanted as we left the locker room for practice.

***

The note hung from my locker just slightly as I went to grab my jacket after practice. As I pulled it out of the vent, I could tell that it was from Pepper, by the way it was folded. I opened it slowly.

It said, "I overreacted. Meet me outside after school," I realized the situation - that since I had gone to practice first, I was about an hour late. I forgot about my jacket and sprung outside.

I didn't care about looking stupid or any kind of risk of falling. I ran straight out of the building, and continued once I was outside. Pepper was all that mattered.

Pepper was already getting into her mom's car when I arrived at the front of the building. "Pepper! Pepper!" I yelled. No response.

I ran up to the car, still yelling as she closed the door. I couldn't get her attention. The car began to roll away. I ran alongside it, though, yelling as loudly as I could. Finally, she turned. I could hear her voice, telling her mom to stop, and then yelling it when her mom didn't hurry to comply. In a moment, she was out of the car.

"Mike," she began, sounding out of breath. "I thought you weren't coming,"

"I didn't see the note... I went to practice first," I replied.

"We have to be going!" Mrs. Harris called to her.

She looked at her, and then back at me. "I'll call you in an hour... we need to talk,"

FREE THROW

"Okay," was all I could say, as she hurried back into the car, and rode away.

***

I picked up the phone at around five o' clock, and it was Pepper on the other end. She didn't bother returning my hello, skipping straight to the brunt of her message. "Look Mike," she said, "I still love you... I was just angry and stupid before. But either way, I'm still going to have to move,"
"I'm sorr..."
"No - don't start with that - it's not your fault or anything..."
"But I still shouldn't have acted the way I did. But, anyway, I've been racking my brain... there's got to be a way that we could still work this out..."
"I wish I could believe that," her voice was straining. "But it's too late," She paused for a moment, and it sounded as though she began to cry. She uttered, "Goodbye," and hung up. I didn't know of anything else that I could say, so I didn't bother calling back. It wasn't anybody's fault, but we had fallen apart.

***

The world wouldn't stop on account of Pepper, though. I played more and more ball on my own and had harder practices, leading up to the championship game. We knew who our opponents would be, just as we had expected - the Jorles Knights, with Timothy Kahn.

Coach had us working on our full court press; it was the speed of their running game that had foiled us to some degree during the regular season. We hadn't been able to beat them before, but they'd never exactly had a convincing win over us either. No-one was looking to fold at this point.

However, some of the guys weren't totally focused on work - namely Greg and George Highman. In the locker room after practice, Greg accosted Chris and I, while we were changing. "Our parents are out of town for the weekend - party at our place, Saturday night. Seven to whenever we feel like,"

FREE THROW

"You've to be kidding," I said, "Remember what happened the last time you two scheduled a party?"

"Yeah, but this time there's no swimming pool. Besides... we'll have you... Mike Weaver... life guard extraordinaire,"

"Ha ha," I said sarcastically.

"Seriously," he went on, "Even if you guys don't want to come, pass the word around to everyone you know. *Everybody* in this school is invited,"

"Yeah, whatever," I said as he walked away. I turned to Chris. "Can you believe..?"

"Hey, this just might work out all right," He paused and smiled. "Yeah, this could be a great opportunity here,"

"What're you talking about?"

"Two things. Since I'm a giving person, I'll tell you the part that benefits you first,"

"Shoot,"

"Okay, you've been on the skids with Pepper lately, right? And even though she's moving in a few days, I know you. If she has to leave, you want it to be with her pining for you, just as much as you are for her,"

"I guess. So what's your point?"

"Well, you guys have proven that you can only make things worse by interacting one on one. Therefore, you can't risk a regular date. But, you can ask her to accompany you to the party. Then you just hang out with her, and if the tension gets too high, you can just go and hang out with other people for a while, and then try again,"

"I'm desperate. And as much as I hate to say it, you may have a point. I'll try it," I paused, before going on, "By the way, what was the second thing?"

"Oh, right. That's for me and Kelly. See, I figure that if we spend this time together, dancing, talking, and groping, I can really get a new outlook on this whole thing, and maybe save the relationship,"

"Well, good luck,"

"You too," he said, and then repeated, softer, "You too,"

***

FREE THROW

Pepper agreed to meet me at the party. So, I came alone, and just waited to find her.

Steve and the rest of his band had stationed themselves on some sort of platform in the living room, and were blasting out music for the party. Greg had said that the whole school was invited to the party, and it appeared that just about everybody had taken him up on that offer.

After searching for Pepper for a while, with no luck, I gave up temporarily, and planted myself on a couch in the living room. I soon saw Chris, with Kelly. They danced closely with each other; both sipping from beer cans as they moved.

It seemed like just about everybody was drinking, though. I'm not even sure where all of the alcohol could have come from, as easily fifty cans were already strewn across the floor.

"Hey Mike!" Travis said, jumping up onto the couch beside me.

"Whoa... careful there, big guy," I said.

"Oh, right," he answered and sat down. "This is some party, huh man?"

"Hey, you haven't been drinking, have you?"

He pretended to think. "Well... just a... hell of a lot!" he suddenly shouted. "You know, I've never even touched alcohol before. And when they invited *me* to this party... you know, I just assumed it wouldn't be that kind of deal. But I think this is just what I needed to clear my head,"

"You needed to get drunk... to clear your head?" I asked slowly.

"Absolutely!"

We sat there, talking for almost an hour, before I finally spotted Pepper. "Hey, look," I said, "I just saw Pepper, so I gotta go,"

"Oh, are you guys getting back together? Because that would be so... awesome man! You guys were like the *best* couple! You just split like that, you know?!"

"Um... yeah," I patted him on the shoulder. "So I'll go take care of that right now,"

"Yes! Go get 'em, tiger!" he shouted, and laughed loudly. I just smiled and walked away.

When I reached her, Pepper was quickly downing a glass of wine, while she spoke with some people I didn't know. "Mike!" she said suddenly, when she saw me arrive. She kissed me on the cheek, sloppily.

"Uh... do you mind if we go and talk somewhere... private?"

FREE THROW

"Sure thing!" she slurred out happily. She turned to her friends, waved broadly, and said, "See you guys later,"

We proceeded to the kitchen. "So, you've been drinking?" I asked.

"Yeah," she said, finishing her glass. "I wanted to take my mind off of everything... you, me, me moving. Because everything just really, really, really sucks,"

"Yeah... yeah it does..." I was cut short as she kissed me on the lips. "Wait a second," I said, pulling away. "We need to talk,"

"Why should we talk," she whispered, her voice still somewhat slurred. She kissed my nose wetly. "We only have a few days left... we can't waste it,"

"Pepper," I sighed, "How much have you had to drink?"

"Just a little here... a little out there... some more over there..." she laughed.

"Come on..."

"Look, seriously," she began more solidly, "I've been thinking... I'm leaving in just a few days. So, I think we should do it tonight," She stopped and kissed me again. I backed up, into the kitchen table.

"Do *it*?" I asked meekly.

"Yeah... you know. We could lose our virginity... here... in this one night of passion," she finished dramatically.

I'm almost ashamed to admit it, but for that one moment, I actually considered going through with it. Naturally, it was something I had thought - even fantasized - about before. However, as she continued to kiss me, I finally pushed her away.

"What're you doing?" she asked, looking up at me.

"This... this isn't right," I said. "Pepper, this isn't you. We can't just do something like this... not without thinking first,"

"So you're saying you're not attracted to me, is that it?"

"No. But I don't want to have sex with you before I know that you really want to do this with me..."

"But, I do..."

"If you hadn't been drinking, maybe I could believe that. But... God... I mean, look at yourself. This isn't you," Neither of us said anything for a while. Then I heard her sniff, like she was holding back tears.

"I'm sorry..." she said, as she did begin to cry. "I'm sorry. I'm so sorry." I hugged her, but she went on, "I don't know what I'm doing. I'm sorry,"

"It's all right," I waited a minute or so, before going on, "Look, I really wanted to just talk to you tonight. I want to know what you're thinking about this whole deal,"

"It sucks... it's ruining my life," She fell silent for a moment. "But, I mean, half of it's all your fault,"

"What?" I was genuinely surprised.

"You know what I'm talking about. You've told me that you've known that you loved me, since back in August. But you waited to say anything. Then, when you asked me to go the Formal, and I said no, you just automatically assumed the worst. If you hadn't screwed up all those times, do you know how much more time we could've had together?"

"All right... I screwed up. I'll admit that. But I never meant to hurt you. You know that..."

We stopped as a huge crashing sound came from the living room Pepper followed me out of the kitchen, as I tried to see what had happened.

"Whoa man! Take it easy!" Greg said. The glass punch bowl had been knocked to the ground - that being the reason for the noise. Travis was the culprit.

"No!" he shouted back. "I'm sick of always playing by all the rules, and trying to make everyone else happy!"

"Travis, you don't have to do this," Karen said, standing in front of him. "Let's just go somewhere and talk, okay?"

"You know, we talk, and talk, and talk!" Travis began, "But it never does anything! I've tried arguing with you... and pouring my heart out... the only thing that I've ever got in return was that one kiss! *One kiss*, for all this damned heartache!" his voice began to crack as he spoke.

"Travis..." Karen began softly.

"Why couldn't you just give me a chance?!" They were both crying at that point, but Travis was too drunk and out of it to give up.

"I did. We had that trial date thing..."

"But you *never* really considered it. You just couldn't get past how I look... and the fact that I'm not as cool, or suave as other guys,"

"Gee, looks and personality. Most people consider those to be somewhat important in deciding who to date!"

"Screw you!" Travis said, and turned toward the front door.
"Oh, so that's the way it is?!" Karen asked, suddenly on the attack. "You can just scream your head off at me, but if I say something *you* don't like, it's wrong?!"

Travis turned around, and grabbed her by her shoulders. He shook her, almost violently. "You ruined me! I loved you! I loved you!" He stopped. Karen was crying and looking up at him in fear. He re-began slowly, "I... *love* you," He released her shoulders, and embraced her. Karen was visibly afraid as Travis began to repeat, over and over, "I'm sorry. I'm sorry. I'm sorry,"

She ducked out of his arms and backed away from him. "No..." Travis said, "I didn't mean any of that..."

"Stay away from me," Karen said, her voice shaking.

"Please... Karen..." Travis said, taking a step toward her.

Karen backed away from him clumsily, stumbling and almost falling over a fallen beer can. Travis reached his hand out to help her, but she only backed away further.

"Karen," Alicia interjected. "Are you okay?" Karen just shook her head and then ran away, up stairs. Travis started to follow, but Alicia stopped him. "Please, just leave her alone,"

"But... but..." Travis looked around, and then held his head. "You're right," he said loudly, at last resigned to his fate.

"Hey guys," Chris said, as he stumbled into the room. Once he had gathered the mood, he went on, "Um... okay... what did I miss?"

"A lot," Steve said, the band having stopped playing when the scene began.

"I kind of gathered that," Chris said, "But, actually, I don't really need any further explanation. I just came in here to ask if anyone had seen Kelly,"

"Uh... no... sorry," I said, as Pepper began to kiss my ear.

"Wait, Kelly Jayne?" Alicia asked.

"Yeah," Chris said. "Have you seen her?"

"Upstairs. She bought a bag of... stuff from some guy, and then went into one of the bedrooms... it was a few minutes ago,"

"Stuff?" I asked. "What do you mean?"

"I think it was marijuana... but I wouldn't really know," she said.

"Wait... pot?" Chris said, angrily.

"Yeah..." Alicia said reluctantly.

"Man!" Chris said, and headed upstairs.

"I'll be back in a second," I said to Pepper, and followed Chris. "What's going on?" I asked when I had caught up to him.

"It's the whole drug thing..."

"Yeah, when did that happen?"

"It's always been happening," Chris said, completely serious. "I asked her to stop... I said I didn't want to be involved with her if she was going to be using any stuff. She promised to stop..." he trailed off as he finished climbing the stairs, and was on the second floor. "Okay," he said at that point. "There's, like, fifty rooms up here. How am I supposed to find her?"

"I guess we'll just have to look," I said, and threw open the first door we came to. Kelly wasn't inside, but the room certainly wasn't empty. "Holy sh..."

"Mike!" Carrie said in surprise, as she covered herself with a bed sheet. Matt was sitting beside her, in nothing but his boxers.

"Oh... oh my God!" I said.

"I can explain..." she began.

"No... I'm sorry," I said, and closed the door. I turned to Chris, "What is going on tonight?"

Chris had already opened the next door he had come to, and didn't bother to respond. A gust of smoke emptied into the hall.

"Hey Chris!" Kelly said, as she came running to him. She hugged and kissed him, while he just stood there.

"No," he said at last.

"What?" she said, laughing.

He removed her arms from him. "This is over,"

"What?" she asked, a bit more seriously.

"This relationship... it's through,"

As he walked away, Kelly began to giggle. "You're silly," she said. Chris just kept walking.

I heard a sound from inside the room, so I went in to check it out. Karen was there, holding a joint. "Karen," I began, "What are you doing?"

"Don't worry," she said flatly, dropping the joint. "I don't even have the guts to smoke the stupid thing,"

"Are you okay?" I asked, suddenly aware of her tear-stained face.

"Yeah," she said, attempting to wipe her face clean with her hand.
"You realize that Travis was drunk... right? I mean, everything he said..."
"Everything he said was what he's been thinking... deep down, but was too afraid to say,"
"Come on..."
"I'm serious," she cut me off. "I know he's hurting from all of this. Getting drunk... it just made him forget to cover that up. He's angry with me... and I don't want this to go on any longer. He scared me tonight... and..."
I sat down next to her and hugged her. "It's okay," I said a few times, while she wept.
"I just want to be friends with him..."
"I know," I said, stroking her hair gently.
"But how can you know?" she pulled away from me. "You've never been put in this position with someone..."
"What about Alicia? It's been, like, the same deal..."
"But you never had to face up to anything. Every night, Alicia whines and cries over the phone, to *me,* about *you.* I have to deal with Travis yelling at me, and trying to avoid me... and doing whatever his damn mood swings dictate each day!" She stopped, looked me in the eye, and started over, less angrily but crying again, "I'm sorry... I shouldn't have said all that..."
"It's okay," I said, and held her shoulder. "You're right... I can't really know how it feels. But you have to know... that you're an amazing person. The fact that you put up with everything and are so nice to everyone... to Travis, to Alicia, to Chris after he screwed up at the Formal..."
"I wasn't that nice to him..."
"But only for, like, a day. Really, Karen, you have no reason to feel bad..." I trailed off as I saw Pepper in the doorway. "I'm sorry," I went on, "But..." I gestured towards the door with my head.
"Oh... yeah..." she said, drying her face with her sleeve. "Thanks for listening,"
"Yeah," I said, "And if you need to talk later..."
"Don't worry about it. Now go on!" she finished with a slight smile.

I nodded and left the room. From there, I followed Pepper back down to the kitchen. "So," she began. "This whole avoiding me all night thing... is it a sign that you don't want to be around me?"

"Pepper..." I sighed. Just then, Alicia entered the room.

When she saw the two of us were alone, and that Pepper was crying, she started, "Oh, sorry. I was just getting..."

"Getting in the way?" Pepper asked, glaring at her cousin. It occurred to me that Alicia didn't know that Pepper had been drinking, and would probably take everything she said seriously. I also knew that in this state of mind, Pepper wouldn't say anything too favorable about Alicia. "It's just because that's what you usually do..."

"Hey, Pepper," I broke in, "Let's not say anything we'll regret, okay?"

"Shut up. This is between the two of us," she shot back.

"Umm... what's going on?" Alicia asked.

"*I'm* just sitting here, talking to my boyfriend. *You're* just trying to get in the way, like usual, and trying to steal him from me,"

There was a tear in Alicia's eye. "I love Mike too, but I've stopped trying to cause trouble..."

"Yeah, and I'm sure that once I'm gone, you'll be celebrating, because I'll be out of the way,"

"Pepper, I respect you, and your relationship... I'm not just going to jump in as soon as you leave..."

"Yeah, you'll wait a week or so,"

Alicia looked over to me, "What's wrong with her?"

"She's been..."

"You're what's wrong with me, you bitch," Pepper interrupted me, and then walked towards her cousin. She shoved Alicia once, startling her.

"Hey, come on..." I said.

"Stay out of this!" Pepper called back to me, and then turned to Alicia, saying "How do you like this?! How do you like this?!" as she continued to push her, before finally shoving her, hard, to the ground. She dropped to her knees, and tried to punch Alicia, but I restrained her, and pulled her back to the opposite side of the kitchen.

Just at that point, Chris entered the room. "Hey, Mike..."

"Help me hold her back!" I cut him off. Pepper was struggling pretty hard, so Chris' helping made my job a lot easier. Gradually, she started to

FREE THROW

slow down, until finally, I was able to say to Chris, "All right, just make sure she stays here, while I check on Alicia..."

"Stop...rewind," Chris began, "It's Alicia she's going after?"

"Yeah... we'll talk about that later," I bent down beside Alicia. "Are you okay?"

"Yeah," she paused to wipe a tear from her cheek. "I'm just a little shaken up..."

"There you go... how typical," Pepper started up again. "You go and check on how Alicia's doing, and leave me standing over here,"

"Pepper..." I began.

"Save it. I'm just gonna go. I'm leaving town on Monday, so goodbye to you all," she said, still crying, and then left the room.

"She was drinking... a lot I guess," I explained to Chris and Alicia.

"Seems to be a theme tonight," Chris said.

"Yeah... I've got to go talk to her, though," I said and followed in Pepper's path.

In the living room, the band had started playing again, and people were back to dancing. I moved through and around the crowds, to catch up to Pepper. I grabbed her by the arm.

"What are you doing?" she asked.

"I'm trying to stop you... we need to actually talk,"

Pepper glanced up at the band. Then she moved towards them. I followed - not sure of what she would do. I found out soon enough.

While Steve strummed his guitar, she embraced him forcefully. He had to stop playing - hence the rest of the band ceased to perform. "What are you doing?" he asked

"Making a point!" she screamed.

"Man, this party blows," someone else said. A number of other people voiced their agreement as they filed out of the house. I ignored them, though.

"Okay... so what are you saying?" I asked.

"I could have had either one of you - Mike or Steve. The only difference was, that I thought I was in love with *you*," she said, pointing at me. "But maybe if I had gone the other way... none of this would have happened. Maybe I could be happy right now..."

"Pepper..." I tried.

FREE THROW

"Shut up!" she yelled, as more people left. "It's like I was saying before... this is all your fault!" At that moment, Steve ducked out of her arms. "What are you doing?"

"This isn't right," Steve said.

"Isn't right? It's what you've always wanted, isn't it?" she barked at him.

"Not this way," Steve said, with complete cool. "I was... infatuated with you. But I'm not Mike. You chose each other... and you're the ones that should be together,"

"But now I'm choosing you..."

"And if you had to get drunk to do that, it only proves my point even further,"

Pepper looked at Steve, and then at me, and then back again. Finally, she just walked out of the house and away from me - perhaps for good.

***

I knocked twice on Carrie's door the next afternoon. After a few seconds, she said, "Come in,"

When I did, there was this awkward silence. We both knew what was on the others mind, but it just wasn't he sort of thing you could just start talking about. Finally, Carrie started, "You know, what... umm... what you saw last night... um..."

"Look, you don't have to explain yourself to me or anything. I mean, it's your life... it's not really any of my business," She grinned a little at me. Another round of silence followed.

"So, how's that novel going?" I asked eventually.

"Not too bad, really. I've got the first two and a half chapters on paper," she gestured toward a blue binder at the corner of the desk she sat at. "It's a start... but, not really anything worth bragging about,"

"Well, still... that's cool... I mean, you've got to start somewhere, right?"

"Yeah. Actually, the hardest part of it all so far is picking a name for the protagonist," she said, with a slight laugh. "I mean, I want something conventional... and easy to remember, but none of the names I've come up with seem to fit her..." she trailed off, and then laughed, and said, "Sorry...

judging by that expression on your face, I guess that was more info than you were looking for,"

"What expression?" I asked, and we both laughed. When all was quiet again, I said, "Well, I guess I'll let you get back to work,"

I turned to leave, but as I turned the doorknob, Carrie said, "Nothing happened," I turned to face her. "You know, with Matt," she went on. "We just made out a lot... that was all..."

"Carrie, you don't have to tell me this. I mean, despite, and throughout, all of that beating around the bush, that's really what I came here to say... that I don't really need to be informed of all the details there..."

"I know I don't have tell you anything... I want to though," she smiled; I smiled back before leaving.

***

"I love you," Pepper whispered into my ear, as she kissed it softly. She was wearing the same perfume that she had been on that night we met - she smelled exactly the same.

"I love you too. I love you too," I repeated. I held her close to me, kissing her lips, her cheek, her neck - kissing everywhere - for that moment, knowing nothing but the taste of her skin.

"But I have to go..."

"No, stay..."

"We both know I can't..."

"Please... I'll do anything... I love you," It was weird, because I was saying the words, but I wasn't, because I was still kissing her. It was like my thoughts were coming out, aloud.

"I'm sorry..."

"No... don't go..."

"I have to,"

I woke up alone, in my room A glance at the clock revealed that it was just after seven o' clock in the morning. It was the day of the big game - but the game was the last thing on my mind.

Chapter 16

It wasn't until the pre-game shoot around that I realized just how much larger the crowd was for this game, than any of the games I had ever played in before. I can't deny that I was pretty nervous. However, in a flash, my mind was taken off of that. I looked up, into the stands and saw -
Pepper?
It couldn't be, and yet, it was. I *saw* her.
There was a tap on my shoulder, and I turned to find Alicia beside me. "Sorry to bug you... but there hasn't been any news on Pepper or anything... has there?"
"Yeah! Look..." I started, pointing up to where I had seen her. Where I *thought* I had seen her. She was gone. Had she been there at all?
"Uh... my bad..." I went on, "I guess... no... there's no news,"
She sighed. "Look, I just want to tell you again how sorry I am about all the trouble I caused... it was stupid..."
"It's okay," I said, "You've been forgiven. Now come on, go do some cheerleading," I smiled. She smiled back, and walked away. As she did, I looked into the crowd again. Still no Pepper.

***

Before the game began, they had everyone line up with their team, to walk by and slap hands with the guys from the other side. However, when Kahn and I came together, and were about to high five, he pulled hand back and smoothed his hair back, saying, "You'd better not be that slow the whole night, Weaver!"
"Come on man," Shawn said, "Show him who's better! Lankford's winning, right?"
"Yeah!" I shouted back, feigning excitement. My head still wasn't in the game, though.
Before the game would begin, Travis tried to approach Karen. "Karen," he began. She walked away from him. "Karen," he repeated. She walked further away.
"Hey man," I interjected. "Maybe you should just save that for later,"
"I just want to apologize," he said, "I was stupid... and..."

FREE THROW

"Look, I know how hard this is... but you have to try,"

"Right," Travis agreed, and we walked away from her together.

"Hey Mike," Chris accosted me, "Guess what this is?" he asked, holding a folded up sheet of loose-leaf paper in his hand.

"Beats me," I said, as we came near the huddle.

"It's a note... telling Erin everything,"

"Are you serious?" I asked, after a short pause.

Chris nodded, and Travis joined in, "You're actually going to tell her how you feel?"

"Yeah," Chris said, "And thank you both so much, for the confidence booster,"

"I didn't mean anything by it," I said, "I'm just surprised. I mean, you just split up with Kelly and all..."

"But that was a long time in coming," Chris interrupted me. "I've known that I feel this way about Erin since... like, forever. It's time to do something about it,"

"It's up to you, I guess," I finished off, as we neared our huddle.

"Don't worry," he said, "I'll at least wait until a little later... you know... make sure I stay focused,"

"Yeah... you'd better," I said. "We all need to put the personal stuff aside, and just focus on basketball tonight,"

"Agreed," Travis said, just as we entered the huddle.

***

Travis won the opening tip, getting the ball to me. I passed to Brad, and he dribbled up court. The crowd was deafening - and nothing worth cheering for had even happened. He signaled a play, and I got into position. But then, I saw Pepper again.

I felt something hit me in the lower back. I turned, and saw that it was the ball - and that it was rolling out of bounds. I had lost concentration, and ruined the play. I looked back up to where I had seen Pepper. She was gone - that is, if she had been there at all.

"This is gonna be easier than I thought," Kahn whispered in my ear. I shoved him down.

A referee signaled for a technical foul for me. Coach signaled for me to come out of the game.

FREE THROW

***

The score was 19-7, in, Jorles' favor, as the end of the first quarter neared. Coach called time out. He turned to me and asked, "Are you ready to go back out there?" I nodded, but wasn't too confident. Twice more, while sitting on the bench, I had thought I'd seen Pepper. Both proved to be hallucinations, like the sightings before them.

When play started, Jorles stole the ball, and began setting up their offense. The ball came to Kahn, and he dribbled past me. However, as he went up for a shot, I blocked him from behind. I grabbed the loose ball; dribbled cross court, ahead of everyone else, and tossed in a finger roll "That's the Weaver I know!" Shawn called out. But I wasn't through.

I intercepted Jorles' inbounds pass, and lobbed the ball up for Shawn, who converted it into an alley-oop dunk. Our opponents scored on their next possession, but Greg made a three-pointer to answer. Jorles missed again, and Shawn rebounded. I was fouled on my shot. As I stepped up to the line, I focused again on basketball. I swished both shots. Jorles scored again, but we got the last laugh, as Brad made a three-pointer at the buzzer, to end the first quarter with us only down by four.

However, as I walked back to our team's bench, I saw Pepper again. I *thought* I saw her, that is.

***

At half time, we were down by just one. While most of us headed to the locker room, Travis went back to Karen. I came along, in an effort to prevent anything regrettable from happening.

"Karen," Travis began once more, but again, she pretended not to hear him. "Look," he went on, "I'm going to say this to you... whether you want to acknowledge it or not. I screwed up. I'm crazy about you... and sometimes... especially when I'm tremendously drunk... I lose control. I really just want to give this one more shot," Karen started to walk away again. "Come on," he continued. "After the game, let's just talk... get everything out. We can work it all out... once and for all, whatever the result may be,"

She turned around at that. "Travis," she began. "I don't want to be mad at you. But I can't take..."

FREE THROW

"I know... I know..."

"Wait... listen," she said, "After the game... we should do that... you know... talk,"

"That's all I ask," Travis said. Karen patted him on the shoulder and they parted ways. "Was that good?" Travis murmured to me.

"It went great," I assured him.

***

Midway through the third quarter, Shawn picked up his fifth foul, so Coach had to put him on the bench. The loss of our star was more than we could compensate for. Jorles was leading by ten by the end of the quarter.

And it was at he end of the quarter when Chris pulled out the note again, and walked toward Erin. I looked on from a distance.

Erin was facing the other way from Chris when he approached. First, he raised a hand to tap her shoulder. Then, he looked as tough he was about to say something to her. Finally, he wiped his forehead with his hand, and walked away. He dropped the note in a garbage can.

"Okay," I said to him as he approached me. "I know that I said we have to stay focused on the game and all... but what just happened?"

"I've been thinking about this whole Erin thing," he said, "And for so long... she's been, like all that I wanted, you know? But then, right when I was about to give her the note... it's like something clicked in my brain,"

"Okay... what is that?" I asked.

"No matter what happens... if she's flattered or freaked out... if she says she likes me too or she laughs in my face... it could never live up to my fantasy. I mean, I really don't even know *her* at all - just my own ideals... installed in her, you know?"

"I have to say... I'm impressed," I said honestly. "It takes a lot of intelligence... and courage to admit that. But... where are you going to go from here?"

"Well, for now, into the team huddle," he said, "We have a game to win,"

"Right," I said, jogging with him, toward our huddle. I stopped dead in my tracks, though, as I looked into the crowd once more. It was Pepper. And then, literally in the blink of an eye, she was gone.

FREE THROW

***

It was as though, with all of the emotional problems taken care of, we were a new team - one with more skill and energy. Of course, Shawn coming back into the game helped too.

Travis got three consecutive blocks to open the quarter, leading to a dunk and a lay in for Shawn, and three free throws being made by me. Next, Chris stole the ball, but Jorles was able to stop us on defense, and Kahn scored.

The quarter continued on a similar note. We would score once or twice, and then they would counter. Things took a turn for the worse, though, in the final two minutes. Jorles went on an 8-2 run, to put us behind by seven.

For the minute and a half that followed, neither of the teams looked like ones vying for a championship. No-one could make a shot. Coach called time out when just twenty-three seconds were left.

When all else had failed, Coach turned to the one strategy that worked for us all season. "Take it to the hole," he said directly to me. "Get the foul," I simply nodded, and we went back out on the court.

Jorles' scoring draught continued, but following Coach's advice, I made four straight free throws. Shawn scored with a dunk. Kahn made a three-pointer. Greg answered with a three of his own - with only 1.6 seconds left.

I stole the inbounds pass, and rose quickly for a lay-up. The tie was within my reach, before Kahn soared up and slammed against me. The shot was impossible, but with merely a fraction of a second remaining, I was headed to the free throw line.

***

I had made every free throw I had taken that season, and throughout the opening rounds of the playoffs. I was the first regular season one hundred percent free throw shooter in Lankford's team history. I had made a greater percentage of shots from the line than any other player in the league that year. And there I was, at the free throw line one last time. It was the championship game, and our team was down, 93-91. I had two shots to bring us into overtime. Otherwise, our championship hopes would end right

FREE THROW

there. Everything rested on my shoulders. There wouldn't be time for the team to score again. This was it.

The referee threw me the ball. I could hear the fans screaming and yelling, almost in unison. I squeezed the grips on the ball, as I began to bounce it on the floor. It was like the sound of a jackhammer to me, while others could barely distinguish it. I swallowed, hard, and then released the ball towards the basket. It bounced off the backboard, off the back of the rim, off the front, and then spun downwards and into the hoop. I heard Coach heave a sigh of relief as about half of the crowd erupted into screams and applause.

There was a screeching like that of a wounded animal behind me. I turned to see the opposing coach, jumping up and down. Beads of sweat ran down his bare scalp as he fired bullets of complaint toward the players on the court. They were the starters for the top ranked team in the league, and they had let a ten point lead dwindle down to a one point advantage, with their opponent's best shooter at the line, and less than a second left to play.

It was showtime. 'Put up or shut up.' as the old cliché goes. The head official bounced the ball to me. I dribbled three times as I stared at the basket. As I got into shooting form, a camera's flash caught my eyes, blinding me for a moment. As I rubbed my eyes, I heard the call from far across the court on the Jorles bench, "Shoot already, ya loser!"

I looked up. I knew everyone was getting testy as they waited to see me shoot. Shawn and I locked eyes. We both knew that this was it. Shawn's last shot at glory at the high school level, and with him leaving, probably mine too. But I wasn't going to squander this moment. If for no other reason than to irritate my detractor from the bench, I used up some more time by bouncing the ball a few more times. As I did this, I gazed throughout the crowd. Mr. Nicholes, or Ray Penner as I then knew him, was sitting in a high up row. I wasn't particularly surprised to see him in attendance. It was the biggest Lankford game since he had played. He winked at me, and suddenly, through that small gesture, I knew that I would drain the shot.

I returned my attention to the basket, dribbled twice more, and got into shooting form again. Then, something caught my eye, just to the left of where I was holding the ball. Standing by an exit, one face emerged from the crowd. It was as though everybody else in the gymnasium turned to shades of gray - like the black and white of old television shows. But she

FREE THROW

was in color. It was Pepper. I closed my eyes, and then looked again. It was real. She was still in town.

"Shoot the ball already, son," the referee said. I realized just how long I had taken at that moment. But really, I didn't care about the game or it's outcome by that point. I just had one thought: go to Pepper. And so, not even looking at he basket, I threw the ball up, toward the backboard, underhanded, with only my right hand.

I knew that I had missed the shot. It just didn't matter to me anymore.

***

As I started to walk toward her, the crowd suddenly leapt to its feet as one, cheering even louder. I had lost sight of Pepper, and then I found myself in Shawn's arms as he hugged me while shouting, "We did it! We did it!" over and over again.

Once he released me, I started to journey forth again, only to be stopped once again. This time it was from my teammates lifting me in the air. "That's gotta be the best pass I've ever seen!" shouted Brad.

"Pass?" My question was answered promptly, as I looked up towards a television monitor in one corner of the gym. My shot bounced off the backboard, and in air, Shawn caught it and slammed it down, through the hoop. I was glad about how things had turned out, but by the time they let me down, I felt I would never find Pepper.

I saw the referees roll a table out to center-court, with a number of trophies on it, and other things. I was sure that I should probably be heading over there, especially once I saw my teammates all going that way. But I was determined to find her, whatever it took.

Then, I felt a tap on my shoulder. I turned around hopefully. But the individual I faced was not the one I'd been thinking of. It was Timothy Kahn. He wore no expression - but I knew that he was thoroughly disappointed. Neither of us moved an inch nor spoke a word, for at least a half minute. I wasn't quite sure what was going on as we peered at each other. Finally, he extended his right hand towards me. I shook it, and then we went our respective ways. I wore a small grin as I started toward the crowd again. Two streaks had been broken - mine in free throw shooting, and his in sportsmanship.

Not long after that encounter, I felt another tap on my shoulder. I was ready for another disappointment. Instead, there she was, standing before me. It was Pepper.

I immediately embraced her. It seemed like an eternity before either of us released. Then, it was time to get some answers. "Pepper, what's going on?!" I began, shouting over the blaring music and noise of the crowd. "Why are you still here?!"

"My parents - well, my dad really - they're letting me stay... I'll be living with my aunt and uncle... with Alicia, until the end of the school year," she answered, absolutely glowing. Next came the moment I thought I would never enjoy again. We started to kiss - the long passionate type that ends all those love movies.

The lights began to dim, as a spotlight was moved to center court. Pepper and I didn't break off, and though I kept my eyes closed, I still heard the announcements being made.

A guy who was introduced as the local athletics commissioner, or something like that, began his presentation. At first, it was the boring rambling that one would expect. Then, he went on to say, "Now, for the presentation of this championship game's MVP. With thirty-eight points, seven rebounds, two assists, one steal, and two blocked shots, I am proud to present this award to Shawn Vetter. You could tell just the moment when he lifted the trophy by when the audience burst into another loud round of cheers.

Following that moment came the distribution of smaller trophies to every member of our team. It was done in alphabetic order, and so, I knew that I would be last - something I didn't mind at all.

Finally, I heard my name called. When I didn't immediately come forth, the guy repeated himself, and then asked if I had left. However, Travis' voice broke through the noise, saying, "He's over there!"

Whoever was operating the spotlight, moved it directly onto Pepper and I. The audience began to clap loudly. We stopped kissing. I saw her face turn a bright red, and I knew that I was probably blushing too. Yet, I whispered into her ear, "Don't worry about it," as I grabbed a hold of her hand, and we walked to center court together.